T0188541

Books by Alyssa Maxwell

Gilded Newport Mysteries
MURDER AT THE BREAKERS
MURDER AT MARBLE HOUSE
MURDER AT BEECHWOOD
MURDER AT ROUGH POINT
MURDER AT CHATEAU SUR MER
MURDER AT OCHRE COURT
MURDER AT CROSSWAYS
MURDER AT KINGSCOTE
MURDER AT WAKEHURST
MURDER AT BEACON ROCK
MURDER AT THE ELMS

Lady and Lady's Maid Mysteries
MURDER MOST MALICIOUS
A PINCH OF POISON
A DEVIOUS DEATH
A MURDEROUS MARRIAGE
A SILENT STABBING
A SINISTER SERVICE
A DEADLY ENDOWMENT
A FASHIONABLE FATALITY

Published by Kensington Publishing Corp.

MURDER AT BEACON ROCK

ALYSSA MAXWELL

KENSINGTON
PUBLISHING CORP.

www.kensingtonbooks.com

KENSINGTON BOOKS are published by

Kensington Publishing Corp.
119 West 40th Street
New York, NY 10018

All Kensington titles, imprints, and distributed lines are available at special quantity discounts for bulk purchases for sales promotion, premiums, fund-raising, educational, or institutional use.

Special book excerpts or customized printings can also be created to fit specific needs. For details, write or phone the office of the Kensington Sales Manager: Attn.: Sales Department. Kensington Publishing Corp., 119 West 40th Street, New York, NY 10018. Phone: 1-800-221-2647.

The K with book logo Reg US Pat. & TM Off.

First Kensington Hardcover Edition: September 2022

ISBN: 978-1-4967-3618-5 (ebook)

ISBN: 978-1-4967-4992-5

First Kensington Trade Paperback Edition: December 2023

10 9 8 7 6 5 4 3 2 1

Printed in the United States of America

Dedication:

To the memory of my grandparents, Paolo and Matilda Amorello, who came to this country in search of a better life and found it, but never could have imagined how well the family would do in later years. I know they were immensely proud of their son, my father, who achieved so much, and I know they would have been enormously proud of me, had they lived to see me become an author. Thank you for having the courage to cross an ocean to an unknown place where you didn't even speak the language, and put down roots, work hard, and do your very best for all of us.

And to my father, for whom my writing was always a priority and a joy, and who would send me home from his bedside in his last months with orders to "go and get that book written."

Acknowledgments:

Prior to writing this book, I had believed nothing could be more difficult than completing a book during a pandemic. I was wrong. Nothing can be harder than writing during the decline of an elderly parent, and sometimes weeks went by when I didn't touch this manuscript. Heartfelt thanks go to my editor, John Scognamiglio, and the entire team at Kensington, for their understanding and their insistence that family comes first.

Chapter 1

❦

Newport, RI, July 1900

The high-sprung carriage, pulled by a matching pair of Cleveland bays, crossed the bridge that spanned a vast, rolling landscape between Harrison Avenue and the estate called Beacon Rock. To either side of the bridge below us, trees in full leaf, a profusion of coastal wildflowers, and flashes of exposed rock spoke of geological phenomena eons in the making. Yet for all its natural appearance, what had once been a series of impassable ravines had been carefully landscaped by Frederick Law Olmsted to create pastoral harmony between the terrain, the bridge, the house, and the sea ninety feet below.

The house stretched nearly the breadth and width of a promontory overlooking Brenton Cove and Narragansett Bay. Its white marble facade gave the image of being guarded by an army of Ionic columns standing tall across its three expansive wings. My breath caught at the sight, and I felt transported to the great hillside Acropolis of Athens that I had seen in paintings.

As the drive turned and we neared the entrance of the forecourt, I understood, as my companion, Derrick Andrews, did not, that although we might enter arm in arm through the front door, I would be venturing into the lion's den alone. Those waiting inside for us readily accepted him, a man born to wealth and pedigree, to power and privilege. But although I could trace my lineage to the first Cornelius Vanderbilt, my pedigree showed wear around the edges and my clan, the Crosses, who were descended from one of Cornelius's daughters, dangled from the nether regions of the family tree.

"Do you remember when they blasted?" Derrick asked as he drew the carriage to a stop after circling the fountain. A fresh, bracing ocean breeze found its way beneath the vehicle's leather roof, stirring the folds of my evening gown and curls framing my face. Moonlight danced across the waves. Several other posh landaus and broughams lined the circular drive, and a groom awaited us, ready to assist.

Derrick didn't need to elaborate. Edwin Morgan had built his summer cottage on what had once been a small mountain that bordered the eastern shore of Brenton Cove. The once-rounded summit had hardly presented a fitting surface for Mr. Morgan's Grecian-inspired, colonnaded masterpiece, so after purchasing the property he had ordered the top blasted away and the land leveled. The former mountain's south slope formed the ravines that made the bridge necessary.

"Good heavens, yes. All of Newport shook that day, perhaps the entire island," I replied, remembering the moment the dynamite had been activated. "I was fourteen and thought, this must be how an earthquake feels—terrifying." I laughed. "The general consensus among Newporters was that Mr. Morgan had lost his mind."

He joined me in laughter, a sound that tripped from his lips in his easy baritone, and then asked, "Ready?"

I nodded, attempting to hide my doubts from him. He handed the reins to the groom, swung down, and came around to my side to hand me down as well. Beneath the glove on my left hand, a diamond caught shards of moonlight through the weblike pattern of the lace. By rights I shouldn't have been wearing such a ring, less than a year after the death of another Cornelius—Cornelius Vanderbilt II, a man I had considered like a second father. Derrick had insisted, gently, sweetly, but nonetheless adamantly, that it was time to let the world in on our secret of the past ten months. He and I were engaged, and whatever skepticism, disapproval, or down-right scorn our situation provoked among the society drag-ons, we would face it together for better or worse.

Tonight was to be an intimate affair, with fewer than a dozen guests. Since I was not an immediate member of Uncle Cornelius's family, I broke no rites of mourning by venturing out to a social occasion. I felt tugs of guilt none-theless. I half expected Derrick to offer words of encourage-ment. *Chin up, all will be well*—that sort of thing. But once my feet touched the ground, he merely bent over me, the stars and inky sky silhouetting his hair and shoulders, and raised my hand to his lips. My heart lifted as I realized his confidence in me was such that it simply didn't cross his mind that I might need such encouragement. Out of his un-questioning faith in me my own grew, so that I held myself tall as we crossed the inner courtyard, were admitted to a spacious central hall, led to the drawing room, and an-nounced to the others assembled there.

As we descended the two steps into the sunken room, Elizabeth Morgan greeted us first. She was a handsome woman in her midforties, tall and fine-boned, her hands long-fingered like those of a pianist, with a cloud of auburn curls arranged to frame her face in a style similar to my own but done with the superior skill of a lady's maid.

"We're so pleased you could come," Elizabeth Morgan said in a voice that had obviously known both elocution and singing lessons. "I understand congratulations are in order?"

"We are engaged," Derrick told her in a low voice meant to convey her special privilege in being among the first to know. He placed his hand over mine, still resting in his elbow.

"How delightful." Her eyes sparkled with enjoyment. "We must help you celebrate. Miss Cross, do you sail?"

"Not with any regularity," I confessed. "I haven't the steadiest sea legs, I'm afraid."

"Oh dear, I'm quite surprised at that," she replied with a quiet laugh. One finely shaped eyebrow twitched inward. "One would think growing up on an island would acquaint one with all manner of water sports."

"I do well enough in a skiff," I said. "As a child I enjoyed rowing about the bay with my brother. And I ride the ferry occasionally. But except for our local fishermen and sailors, most Newporters are landlubbers. And don't forget, ma'am, I'm busy working for the *Messenger*. That doesn't leave much time for sailing."

"How extraordinary." Mrs. Morgan's gaze shifted to include Derrick. "We must remedy that immediately, mustn't we?"

"That's up to Emma," he replied without hesitation. In a gesture that was both protective and a show of solidarity, the warmth of his hand moved to hover at the small of my back.

"Nonsense. It sounds as though if we leave it up to Miss Cross, she might never venture out upon the seas." With a teasing toss of her head, Mrs. Morgan went on. "Do you not own a yacht of your own, Mr. Andrews? The *Polaris*, I believe, a small but smart vessel. And are you or are you not a member of the New York Yacht Club?" She didn't wait for his reply. "Of course you are. Your wife-to-be, then, must sail."

I suddenly felt as though I was no longer there, as though I had become the absentee subject of conversation.

"Elizabeth, please, they've only just arrived. Don't hound them." Her husband, a trim, robust-looking man also in his mid to late forties, came up beside his wife. "If Miss Cross wishes to sail, she'll sail."

Elizabeth Morgan would not be daunted. "We'll take them on the *May* this week, won't we, Edwin? We'll have luncheon on the water." It wasn't a question, but a silken command, issued as only a genteel woman of the Four Hundred could utter. By the mild acquiescence on Mr. Morgan's face, I deduced her demands were always met.

"If Miss Cross and Andrews here are available, we'll plan it for Tuesday or Wednesday." He clapped Derrick on the shoulder, kissed my hand in welcome, and led us across the Persian carpet. I followed with a distinct sense that I had failed my first test as Derrick's future wife.

I had never been inside Beacon Rock before, though the view of it from the water had become familiar enough. The house's interior showed little sign of its outward Greek influence, but instead comprised an array of European design elements. The rooms flowed from the central hall, one leading into the next, allowing guests to circulate throughout the house with ease. On the way in, I had glimpsed an oval reception room decorated with gilded pilasters, each pair framing a mural depicting an outdoor scene of coaching and riding in the English countryside. Opposite that, an octagonal dining room paneled in rich, burled walnut held a gleaming inlaid table and at least a dozen Hepplewhite chairs. A crystal vase at the center of the table held a profusion of pristine white lilies.

Here, in the sunken drawing room, the dark paneling and pilasters continued, interrupted by bookcases and crowned by crenelated molding. The room ended at a semicircular bank of windows, which had been thrown open to the night air. In the distance, lights twinkled from vessels on the water. I could hear the distant rush of the ocean where it fed into the bay, and could only imagine the spectacular views in daytime.

By the standards of the Four Hundred, it was indeed a small gathering; Derrick and I rounded out a group of ten. Mrs. Morgan made the introductions, presenting first her husband's cousin, John Pierpont Morgan, and his wife Fanny. I had seen portraits of J.P. Morgan—industrialist and financier, with a leading role in steel, railroads, energy, and countless other enterprises—and had glimpsed him from a distance, but as the couple only frequented Newport for the sailing, they usually stayed on their yacht, the *Corsair.* He was a good two decades older than his cousin Edwin, with a broad figure well-disguised by his tailor's skills, bold eyebrows above discerning eyes, a large nose, and a handlebar mustache that bisected the sagging lines of his jowls.

My hand disappeared inside his as he shook it. "Miss Cross, yes, yes, the lady journalist. Here to ferret out our secrets and sell them to the enemy?"

"I'm sorry?" His insinuation baffled me, and I found myself unable to parry in response to his advance-lunge. Yes, I had come, in the past few moments, to think of the evening in terms of swordplay. "The enemy?"

"The other yacht clubs we're likely to face in the run-up to next year's America's Cup challenge," he clarified. He puffed out his considerably barrel-shaped chest. "Not to mention the Royal Ulster Yacht Club. No one stands a chance against my *Columbia.* No one. That's a promise and you can quote me in your newspaper, Miss Cross. That goes for you, too, Andrews." With that, the man pulled a cigar out of his breast pocket and stuck it between his teeth, though he did not light it.

"Oh, John, leave the poor child alone. Stop frightening her." Fanny Morgan, a pleasant-looking woman who wore her dark hair in a simple braid arched across the crown of her head, shook my hand. Large diamond earbobs dangled above her shoulders. Despite her even countenance, I believed I detected genuine annoyance in her gaze, but whether aimed at me or her husband, I wasn't certain. Her next words suggested the latter. "You mustn't pay any mind to my husband, Miss Cross. He rather enjoys playing the bully with unsuspecting young damsels."

I nearly laughed aloud at being called a damsel. If only Mrs. Fanny Morgan knew the truth of it; if only she had witnessed some of what *I* had witnessed these past years. "I'm not frightened in the least, Mrs. Morgan."

"Hmm." She looked me over, a slight smile turning the corners of her mouth upward. "That certainly sets you apart, Miss Cross. Incidentally, I overheard that you do not sail. Do you ride?"

"Not with any great expertise, I'm afraid."

"What do you do to amuse yourself, then?" she wished to know. Ah, another test failed.

A twittering laugh came from nearby, and then Elizabeth Morgan set a hand on my shoulder. "Fanny," she said to her cousin-in-law, "you and I shall take Miss Cross under our wing and teach her all she'll need to know as a wife of the Four Hundred." A small frown marred her brow, still smooth for a woman of her age. "Then again, I suppose Mr. Andrews isn't technically of the Four Hundred, considering his family hails from Providence and not New York. Still, they are good old New England stock, and Mr. Andrews . . . well . . ."

She left off, never completing whatever thought she had concerning Mr. Andrews. Perhaps that, as good old New England stock, he deserved better than a local Newport girl who neither sailed nor rode, nor boasted any other refinements that might offset the vulgarity of her workaday ambitions.

I was being sensitive, perhaps even peevish, though I let the others see no sign of it. Typically, I allowed society's disapproval to roll off me without effect, but for some reason my engagement had left me vulnerable, my sensibilities closer to the surface than ever before. Perhaps it was because now I hadn't merely my own social position to consider, but Derrick's as well.

That left one final couple to meet, the Delafields, whom I recognized but had never had reason to speak to directly. That didn't mean I knew nothing about them. They were younger than the others, closer in age to Derrick and myself, and made a handsome couple—she a shapely, dark-haired beauty with impeccable taste in fashion and furnishings, while he was tall and elegant, with a sportsman's physique and impish green eyes. Through the grapevine I had learned that while he might be an investor in the next America's Cup Races, she had brought the money to the marriage—nearly all of it. Her family had made its fortune in the Colorado silver mines before settling in New York, so one would imagine her dowry had been considerable.

I also understood the reason for Ruth Delafield's sulky expression when Bernard Delafield bent over me and pressed a lingering kiss to my hand—until I nearly yanked it out from beneath his lips. I darted a glance at Derrick; he had noticed, too, and looked on with a steely-eyed calculation.

Rumor had it Ruth Delafield had asked her husband for a divorce, which he had denied her. Yes, divorce among the Four Hundred had once been strictly taboo, and yes, my aunt Alva Vanderbilt, now Belmont, had changed all that five years ago by divorcing my uncle William, *but*, Uncle William had gone along with her wishes, even so far as to claim responsibility for the marriage falling apart due to his infidelity. Whether or not he had been untrue to his wife didn't matter. He had acted the gentleman and taken the blame.

Apparently, Bernard Delafield didn't possess as generous a nature. Whether he had threatened to keep the children from her, smear her reputation, or employ some other means of retaliation, I didn't know, but it was plain to see from their expressions and mannerisms that they held little esteem for each other.

Ruth Delafield soon drew me aside. "Congratulations. Derrick Andrews is quite a catch for you, Miss Cross." She smiled and darted a glance at her husband from beneath her lashes. "But are you quite sure you wish to spoil a good thing by marrying the man?"

I chuckled and pretended to know nothing of her familial woes. "What would you suggest instead, Mrs. Delafield?"

One eyebrow, thin and sculpted, rose in a perfect arch. "Hold him at bay, keep him wanting. It's the only way to keep them from wandering."

This was far more candidness than I would have expected from a woman of her social class. Of any woman, to be frank. I fumbled for a response, but was saved from having to give one when Derrick returned to my side.

Further relief from the tensions of the gathering came in the form of footmen, uniformed in gold-trimmed livery, circulating through the room with platters of seafood canapés and tiny pastry shells filled with pâté and truffle paste. A glass of champagne found its way into my hand. I remained with the women when the men—Derrick, the two Morgan cousins, Bernard Delafield, and another gentleman, introduced to me as Tyrone Kerr—moved off to a bridge table at the far end of the room. Each of them was a principal investor in the upcoming America's Cup Races, having formed a syndicate backing John Morgan's *Columbia.*

Seated around the table, they discussed whatever strategies they would employ over the coming months to prepare for the next year's challenge. I had known this to be the reason for tonight's soirée; known that the women would be left to amuse themselves for at least part of the evening; known, also, that whatever I heard discussed here must be kept in strictest confidence. But each time I thought of John Morgan fairly accusing me of gathering information for the *enemy*, a chuckle rose in my throat and I had to resist the urge to shake my head.

In truth, only one detail about those gathered around the card table caught my attention: the presence of an older woman, perhaps nearing fifty, who seemed to have as much to say about racing strategy as the men. We had met only briefly before she had excused herself to me and the other women and seated herself at the card table as though she had every right in the world to be there. Her voice carried across the room, sometimes drowning out the lower tones of the men. I half expected them to send her on her way, but they didn't.

I had heard of Lucy Carnegie but had never met her previously. The widow of Andrew Carnegie's brother Thomas, she had become an avid yachter in her own right and six years ago had gained membership in the New York Yacht Club—something no woman had ever done before. Though a diminutive five feet tall at most, she had nonetheless projected a lofty stature and a jaunty self-assurance when we shook hands. Unlike the other two women present, Mrs. Carnegie didn't offer any subtle frowns or make a friendly fuss about my lack of experience either in the saddle or before the mast. And for that, I silently thanked her and was determined to know her better.

The yacht club meeting broke for dinner. We gathered at the lengthy table in the octagonal dining room and enjoyed a several-course meal of seafood and game birds served in a variety of sauces. A lovely Charlotte Russe followed for dessert. I sat across from Derrick, and between J.P. Morgan and Tyrone Kerr. Mr. Kerr, it seemed, was a dedicated bachelor who spent nearly all his time sailing, racing his yachts, and hunting in the mountains of both this country and Europe. I found myself forced to add a lack of hunting know-how to my multitude of sins. Honestly, in these people's estimate, Derrick and I could have nothing in common. I redeemed myself slightly in Mr. Kerr's eyes when I told him I possessed a sharp eye and a steady hand when it came to a bow and arrow, and he suggested I might try that method of hunting. I didn't bother to explain that, while I enjoyed a hearty meal as much as the next person, hunting for sport held no appeal for me.

Finally, Elizabeth Morgan came to her feet, prompting the rest of us around the table to do the same. The footmen held the ladies' chairs while the men bowed politely to us, and Elizabeth Morgan led us—Mrs. Carnegie included—out of the room and back to the drawing room. Derrick winked at me as I turned away from the table, and I went away grinning.

Conversation turned to the coming weeks of the summer Season. It had once been my job to keep track of who wore what gowns to whose parties and balls at which cottages along Bellevue Avenue, but I had since graduated from society columnist to news journalist, and I found the discussion not only inconsequential, but disheartening. Such was the society I would enter as Derrick's wife, unless I could manage to inhabit both worlds—theirs and mine—simultaneously.

The terrace doors stood open, proving too much of a temptation for me. I drifted to them and, after pausing for a half glance over my shoulder, stepped out. The voices of the ladies behind me faded as the sounds of the breeze and the waves filled my ears. Clouds had moved across the sky, blotting out most of the stars, and a low fog crept across the bay.

I turned the corner of the house, now walking beside the wing that held the kitchen and servants' quarters. I could just about make out the muted lights of Fort Adams across Brenton Cove. Beyond it, across the bay, Jamestown lay invisible, its lamplights unable to pierce the murky night. I breathed the salty air deep into my lungs and held it there while I savored the taste of it on my tongue. At the same time, I tugged the gloves from my hands and draped them over the low wall before me.

Always here, in close proximity to Aquidneck Island's briny waters, did I find my balance, my steadiness. I might not be much of a sailor, but that didn't mean I didn't understand the ebb and flow of the tides, couldn't read the sudden quickening of the winds that whipped the waves to a froth, or recognize the doldrums that flattened the water to a glossy, undulating mirror.

Those people in the house loved their yachts, their adventures across the world's oceans, but I couldn't help feeling that I loved something deeper and more lasting, and that I belonged to it—belonged to this rocky, windy, salty island I called home, and to the waters that struck its shores unendingly, year in and year out.

The side terrace led down to the driveway, and then a walkway along the edge of the promontory. Little separated the path from the rocky descent but the sculpted hedges that ran its length. I kept going, all the way to the service driveway and the entrance of a wooden staircase that zigzagged downward to the water's edge at the base of Beacon Rock.

Intertwined with the sounds of the sea came the toll of buoys, marking the rocky dangers at the mouth of the harbor. Through the fog, dull circles of illumination from several yachts anchored within Brenton Cove rose and dipped in a leisurely rhythm on the waves. Derrick's *Polaris*, which he had purchased this past autumn, was not among them, but these belonged to Edwin Morgan and his guests, their private steamers on which they had traveled to Newport. Their sails were furled, their decks quiet, yet on the lower levels, activity remained constant as the crews conducted never-ending maintenance and cleaning. One yacht stood alone, closer in toward the Morgans' boathouse and pier: the *Columbia*, the object of tonight's gathering. Far sleeker than the others, clearly intended to cut knifelike through the surf, this vessel carried the high hopes of the yacht club members in the house behind me.

I lingered at the top of the stairs, enjoying the evening, when a voice called to me. I'm not sure I had intended going down. I had only wished to put a bit of distance—breathing room—between me and the effort of maintaining a suitable expression for the four Morgans and the others, when, really, I wished to roll my eyes and go home.

"Miss Cross, do wait. Are you going down? I'll join you if you are."

I needn't have turned around to recognize the speaker as Lucy Carnegie. Though one could not say her voice lacked the refinement of the other wives, she nonetheless spoke with . . . I suppose one might call it authority. Directness. She reminded me somewhat of Mrs. Stuyvesant Fish—Mamie to her friends—who never minced words or hesitated to speak her mind.

She came to stand at the rail beside me. Her head barely reached my shoulder, making me feel giantlike, though I had never considered myself particularly tall. "It's too nice a night to spend it cooped up inside. Wouldn't you say?"

"Yes, it's a lovely evening," I agreed, and gazed out over the darkened waters with what I hoped appeared to be an appreciative expression. "And I can't help admiring the boats."

She studied me a moment, then grinned. "Fiddlesticks! You were as bored in there as I was."

"No, really . . ."

"It's quite all right, my dear. I thought my eyes would cross just now when they started talking about which parties they'll attend this summer. I tell you, I'll go or not go if invited, but with hardly a second thought. It is industry and personal challenges that I thrive on. Give me a yacht to sail or a home to design any day of the week, and I'm happy."

"You've an interest in architecture, then," I commented with genuine appreciation. When she nodded, I continued, "My aunt Alva Vanderbilt, now Belmont, worked very closely with Mr. Hunt in designing Marble House."

"Yes, and good for her. Me, I'm setting my sights on building a recreational camp for my family up in the Adirondacks. Horses, swimming, golf, hiking, boating—you name it, we'll have it there. A body must be active at all times to be healthy. Ever been to the Adirondacks, Miss Cross?"

"Actually, no, I haven't."

"God's country, up there. Wild, rugged, magnificent. You must go at the first opportunity. Your honeymoon, perhaps? When is the big day?"

"Oh, not for another year, probably. We haven't set a date yet."

"Whyever not? My dear, one mustn't leave these things to happenstance. Scrupulous planning—that's how one gets things done. I suggest you and Mr. Andrews decide on a date tonight. No more delays."

Such different advice than Ruth Delafield had offered. "I'll think about it."

"You do that, and give the Adirondacks serious consideration for at least a portion of your wedding trip. Unless you've set your sights on Europe?"

"I haven't thought about it, to be honest."

She shook her head at me, her amused smile letting me know she didn't disapprove of me, but perhaps didn't quite understand me, either. In the ensuing pause, I became aware of a *slap-thumping* sound from below, like that of some large ocean debris caught against the pilings of a pier. It was a common enough sound along the wharves, but here, away from the commercial endeavors of the main harbor, it struck me as unusual.

"What could that be?" I mused aloud.

"What? I don't hear anything. Just the waves and the beat of the rigging against the masts." She pointed out over the water. "Speaking of which, that one there is mine. The *Dungeness*. Can you make her out against the mist? Steel construction, one hundred and thirty-five feet long, and superbly appointed. Named for the estate my husband, God rest him, and I built in Georgia. I understand you don't sail, Miss Cross, but even you must admit, she is a beauty."

"That she certainly is, Mrs. Carnegie. I might not sail, and it might be nighttime and foggy, but I can see she's a fine ship." I spoke earnestly, yet that thumping tide still held my attention.

The woman beside me nodded vigorously. "She helped me become accepted as a full-fledged member of the yacht club. For one, she's a finer ship than most of those old buckets owned by the men. And two, I've entertained enough of them on her decks that they couldn't but return the favor by opening the club doors to me."

"I'm glad. I can't see what difference it makes who owns a craft, man or woman." I pricked my ears. *Whap, thud, thump*. What *was* that sound?

Mrs. Carnegie said something I missed, for she then asked with concern, "Miss Cross, are you quite all right?"

My eyebrows gathered as I held the railing and leaned forward to listen. Mrs. Carnegie was probably right. The bay carried a symphony of sounds, especially at night. But something about this particular *thud-thud*, clearly just below the waterline, accompanied by a hollow echo, ran beneath my skin and spiked the hair at my nape. Whatever was caught by the tide had clearly lodged against one of the vessels, the *Columbia* itself, perhaps, and was certainly heavier than the usual flotsam or jetsam.

"I'm going down." I placed my foot on the top step, but Mrs. Carnegie put a hand on my wrist.

"I'm sure it's merely driftwood."

I held her gaze an instant, and then continued down. Behind me, I heard her footsteps on the treads, following my own. Upon stepping onto the dock, I realized the thumping was not coming from the *Columbia*, but much closer, practically on the dock itself. Years ago, an old, three-masted barque had run aground on the shoals just beyond Brenton Cove. They had tried to put into the cove but had taken on too much water too quickly. They'd sunk, but when Edwin Morgan had Beacon Rock built, he'd raised the *Bessie Rogers* and had her placed beside his boathouse, in the crook of the dock and the longer pier, as a kind of picturesque feature harkening back to Newport's past.

I leapt from the dock onto the deck of the barque and paused to listen. The thumping sounded like slow, steady drumbeats now, the vibrations tickling the bottoms of my feet and traveling up my legs. The regular, pulsing quality of it seemed to control my own heartbeat. A lifetime of living beside the sea had taught me when to dismiss a sound and when to take notice. I was positive that if my dog, Patch, had been here, he would be barking up a storm.

Mrs. Carnegie went farther down the dock, closer to the boathouse, where a short gangplank connected the dock to the *Bessie Rogers*. She came aboard, holding her skirts aloft, pausing in a silver shaft of moonlight that had made its way through the clouds. A swirl of fog swallowed the details of her jeweled pumps. "Well, Miss Cross?" Then she, too, frowned. She turned her head aside, listening. Her forehead tightened. "Yes, I hear it. I see what you mean."

She turned her head this way and that, as I was doing. Then we both froze, our attention riveted on the same spot. In the next instant, we crossed to the starboard side of the *Bessie Rogers*, gripped the gunwale, and leaned over. Through wisps of fog, an object took shape below us.

The blood rushed to my head, rendering me dizzy. I tightened my grip until my fingers ached and a splinter pierced my forefinger.

"Dear God," Mrs. Carnegie murmured. "Oh, dear, dear God."

Chapter 2

What had first appeared as a bundle of seaweed floating on the tide rearranged itself into the shape of a woman, her skirts billowing with the current, her hair streaming out around her like the graceful tentacles of a sea creature. She lay face down, her arms and legs akimbo.

"We must get her out." Mrs. Carnegie leaned farther over, prompting me to clutch her arm.

"Don't. She's beyond our help and we don't need you going over, too."

"I can swim," she brusquely replied, and before I knew it, a splash announced her arrival in the water.

"Mrs. Carnegie!" I cried out, then immediately backed away from the railing. "Hang on! I'll run for help."

"No, ring the bell beside the boathouse door," came her sharp reply from the inky water below me. "I'll hold on to her and make sure she doesn't break loose. And you're right, Miss Cross, she's quite beyond our help."

I ran to the end of the barque and took the gangplank in two strides. With my skirts bunched in my fists, I ran to the boathouse door to find the bell mounted between two carved wooden posts. I tugged the chain—over and over and over, raising a jarring cacophony that echoed against Beacon Rock and across Brenton Cove.

Moments later shouts and pounding steps echoed down from the house as the men came running outside. I stilled the bell and ran back along the dock until I reached the base of the steps.

"There's a woman in the water! Come quickly." Even as I spoke, I realized the futility of hurrying them to the scene. What could they do, other than relieve Mrs. Carnegie of her charge and help them both out of the water?

Derrick reached me first, grasped my shoulders and held me at arm's length. I saw the relief in his eyes when he realized I was in sound health. "What the devil has happened?"

"Miss Cross, what is this all about?" Edwin Morgan came up quickly behind Derrick, followed by his cousin, J.P., Tyrone Kerr, and the others. Moments later, servants in livery and men from the house I hadn't seen before crowded onto the steps. They amassed on the dock, suspended in uncertainty.

I thrust out my arm to point to the barque. "There's a woman washed in from the bay. Drowned. Mrs. Carnegie is in the water, holding her fast."

"I need a pair of swimmers pronto to help lift her out!" Lucy Carnegie's voice echoed against the hull and ricocheted against the nearby vessels, magnifying the sound several fold.

Elizabeth Morgan ran to the gangplank and onto the barque. When she reached the starboard side, she leaned over and stretched out an arm. "Lucy, what have you done? Take my hand, I'll hold on to you."

"I'm all right, Lizzy. Just get someone down here to help me."

Two men I didn't recognize, but clearly not footmen, shed their coats and kicked their shoes from their feet. A moment later they were on the pier and dove in. Derrick and the other men from the party hurried onto the barque. They lined up along the gunwale, shouting directions. I followed, leaning over Derrick's shoulder to see the two men in the water gather the body from Mrs. Carnegie's hold. She immediately kicked off and swam for the boathouse. I ran to meet her there, knowing that no matter how strong a swimmer she might be, in petticoats and evening gown she would need help emerging onto the boathouse steps and onto the dock.

Derrick had followed me, I discovered, and together we each grasped one of Lucy Carnegie's hands. They were slippery and cold, but we held fast as she gained a foothold and swung herself up toward us.

"Hang on," she advised, "or this dratted train of mine will drag me back in."

"We've got you, Mrs. Carnegie," Derrick said, and a moment later she stood beside us on the dock, water streaming in wide rivulets from her hair and skirts. Derrick and I were rather damp as a result as well.

Mrs. Carnegie let out a whoop. "Thank goodness you all got here when you did. Next time, I'll bring my bathing costume." She was breathing heavily, and her shoulders sagged with each indrawn breath. A pair of benches sat on either side of the boathouse door.

"Come and sit, Mrs. Carnegie." She came with me docilly and sank onto a bench. I sat beside her, the slap of the waves continuing against the *Bessie Rogers*'s hull as the men brought the body to the steps. Derrick and Edwin Morgan helped lift the body out of the water.

"I'm sorry I said that." Mrs. Carnegie laid a cold, sodden hand on mine. "About bringing a bathing costume. I should not have joked like that. It was callous of me." She glanced toward the steps. Derrick and Mr. Morgan had the drowned woman laid out on the dock now. The two who had dived into the water to retrieve her were on the dock as well. Their clothing clung to their bodies, slick like the coat of a seal. "Poor soul."

"You've been through a shock, Mrs. Carnegie. I certainly didn't expect you to jump in the water like that."

"One thought propelled me: that if she broke away and floated back out into the bay, she might never be found again. Whoever she is, her family might never know what happened to her."

I nodded, feeling forlorn. "I do hope we can identify her."

While the others milled on the dock, the two Morgan women and Ruth Delafield exclaimed over this unexpected interruption to the party. More people came running down from the house. A maid carrying towels offered two to Mrs. Carnegie, which she accepted gratefully. She had begun to shiver. I helped drape them around her and did my best to cover her damp hair. "We must get you back to the house," I said, and readied myself to help her stand.

She shook her head. "Not yet. Not until we know. . . ."

The woman lay faceup on the deck, her hair like a halo of sodden ribbons surrounding her face. Someone had gone into the boathouse, Edwin Morgan presumably, and turned up the gas on the dock lanterns. I rose and went to the body. Despite Elizabeth Morgan's admonishment to come away and Ruth Delafield's gasp, I stared down at the woman, studying her features through the mist. Her eyes were wide open, glassy and blank. She was young—very young. Even mottled by water and death, her face was smooth and softly formed, that of someone who had been a mere child not long ago.

Suddenly overcome by the tragedy of one so young meeting her end, I fell to a crouch beside her. "Who are you?" I whispered, staring into those empty eyes. "How did this happen to you?"

"Miss Cross, please." Elizabeth Morgan leaned to place her hands on my shoulders and grasped them firmly. She tugged, gently but adamantly, to coax me to my feet.

Fanny Morgan added her persuasion, and Ruth Delafield implored me as well. I ignored them all.

The woman lying prone before me wore a traveling suit consisting of a short jacket with wide lapels and a matching skirt, both gray and trimmed in black silk. The tailoring suggested good quality, of a kind only the well-off could afford. She wore black lace gloves. I saw no handbag, of course, and her jacket appeared to have no pockets. But her skirt did. I reached for the one closest to me.

A gasp came from behind me. "No, Miss Cross, you mustn't." The voice once again belonged to Elizabeth Morgan. Again, I took no heed.

One of the men who had retrieved her from the water knelt on the other side of her. His clothing oozed seawater onto the planks; his dark hair was plastered to his head. "I'll do it, miss, if you'd rather not."

But I had already dipped the fingers of my right hand into the pocket. They came out empty. My companion began searching the pocket nearest him. Like me, he found nothing. I contemplated what to do next, hesitated, and then a thought prompted me to undo the silk-clad buttons of her traveling jacket.

"Good gracious, Miss Cross." Mrs. Fanny Morgan's disapproval drifted on a tuft of fog, muted but nonetheless indignant. "Is this poor child to be afforded no dignity?"

I glanced up at her briefly. My gaze darted to the Morgan cousins and Mr. Kerr. They stood back a little, looking indecisive, as if they believed they should take charge but weren't sure how to go about dislodging me from the woman's side.

On the other hand, Bernard Delafield's bright green eyes nearly glowed with anticipation. Derrick knelt beside me, his hand on my shoulder. He made no move to urge me aside.

"There is no dignity in dying an anonymous death," I said bluntly, and opened the jacket's last button. I peeled the two halves away and studied the lining. In the murky light, I made out what I had been seeking—an inner pocket. Chances were, I knew, she had kept anything of significance in her handbag, lost to the bay waters. But perhaps . . .

My reach was rewarded when my fingertips came in contact with a sodden object, flat and pliable. I caught it between my first and middle fingers and ever-so-gently drew it out, careful not to tear what I determined to be thick paper, or perhaps cardboard.

"Is it a photograph?" Derrick asked, and reached out to lightly touch the edge of what did turn out to be cardboard, though limp and fragile from its sojourn in the water.

"Yes. A *carte de visite*." I held it closer. "The image is still clear." I glanced back at the lifeless face. "I believe it's her."

Indeed, the photograph revealed the head and shoulders of a young beauty, her wavy hair loosely piled in a knot at the top of her head, her eyebrows bold above penetrating eyes that gazed directly at the camera. She held her head at a tilt, her chin lifted, her lips slightly pursed into a hint of a smile. Her shoulders were nearly bare, but for an airy wrap draped lightly around them. She wore a simple chain necklace from which a pearl dangled. I was immediately gripped by a sense of intimacy, by a conviction that this photograph had been meant as a message to a special man in her life.

Was she married? No, I didn't think a married woman would go to the trouble of having such a picture taken. Perhaps engaged. Obviously, in this picture she had been happy, filled with hope and plans for her future. With whom? And what happened—what had sent her into the water? An accident? Some sudden sorrow? The hand of another?

"There's something written on the front," I said, "but I can't make it out."

Derrick touched my hand. "Is there anything on the back?"

I flipped it over. "Yes. I think it's the photographer's stamp."

"That should give a clue as to where she's from."

I nodded and handed the photo to him. The notion of an engagement had sent me gazing down at my own hand. I had pulled off my gloves upon coming outside, and the ring I wore on my left ring finger flashed in reply to the lanterns' glow. After an initial hesitation, I reached for one of the young woman's hands, the one that lay closest to me. As I did, the man still crouching opposite me saw what I was about to do and took up her other hand. Together we slid off her gloves.

"She's wearing a gold bangle," he said. "Nothing else on this side." He glanced over to her other hand, clasped in both of my own.

"There's a ring," I said. But not an engagement ring. At least, I didn't think so. There were no diamonds or other stones. The thin gold band had been twisted into a knot, and from it two hearts dangled from tiny chains. I could make out no details, but a light graze of my fingernail confirmed there were small engravings on each heart. Even so, it appeared too simple for an engagement ring, especially since, judging by her costly clothing and the photograph, a suitor would have gone to much more effort, financially, to seal a marriage pact between them. A promise ring of sorts, perhaps. Or a gift from her parents or a friend.

"Miss Cross, the police have arrived." With her towels draping her head and shoulders, Lucy Carnegie stood between John Morgan and his wife, Fanny. I looked up first at her, then raised my gaze to the summit of the promontory. Voices echoed against the house, and then officers in uniform started down the steps. Moments later two men in street clothes followed them.

The sight of those men heartened me, for it meant that my friend on the police force, Jesse Whyte, had been assigned to investigate. Last summer, due in large part to my own interference in police business, Jesse had been taken off Newport's most serious crimes and relegated to burglaries, civil disturbances, and misdemeanors. A new man had been brought onto the force to investigate homicides, one Gifford Myers, who had no tolerance for nosy female reporters such as myself. Not even when said nosy female reporter turned up hard evidence and creditable leads.

By the end of last year's summer Season, however, I had learned the art of subtlety and Jesse had been forgiven, not to mention reinstated. He and Gifford Myers now worked as partners.

Derrick stood and offered his hand to help me up. We stepped away from the body to allow the uniformed men to do their job, but I held on to the *carte de visite* until Jesse and Detective Myers stepped onto the dock.

"What have you got there, Emma?" Jesse said in greeting. I ignored the other detective's sardonic expression and handed Jesse the photograph. He brought it beneath one of the lanterns and studied it while Gifford Myers approached the body. Jesse wrinkled his nose as he strained his eyes to make out the stamp on the back. "Interesting. Says here this was taken in Great Neck, New York." He looked up. "I believe that's on Long Island." He bent his head over the photo again to read, "Edward Gorman Photography."

He flipped the photo over. I already knew what had been inscribed in the lower righthand corner of the image, over part of the wrap draped around the young woman's shoulders. But I stayed silent as Jesse read, "To Wally darling, from L."

Detective Myers came up beside him and took the photo from him. "Anything important?"

"Could be," was Jesse's brief reply.

Gifford Myers ran his fingers down the handlebars of his mustache as he bent his head to study both sides of the photograph. "Wally darling, eh? From a photographer in New York . . ."

"We'll want to contact him," Jesse said.

Detective Myers held me in his sights. "Is there any other evidence you should turn over to us, Miss Cross?"

I heard his sarcasm plainly and shook my head.

"Tampering with evidence is a criminal offense," he warned me.

"I didn't see the sense of letting it continue to be water damaged in her pocket." I wanted to ask him if he had seen her ring, and what he thought of it, but there would have been no point in my questioning him.

Edwin Morgan joined us beneath the lamplight. "Detectives, I see no further need for my guests to be out here. May we return to the house now?"

"We'll need to question everyone about what they might have seen," Gifford Myers said, but then nodded. "Yes, you can all go back to the house."

"I can answer that question for you." Edwin's cousin, John, escorted his wife and Elizabeth to the foot of the stairs. "None of us saw anything. This poor woman evidently washed up from the bay. Probably fell off a vessel. Tragic, but we were all up in the house when she was found."

"Not everyone, apparently," Detective Myers countered. "Miss Cross seems to always be on hand in situations such as these, don't you, Miss Cross?"

Before I could answer, Lucy Carnegie strode to my side and tossed an arm around my shoulders, half covering me with the damp towel she still wore draped over her own. "I was with Miss Cross as well. We were talking on the terrace when we heard an odd slapping. An ominous sound it was. We of course came to investigate and . . . well . . . this is what we found."

"And you jumped in to hold on to her, I understand," Jesse put in.

"Foolish, especially for a woman," the other detective murmured.

Mrs. Carnegie's hold on me tightened, her still-sodden skirts transferring moisture to mine. She pulled up straighter, which brought the top of her head just a shade above my shoulder. "I'm a strong swimmer and the water doesn't frighten me, even at night. I didn't wish to risk letting the body—this poor woman—drift away while Miss Cross sounded the alarm. I was never in the slightest bit of danger."

With a twist of his lips, Detective Myers *hmphed* and turned toward the others. "You may all go home if you wish. We'll contact you if we need to speak to you."

"I believe with the exception of Mr. Andrews and Miss Cross, we're all staying either at Beacon Rock or out in the cove." Tyrone Kerr raised an arm to point in the general direction of the vessels moored nearby. "It won't be much effort to round us up if you need to speak with us. But as Mr. Morgan said, none of us will know anything more than you do now."

"We shall see," the detective replied, and turned away to return to the body, effectively dismissing several of the richest men in the world.

Chapter 3

Derrick and I were at the Newport Hospital early the next morning and used our reporters' credentials to gain admittance to the makeshift morgue in the basement. That is to say, I used my reporter's credentials, which in truth would not have gotten me much farther than the hospital's front door, if one judged by the gaggle of fellow journalists gathered inside the lobby. They all spoke at once in an effort to obtain information about the drowned woman, while a beleaguered nurse held up her arms and protested that she couldn't make out what any of them were asking. I weathered more than one disparaging glare, owing to word having gotten out that I already had a scoop on the story.

"How does she do it?" more than one grumbled as I passed them by. "How does she always manage to be in the right place at the right time?"

Though I wouldn't term it as such, in truth I didn't know the answer. At any rate, it was Derrick who got us as far as the basement—with his clout, connections, and yes, the donations he had made to the hospital since becoming a Newport resident.

Jesse and Gifford Myers were already standing in the doorway of the morgue, while a team of four men, the coroner—who examined the body and pieced together the medical evidence—and three assisting examiners, who determined, based on the coroner's findings, whether a crime had been committed, conferred with one another.

Derrick shook hands with the two detectives. "Have they discovered anything new from last night?"

I had pointed out the woman's ring to Jesse while we were still on the dock—not that he had needed my help in finding it. He said, "There are two initials engraved on her ring, an *F* and *R*, one on each heart."

Detective Myers exhibited his habitual scowl as I remarked, "Odd. Neither of those matches the name or the initial inscribed on the photo."

"Whether there is any connection between the ring and the photo is for the police to determine, Miss Cross." Mr. Myers tried to stare me down. I smiled back at him. "Chances are, they are completely unrelated."

"That seems unlikely," I couldn't help replying, knowing I was baiting him and cementing an already contentious relationship between us. He had no reason to dislike me, other than that last summer I had helped solve another case, and Jesse had been reinstated in his position of homicide detective. Apparently, Gifford Myers didn't admire assertive women, but he had very much enjoyed being Newport's chief investigator.

"What about the photo?" Derrick asked Jesse. "And the address on the back?"

"A telegram was sent this morning." Jesse switched his derby from one hand to the other. "Hoping for a reply soon. We're hoping she not only had the photo taken there, but that the photographer—or someone who works there—actually knew her."

"Or at least can furnish us with information about where

she lives," Gifford Myers added, then blinked. "Or lived, I should say."

The four of us waited just outside the doorway, not wishing to distract the process going on inside. The coroner and the others kept their voices to whispers and murmurs, and though I pricked my ears, I could make out none of what they discussed. Finally, the three examiners filed from the room, walking past us without a word and making their way upstairs. The coroner came out, untying his apron and removing his gloves.

"We detected no sign of foul play. We estimate she had been in the water two to three hours, which, if you check with last night's schedule, might coincide with the time of the last ferry to leave the island."

"An accident, then," Detective Myers pronounced, as though he spoke the final word on the matter.

"It doesn't mean she wasn't pushed," I pointed out, then wished I hadn't—not only because of the look the detective sent me, but because, like him, I too had jumped to a conclusion with no evidence to support it. Yet, if she had been pushed, she'd likely not bear any evidence of the crime. One quick shove over the railing in a dark corner of a sparsely occupied ferry would leave neither bruises nor witnesses.

"She might have dropped something over the side, impulsively leaned over to catch it, and . . ." The coroner made a hand over hand motion to indicate a body tumbling over the side. "At any rate, as I said, there is no indication of foul play, or that this was anything other than an unfortunate accident."

"Well, that pretty much settles that." Detective Myers shrugged and headed for the stairs. His foot on the bottom step, he half turned to glance over his shoulder. "Whyte? You coming?"

"You go on ahead. I'll catch up with you at the station."

"Suit yourself." Yet the look on Jesse's partner's face belied his nonchalant reply. He didn't like that Jesse would remain behind to speak with Derrick and me. I was glad he did. Gifford Myers was too quick to dismiss this case—if indeed it was a case. I couldn't help feeling he was being quick to dismiss a woman, that if the drowned individual had been a man, he would be more intent on finding out how it had happened.

"The ferry schedule will have to be checked," Jesse said, reading my mind and speaking the words I'd intended to say next.

I had more to add. "Not only the schedule, but the ticket sales. How many people boarded the last ferry—you'll want to know that. Could someone have accidentally fallen overboard without being seen? There were no reports of such an incident last night, were there?"

"No," Jesse admitted, "there weren't, and you're right. Had the ferry been crowded, there is no way anyone could have fallen into the water without at least one other person noticing. I'll check on it while we wait for that return telegram."

"We'll have an article in today's *Messenger* describing her and asking for information from anyone who might know her or had at least seen her. In the meantime, I think we should double our efforts with a midmorning extra." I appealed to Derrick. "We should be able to get that out quickly, yes?"

"I'll make sure it happens."

Within the next hour, Derrick and I personally loaded our newsboys' arms with a single-sheet extra as it came off the press. He had bought the newspaper two years ago, when it had been a struggling broadsheet in danger of closing, and turned it into a respectable local enterprise with a growing number of subscriptions. I had served as editor-in-chief for a year, but realized my calling lay in reporting the news, in following the trail of a story, not managing an office and worrying about paperwork.

When word came from Long Island several hours later, Jesse brought it to us himself, making the short trek from the police station on Marlborough Street to our offices on Spring Street. His partner was nowhere in sight, but that didn't surprise me.

"I hoped I'd catch you before you left for the day," he said upon entering through the street door, swatting the dust from the street off the shoulders of his coat. He removed his derby and shook a fine layer of particles from its crown and his auburn hair as well. No wonder—a streetcar had rumbled by only moments ago, raising clouds from the dry roadbed. We badly needed rain.

"We weren't going anywhere until we heard from you," I assured him. Muted voices and the ever-present rumbling of the presses in the back rooms made their way through the building, but we had the front office to ourselves, as Stanley Sheppard, the current editor-in-chief, had left for the day. Not that his presence would have been a hindrance to our discussion. Mr. Sheppard was an often blunt taskmaster around the office, but he was a good man, intelligent and fair, and Derrick and I trusted him.

Jesse was under no obligation to share information with us, and Gifford Myers's reticence was perfectly understandable, if a trifle inconvenient. Several years ago, Jesse would not have gone out of his way to enlist our confidence on a case, but both Derrick and I had long since proven our worth in examining clues with an objective eye. And where sometimes Jesse's hands were tied by department regulations or the influence of powerful men, ours were not. Truth be told, the three of us made an excellent team.

"Well, Whyte? Who is she?" Derrick sounded impatient—as impatient as I felt but tried not to express.

Jesse smiled slightly, acknowledging our eagerness for answers. "Her name is Lillian Fahey, and you were right, Emma—she was young. Only eighteen."

"It's not a name that is familiar to me," I mused aloud. "She could not have been a regular visitor to Newport. At least, not one who mixed with the Four Hundred."

"The photographer, Edward Gorman, had no trouble identifying her from the description in the telegram," Jesse went on. "Said the photo was taken about a month ago. She was very specific about the type of pose she wanted, which is why he remembers her so well. It wasn't typical of ladies of her age. Or any age, really."

I nodded, recalling the sense of intimacy projected by the tilt of her chin and the directness of her gaze. "Looking at that photo, I had the sense it had been meant as a message, or a declaration, to a special person—the Wally mentioned in the inscription—and was not something she handed out to casual friends. Have you tracked down her family yet?"

"The photographer didn't know her," Jesse said, "but we're in touch with the Great Neck police and they're working on it."

Derrick groaned. "Everything takes so long. Meanwhile this poor girl lies in a morgue, unclaimed."

"They're doing the best they can," I reminded him.

"I hope the family can identify this Wally person." Derrick stared out the office windows at the passersby on the street. "One can't help but wonder if he had anything to do with her death."

"Or can at least enlighten us as to why she came to Newport. By all appearances, she traveled here alone." Jesse absently twirled his derby on one finger. "That's not typical of a young woman of her background—judging by how she was dressed."

"Not at all," I agreed. "Unless we're mistaken about her background, but I don't believe so. The fabrics, the tailoring—clothing like that isn't easily come by. Jesse, you'll let us know when you learn more?"

"Be assured I will."

Jesse telephoned over to the *Messenger* the following afternoon, asking me to come to the police station.

"Leaving yet again?" Stanley Sheppard said when I'd made my way to the front office. I didn't imagine the sardonic tinge to his voice, but I also didn't take offense, as I knew none had been intended. He had grown accustomed to my leaving at odd times during the day to follow a story, often with no notice or explanation of my errand. But just as I trusted his instincts as an editor-in-chief, he trusted mine as a reporter. Gruffness was simply his way, and we had both grown comfortable with it.

"I'm meeting Jesse Whyte at the police station." I pinned my straw boater into place as I crossed to the street door. "When Derrick returns, would you tell him where I've gone?"

"Do I look like your private messenger, Miss Cross?" He sat back in his rolling office chair, snatching up the pipe that always sat in its holder at a corner of his desk, though he never lit it inside the building. "Did Detective Whyte at least give you any hint why he wants to see you?"

I could see by the gleam in his eye that he was as keen as I to know more about what had happened to young Lillian Fahey. "I'm assuming it's about the drowned woman, but I wouldn't expect him to discuss police business over the telephone."

"No, not with our intrepid Gayla Prescott listening in."

"That's not true." I sprang to the defense of Newport's main daytime operator, whom I had known all my life. But even I knew better to discuss anything over the wires I wished to be kept secret. "I don't know that she listens in, exactly. She's just ensuring the proper connections are made."

That brought an amused chuckle to Mr. Sheppard's lips.

"You know, you're downright handsome when you smile," I teased.

He used his pipe to point the way to the door. "Get along to your appointment, Miss Cross." Before the door closed behind me, I heard, "I hope you learn something of value." The sarcasm had faded from his voice.

When I arrived on Marlborough Street, I discovered an older man sitting opposite Jesse at his desk in the large station room. They appeared to be deep in discussion, both leaning toward each other across the desktop. In the general din of voices, telephones, and typewriters, I could not hear any of their conversation. I wondered why Gifford Myers wasn't with them; a brief glance around the room found him at his own desk. His gaze met mine, and his lips turned downward.

As I approached Jesse's desk, he came to his feet, as did his visitor. Of short stature, with thinning, curling gray hair and round spectacles sitting halfway down a fleshy triangle of a nose, the individual bobbed his head in greeting.

I saw that Jesse had already moved an additional chair before his desk—perhaps Gifford Myers had sat there previously, vacating when he saw me enter the room?—and now he motioned for me to sit. Once the men had resumed their seats, Jesse gestured at the man in the spectacles. "Emma Cross, this is Eben Fahey. He traveled up from Long Island this morning and arrived here about an hour ago."

I couldn't help replying with a gasp. "Oh!" Then, recovering, I offered my hand. "You're Lillian Fahey's father?" He shook my hand lightly and nodded. "I'm so sorry for your loss, sir."

"Yes, thank you." A faint Irish accent laced his words—no, when he spoke again I realized he was Scottish. "I understand it was you who discovered my daughter, Miss Cross. In the water."

I glanced down at my handbag and nodded before meeting his solemn gaze. "Yes, sir. Has Jesse told you all the details?"

"That she was found near an estate . . ." He frowned, as if trying to remember.

"Beacon Rock," I supplied. "Yes. I was there for a dinner party and happened to wander outside for some air."

"The detective says the house is some distance above the water, and yet you heard her."

I felt a moment's hesitation. Was he about to accuse me of something? I gripped my handbag and remained calm. "I heard . . . something . . . that didn't sound right. I can't quite explain it, but I felt compelled to go down to the dock to investigate."

"Thank goodness you did, Miss Cross." He reached for my hand again and this time held it fast. "If not for you, my Lillian might have drifted out to sea, never to be seen again. And I might never have known what happened to her. That is why I told the detective I wished to meet you, to thank you personally."

"There is no need to thank me, Mr. Fahey. I'm only sorry we weren't able to help her."

"I simply don't understand what she was doing so far from home." He spoke to both Jesse and me now. "She was not the kind of girl to run off, especially without telling me. She had never done anything like that before. And that photograph . . . I don't know what to think about it."

"You didn't know she'd visited the photographer?" When Mr. Fahey shook his head, Jesse absently placed the palm of his hand on a cardboard folder on his desk, which must have contained the photo.

"Do you know who Wally is, Mr. Fahey?" I asked.

He shook his head. "I've no idea. She would not have kept company with a man without my knowledge. Not my Lillian."

Yet apparently, she had. How well had this man known his daughter?

"Are you completely certain, Mr. Fahey?" I gently prodded.

"As certain as I can be." He stared down at his hands. "Since her mother died, she and I have been—*had* been—very close. She never attempted to deceive me before. Why would she now?"

Because Lillian Fahey, at eighteen, had no longer been a little girl. Because when young women met intriguing men—*designing* men—they often believed or were led to believe that secrecy was best, to prevent families from interfering. Such had been the case with my cousin Consuelo several years ago, when her mother's plans for Consuelo's marriage had driven the distraught girl into the arms of a dangerous scoundrel. Had something similar happened to Lillian?

Wally darling obviously existed, had been part of Lillian's life in some way. "Are you sure she couldn't have met someone you were unaware of?"

He held up his hands. "Where? When? She was rarely from home. She helped me with my work. A brilliant girl, my Lilli—" The rest choked off, and he buried his face in his hands.

I reached over to pat his shoulder. When he raised his face and seemed more composed, I asked, "She was rarely from home. But were you also always home?"

"Why, no. Business sometimes took me to meetings. And

I am a lecturer at New York University, twice a week. But my housekeeper would have been there."

Ah. I didn't say it, but housekeepers could sometimes be persuaded to keep secrets, especially by motherless girls. "May I ask what your profession is, Mr. Fahey?"

"I am an engineer, specializing in aerodynamics as it relates to the speed of mechanical objects."

"I see. And you said your daughter helped with your work?"

"She is—was—a brilliant mathematician. She often helped me with my formulae."

"And how do you apply your formulas, if I might ask?"

"These days, I work mostly with watercraft. My services are in high demand for racing yachts and I often collaborate with Nat Herreshoff."

My gaze darted to Jesse. He had suddenly gone as pale as I felt. Nathanael Herreshoff designed many of the racing yachts belonging to New York Yacht Club members, including the *Columbia*.

Chapter 4

Two uniformed officers arrived at Jesse's desk to escort Mr. Fahey to Newport Hospital. The time had come to officially identify the body.

"Mr. Fahey," I said, coming to my feet beside him, "if you wish, I'll accompany you." He looked so forlorn, so grief stricken, I hoped to be of some comfort to him. But the suggestion took him aback.

"Goodness, no, Miss Cross. You've done enough for my Lillian and for me. I would not subject you to any more unpleasantness."

"Truly, sir, it would not be an imposition." I reached out, my fingertips lightly touching his sleeve. "No one should have to go through this alone."

He shook his head, letting his eyes fall closed. "No. I shall be all right. I understand you are a reporter. All I would ask of you now, Miss Cross, is to be kind to my daughter in what you write about her."

"I will, Mr. Fahey, I promise." I shook his hand again. "And I'll help find the truth of what happened to her."

He started to say something, but then only nodded and walked away with the two policemen.

I resumed my seat and asked Jesse a quick question, one I could not ask in front of Lillian Fahey's grieving father. "Had she been interfered with?"

"No." He looked away, clearly uncomfortable discussing the unseemly topic with me, but willing to give me an answer. "The coroner found no evidence of any form of violation."

Lillian Fahey hadn't suffered that indignity, at least. Seconds later, Detective Myers appeared at Jesse's desk. He flopped down on the chair beside me. "Poor man. I feel for him. He's simply not up to facing the truth about his daughter."

"And what truth is that, Myers?" Jesse raised an eyebrow in mock curiosity.

Mr. Myers glanced around the station room, seeming to search for something or someone. A door opened across the way and Chief of Police Rogers stepped out. He held a sheaf of papers in one hand and strode briskly in our direction. His features were set, his jaw squared. Detective Myers watched his progress with a satisfied air. When the police chief reached us, he tapped the papers with his other hand.

"Miss Cross, Whyte," he said in greeting, "Myers and I have been going over the evidence, including the girl's father's statement. And we've reached a conclusion."

I knew by Detective Myers's nod that this *conclusion* they had reached coincided with the *truth* he mentioned moments ago. I was not wrong.

"Lillian Fahey appears to have been a misguided girl believing herself in love with a man who apparently didn't share her sentiments." Chief Rogers gave a decidedly uncomfortable cough and cleared his throat. "It's a delicate subject, an unpleasant one." His gaze landed on me; I gestured for him to continue. "From what we can gather, it seemed she traveled up to Newport to be with this individual, who instead broke off the attachment. An ungentlemanly act to be sure. One that prompted Miss Fahey to throw herself from the ferry into the bay."

It took me several moments to digest this. The look on Jesse's face told me this scenario left him dumbfounded as well. I said, "And how did you reach this very specific conclusion?"

A muscle in Chief Rogers's cheek bounced in clear annoyance. It was instinctual, as the man didn't appreciate when I or any civilian questioned him. Still, he opened the folder on Jesse's desk to reveal a stack of papers. Secured to the topmost one with a Gem bent-wire clip was the photograph of Lillian, inscribed to *Wally darling*. "Isn't it obvious? She had given him that photograph as a keepsake, which he returned when he broke off their association. Otherwise, why would it have been in her possession?"

"She was still wearing the ring," I reminded him. We now knew one of those initials on the tiny hearts, the *F*, stood for Fahey. But what about the *R*? And did Wally stand for Walter, Wallace, or perhaps something less common such as Walden or Walford?

"Perhaps in their quarrel the ring went forgotten." The police chief gave a shrug. "Or the gentleman didn't ask for it back."

Detective Myers came to his feet. "This is the most likely theory."

"But still only a theory," Jesse said dryly. "Speculation based on very little evidence."

"Are you saying someone murdered this girl?" Chief Rogers challenged. "A young woman unknown in Newport, with no enemies her father could name?"

"Just because Mr. Fahey couldn't name any enemies doesn't

mean they didn't exist," Jesse persisted. He kept his voice down, but his insistence nonetheless carried force. "He didn't know about this beau either, did he?"

"Whyte," Chief Rogers said with feigned patience, "why would a man wish to kill an innocent young girl? Who knows why he broke off their understanding? Perhaps his family objected to her. Perhaps he realized they simply didn't suit. I understand she was something of a bluestocking, a female intellectual, according to her father's description." I nodded at that, as Mr. Fahey had indicated as much to me as well. But my own experience had taught me that not all men feared or objected to intelligent women. Chief Rogers went on. "Having her hopes dashed more than likely sent her overboard—in fact, I'm sure of it. Women are fragile creatures—if you'll pardon me for saying so, Miss Cross. But it's true. They are easily overset and thrown off balance, so to speak."

Anger made my fingertips tremble. "Women are not as fragile as that, not by half. I've certainly proven time and again that I'm not."

"You are an exception to your sex, Miss Cross." Chief Rogers conferred silently with Detective Myers, who nodded his agreement with a reluctant twist of his mouth.

"The only exceptional thing about me is that I refuse to allow myself to be held back." I came to my feet, prompting Jesse to do the same. To the rest of the stationhouse we probably looked like four amiable people about to end their discussion and go their separate ways. But I seethed so hard my stays pierced my sides, and if Jesse held his jaw any tighter it would shatter. Very quietly, using every shred of patience I possessed to hold my features steady, I said, "Is this because she was found by Beacon Rock?"

"What do you mean?" Detective Myers demanded before Chief Rogers had a chance to speak.

MURDER AT BEACON ROCK   43

I stepped closer to the two men. "Did the Morgans ask you to close this case quickly to avoid the publicity? To prevent gawkers going by in boats to view the scene where she was found?" Or, I thought, was there yet another reason—one much closer to home, and to the truth of how Lillian Fahey ended up in the water that night. Did she fall from the ferry, from somewhere closer to shore—or from the shore itself?

The chief puffed up his chest, straining the brass buttons of his captain's uniform coat. "I not only resent your implications, Miss Cross, but I could have you brought up on charges of interfering in an investigation."

"I'm doing no such thing," I said, crossing my fingers in a fold of my skirt. "I'm simply asking why this case is being rushed to its conclusion."

"Miss Cross, think about it." Detective Myers paused, presumably to allow me to do just that. I tapped my foot and waited. He said, "Even if this beau of hers pushed her from the ferry, he would have done so out of frustration, not true malice. We know how spurned women can be. Especially the type of woman who would pursue a man across many miles." He shook his head and tsked. "Perhaps he intended only to push her away—to put distance between them—and pushed too hard. Even if that occurred, it's unlikely he'd ever kill again. It was a crime of passion, an accident, really, and not what one would call murder."

"You certainly have this all figured out, don't you?" My throat closed and my vision blurred. The fury coursing through me ran hot and cold as my resolve hardened. The chief's next words cemented my intentions.

"We only included you in this discussion out of curtesy to Mr. Andrews. Thought we'd toss you the scoop on the story. I see that was a mistake." The chief tugged his coat to straighten it and retrieved the papers. "Good day, Miss Cross. As for you, Whyte, you're to let this drop. We have our answers."

Stiffly, Jesse replied, "Sir."

Jesse wouldn't let the matter drop. And neither would I.

After leaving the *Messenger* later that afternoon, I went the long way around the southern portion of the island. Rather than taking the interior roads that cut across to my home on Ocean Avenue, I drove my buggy along the shore of Narragansett Bay and traveled along Harrison Avenue until I reached Beacon Rock.

Daytime revealed what I could not see the night before: the northward peninsula across Brenton Cove that housed Fort Adams and, beyond it, the rolling, misty green shore of Jamestown. I could also better appreciate the lovely terrain created by Frederick Law Olmsted—premier gardener to the Four Hundred—but, given my current errand, I had little time to appreciate it.

I had called ahead, so when I arrived in the forecourt, a groom waited to secure my carriage and a footman escorted me through the courtyard. We crossed the spacious central hall into the dining room and exited to the rear terrace, where Elizabeth Morgan and Ruth Delafield greeted me. Mrs. Morgan bade me sit with them at the garden table on the covered veranda.

From this north-facing vantage point, all of Brenton Cove and Newport Harbor beckoned with a dazzling display of crisp white sails against a backdrop of deep blues capped by lacy foam. The clouds above us were kissed golden by the afternoon light. Without asking if I desired any, Mrs. Morgan poured me a cup of tea, handed me the cup and saucer, and offered me a tiered tray of petit fours. I wished for neither, but I accepted out of politeness.

"Thank you for seeing me on such short notice," I said after a sip. I had hoped to speak to Mrs. Morgan alone, but I couldn't very well ask Mrs. Delafield to leave us. Both women wore tea gowns in lovely pastel prints embellished with cascades of ivory or white lace. Mrs. Morgan's hair had been swept up and piled in a loose chignon at the top of her head, the curling tendrils escaping the pretty little silk hat and sheer veil she wore. Ruth Delafield, in deference to her younger age, wore the front of her hair pulled back and held with clips, while the back had been left to spill in dark, glossy waves between her shoulder blades. A casual style but perfectly acceptable when having informal tea with friends.

"You're quite welcome, Miss Cross," Mrs. Morgan said graciously. "You happened to catch us at home and on our own this afternoon. My other guests—our Morgan cousins and Mrs. Carnegie—are on their respective yachts. And my husband and some of the *Columbia* crew are off somewhere in town, overseeing the dispersal of some incoming supplies."

"I see. Those men who helped remove the body from the water last night—are they crew members?" I had wondered who they were at the time, as they had not been present at dinner, nor did they appear to be dressed as servants.

Both women flinched at my mention of *the body*, but Elizabeth Morgan quickly recovered. "Yes. Some of the crew are staying here at the house for when my husband and his cousin take the *Columbia* on practice runs. They're quite accomplished sailors, and strong swimmers, thank goodness." She glanced out over the water. "At any rate, seeing you is the least I could do after the shock that occurred here last night."

"That's why I've come, actually." This drew from her a flash of wariness. She darted a glance at Mrs. Delafield. I saw immediately that neither wished to discuss last night beyond what we had already said, but I plunged on. "I've just come from the police department."

"Oh?" With a tilt of her head, Mrs. Delafield stirred her

tiny silver spoon around inside her teacup, making little tin-kling sounds. "As a reporter, we must presume?"

"Yes, partly," I admitted. "But there's more to it. I wish to know the truth of what happened to Lillian Fahey." At their puzzled frowns, I explained, "That is the deceased woman's name. Lillian Fahey, and she was eighteen years old. From Long Island."

Mrs. Morgan's face became shuttered, as if she didn't wish to learn more. Mrs. Delafield's plump lips pouted in distaste.

"The police have already decided to close the case," I continued. "They're calling it a suicide."

"Oh, dear. That *is* dreadful. The poor child." Mrs. Morgan lifted the veil away from her face and raised her cup to her lips. Upon returning it to its saucer, she eyed the petit fours before selecting one. I noticed her hands had been freshly manicured, probably that morning.

"I don't believe it was suicide," I said, ignoring the confection on my own plate. "At least, I don't believe there is enough evidence at this point to support such a conclusion."

Mrs. Delafield remained silent, but Mrs. Morgan glanced up at me with a look of surprise. "No? I should think the police know what they're about."

I very nearly laughed. *Yes*, I wished to say, *they know what they are about, but it isn't necessarily finding the truth.* Aloud, I said, "As a woman, I find their theories lack the ring of truth."

Mrs. Delafield wrinkled her nose in puzzlement. "What do you mean, as a woman?"

"Based on the photograph found in her possession, they suppose Miss Fahey to have been disappointed by a suitor, and in her distress she threw herself from the evening ferry."

"It's possible, isn't it?" The younger woman bit into a petit four with a flash of her even, white teeth.

"It could be possible, yes." I watched her chew the morsel

of chocolate and raspberry. "But so could several other possibilities."

"Such as?" Mrs. Morgan demanded airily. We might have been discussing drapery or wallpaper options.

"Murder," I told her bluntly. The color leached from her face. I decided not to spare them further unpleasantness. "Her father, you see, is Eben Fahey. Are either of you familiar with him?"

"The name *is* vaguely familiar," Mrs. Delafield said with a frown. "Who is he?"

"Mr. Fahey is an engineer who specializes in the field of aerodynamics. As in racing yachts. He has worked with the designer responsible for the *Columbia* and perhaps even your steamer yachts."

Mrs. Morgan stared at me for several long seconds. "Are you implying there is a link between this girl's death and . . . and *us*?"

"I don't know, Mrs. Morgan. Could there be?"

"Of course not." She pushed her cup and saucer away from her. "None of us last night had any idea who that girl could be. Or why she had come to Newport. Or how she drowned. Isn't that so, Ruth?"

Mrs. Delafield concurred with a nod, her lips pinched.

I studied the still-uneaten confection on my plate. "Then why were the police encouraged to close the case as soon as possible?"

"Miss Cross, if the police are satisfied with the conclusion they have drawn, why shouldn't you be?" Judging by Mrs. Morgan's tone, I half expected her to have me escorted out, but she went on. "Surely you see that raising such doubts will cast a long shadow over the racing world, the New York Yacht Club, the *Columbia* and its continuing future as a champion vessel, and on our home here at Beacon Rock. What purpose can it serve to put such a stigma on so important an event as the America's Cup Races, and yachting in general? I do not need to remind you that the sport of sailing brings untold dollars to Newport each summer. Causing a stir cannot bring the poor girl back."

"So you admit the police have been stifled in their efforts." I didn't wait for her answer. "Lillian Fahey deserves justice, and I had hoped that, as a woman, you would wish to see justice served."

She flattened her lips into a thin line. In that instant, a voice called to us from inside the house. "Lizzy! Oh, Lizzy, I'm here to whisk you and Ruth away to the *Dungeness*. Cocktails on the top deck?" With those last two exuberant words, Lucy Carnegie bustled out onto the patio. She stopped short upon spotting me. "Oh, good afternoon, Miss Cross. How are you today?"

"Quite well, Mrs. Carnegie," I replied stiffly, "all things considered."

"Well, I'm glad you're here. I shall whisk you all to the *Dungeness*. We can begin your tutorials in yachting this very day, Miss Cross."

"I'm afraid I cannot join you today." Elizabeth Morgan avoided Mrs. Carnegie's gaze by staring out at the view beyond the veranda.

"No, nor I," her younger friend concurred.

Mrs. Carnegie looked from me to the other two ladies, back and forth several times. A slight curl of her lips revealed that she sensed the tension between us, not that it was easy to miss. "Oh, come now, Lizzy. You too, Ruth. Don't be like that. What else can you have to do before the Astors' musicale tonight?"

"I don't know that I'm going to the musicale, Lucy," Elizabeth Morgan said with a petulant shrug.

"Don't know?" Mrs. Carnegie set her hands on her hips, once more projecting, somehow, a larger image than her actual five-foot stature. "What on earth has gotten into you?"

"A dead body, right here in our cove, Lucy. That's what." Mrs. Morgan crossed her arms over her bosom. Ruth Delafield pouted.

Mrs. Carnegie's face fell. "Oh. Yes, yes, of course. Don't think I've forgotten. After all, it was I who jumped in first to prevent the tide from taking the poor girl away again. But what good will it do to sit and brood over it? It won't bring the girl back." It struck me that Mrs. Carnegie had echoed Mrs. Morgan's very words. Could the Four Hundred dismiss a life so easily? "A distraction is what we need. And a musicale is just the thing."

"I'm afraid I've no heart for it." Mrs. Morgan slid her chair back and came to her feet. Ruth Delafield jumped up beside her, straightening the wide satin sash at the waistline of her tea gown. The two women linked arms. "Excuse us, please." With that, they went into the house.

Lucy Carnegie watched them go with a look of astonishment. "Well, I never. What's gotten into them?"

"I'm afraid I have," I confessed.

"How on earth did you do that?" As I gathered breath to respond, she held up the flat of her hand. "Wait, not yet. I still intend to convey you to the *Dungeness*. My oarsman is waiting in the skiff down at the dock. Shall we?"

Mrs. Carnegie conducted me on a brief tour of her beloved *Dungeness*. We passed through a parlor decorated in blues and beige, a dining room in green and gold, and two of its guest staterooms. Each rivaled rooms in houses like The Breakers and Marble House in ornateness. Next, she showed me the galley, where several-course meals were cooked on a regular basis, and even the engine room with its many pumps, valves, and pistons, quiet now with the vessel moored in Brenton Cove. We didn't enter the adjoining furnace room because, as Mrs. Carnegie declared, coal dust is all but impossible to remove from one's hems.

As I'd already had tea up at the house, I wasn't offered that type of refreshment. Instead, Lucy Carnegie led me aft of the main stack, where a long overhang provided cooling shade. There we sat side by side in chaise lounges and were brought champagne cocktails. I sipped mine tentatively, not wishing the spiritous bubbles to fuzz my brain. I gazed out at the other vessels anchored nearby: Edwin and Elizabeth Morgan's *May*; John and Fanny Morgan's private yacht *Corsair*, as well as the *Columbia,* which swayed gently on the waves closer to the boathouse. There were additional craft, none as large as either the *Corsair* or the *Dungeness,* but equally as posh. I assumed these belonged to the Delafields and perhaps Mr. Kerr. The rest, much more ordinary looking, perhaps belonged to members of the *Columbia*'s crew.

In due course, Mrs. Carnegie bade me tell her what I had said to upset Mrs. Morgan and Mrs. Delafield. She nodded as she listened. When I explained the police's theory, her face took on an angry shade of pink.

"Fools, if you ask me. Assuming women are as delicate as all that. Killing oneself over a man. Bah!"

"Not only that," I said, "but you saw her clothing. It was of good quality, yes, but also in the latest style of menswear for women. The jet-black adornments on the otherwise plain skirt and Eton jacket, the severe lines of the shirtwaist, even a necktie."

"What are you getting at?"

"Delicate women don't dress accordingly. Such fashion is for the independent minded. Women who value assertiveness and self-reliance. Her father described her as highly intelligent. She used to help him in his work."

Mrs. Carnegie sat up, swinging her feet from the chaise to the deck between us. "You believe she was murdered, don't you, Miss Cross?"

"I believe it's a possibility. Too much of one to allow the police to label her death a suicide and besmirch her character for all time."

"No, indeed. The truth must be revealed. Her death must be fully explained, if that is possible. She is owed that much." Mrs. Carnegie relaxed slightly, crossing one leather-booted ankle over the other. "You said she helped her father in his work. What work was that?"

When I told her, her eyes popped wide, but only for an instant.

"Do you know him?" I asked after a moment. "Perhaps he worked on improvements to this very boat?"

"Oh, no, not to my knowledge." She waved the notion away. "Although my captain might have consulted with him."

That struck me as odd. Mrs. Carnegie was involved in every aspect of yachting life, from the design details of the craft to the supplies and maintenance needed to keep her afloat, to the subtleties of the winds and currents in sailing her. I doubted the *Dungeness* could make so much as a vibration she could not decipher. Her expertise was part of the reason she had been admitted to the New York Yacht Club as a member in her own right. It seemed highly unlikely her captain made any decisions, or consulted with anyone, without her knowledge and approval.

I let it go for now and told her of the coroner's conclusion that Lillian hadn't been violated, which, if she had, could have driven her to take her own life. "But that was not the case," I said. "However, there was a man involved in her life, one she had apparently cared a great deal for."

Mrs. Carnegie had seen the photograph last night. Now I told her about the ring and the initials on each of its hearts. Once again, her eyes nearly bulged in their sockets and her mouth dropped open for an instant.

"An *R* you say?"

"An *R* and an *F*," I replied. "The *F* obviously being for Fahey."

Mrs. Carnegie set down her champagne coupe and sprang to her feet. "Miss Cross, I believe I might know who this Wally person is." Her agitation set my own nerves buzzing. "There is a man right here in our midst, one of the racing crew. His name is Wallace Rayburn."

Chapter 5

"I wish I could tell you more, Miss Cross." Mrs. Carnegie tugged her sun hat lower and ducked her chin to the breeze circling the cove. We were back in the skiff for the short row back to Beacon Rock, sitting beside each other at the rear of the small boat. If the oarsman heard our conversation, he gave no indication as he threw his shoulders into his task. "I'm afraid I didn't know Miss Fahey existed previous to last night, and I've had precious little interaction with Wallace Rayburn. If he and Miss Fahey had an understanding, he never mentioned it, or even hinted at it, in front of me."

"And one must allow that his name is merely a coincidence and that he had no acquaintance with Lillian," I mused, somewhat more to myself. "But it seems an unlikely coincidence."

"It does indeed." As we approached the *Bessie Rogers*, Mrs. Carnegie gestured to her oarsman, who made a subtle change in direction that swung us wide around the barque and to the boathouse steps. Apparently, Lucy Carnegie had no desire to revisit the scene of her attempted rescue last night.

Once on the dock, we stood and surveyed the waters of the cove that fed in from the bay. Mrs. Carnegie had gone uncharacteristically quiet. Then she cleared her throat. "I should have mentioned this right away, but I only just remembered."

"Yes?"

"Wallace Rayburn was one of the men who brought Miss Fahey out of the water."

Despite my astonishment over this bit of news, I took a moment to consider. "Neither of those men showed much emotion at the time," I said. "At least no more than the rest of us. I wouldn't have thought either of them knew her."

"No, but if Wallace Rayburn killed her, he wouldn't want to show any recognition. However, if he *did* kill her, it must have been quite a shock to see her again so soon."

"Indeed . . ." I sighed as I mulled this over. "We assumed the tide brought her into the cove." I added my hand to the brim of my hat to shield my eyes from the sun. "The police believe she fell or jumped from the last outgoing ferry. But what if she didn't fall from a boat at all?"

"You mean she was pushed in from somewhere along the shore?"

"There are plenty of places where it could have happened. A dock, a wharf. Along the harbor's seawall." I turned full around to gaze up at the Grecian-inspired house perched imperiously upon Beacon Rock. "Perhaps from this very place."

She pressed her hand to my wrist. "Miss Cross, perhaps I spoke overhastily. I do not wish to implicate a young man simply due to the misfortune of his initials. When you spoke of the *R*, that, together with the first name, Wally, made me immediately think of Wallace Rayburn. But I could be entirely wrong."

"You could be," I readily agreed. "And I have no desire to

see an innocent man accused, either. But it is a start, a place to begin exploring Lillian Fahey's life. I don't believe in coincidences, Mrs. Carnegie. Names, initials, places, occupations . . . All lead here to Beacon Rock and the yachting concerns that brought you, the Morgans, and the others here. And Lillian Fahey. She might have been anywhere in Narragansett Bay, but she was found here, just as the rest of you convened to discuss the races. It's too significant to ignore."

"But we will proceed with caution?"

It didn't escape me that she had used the word *we*. I had acquired "helpers" in the past, and I must be careful now not to endanger this woman. "Of course. I always do."

At the top of the staircase, I said, "Mrs. Morgan won't be pleased to see me again."

"She probably won't know we're here. Anyway, you're with me now. I shall protect you from Lizzy's wrath. Come."

As we had planned on our way across the cove, we slipped into the house through the servants' wing, and were stopped almost immediately by a young maid. "Pardon, but may I help you ladies? Surely you must be lost."

"No, we'd like to speak with the housekeeper, if we might," Mrs. Carnegie said, affecting an imperious air. This had the effect of turning the maid milky white. She bobbed a curtsey and scuttled away. Soon, an older woman took her place and invited us into her parlor.

"What might I do for you, Mrs. Carnegie?" The woman held her hands folded at her waist and spoke with a blend of familiarity and deference.

Mrs. Carnegie got right to the point, without introducing me. "Mrs. Gage, are you familiar with Wallace Rayburn? He's staying here."

"Why, yes. He's bunking with one of his yachting mates here in our servants' quarters. Several of our footmen have had to squeeze into two rooms to accommodate the crew. I suggested they stay in town, but those were Mr. Morgan's orders."

"Is Mr. Rayburn here now, or any of his associates?" Mrs. Carnegie asked.

"They left with Mr. Morgan and Mr. Kerr some time ago. I don't know when to expect them back."

Mrs. Carnegie continued her questions in a blunt manner. "Has he had any visitors?"

"Mr. Rayburn?" The woman frowned. "Not to my knowledge."

"No young women have come to see him?"

"Heavens, no. That would not be allowed under this roof. If Mr. Rayburn or any other employee of the Morgans wishes to associate with women, he shall have to do so elsewhere."

Mrs. Carnegie and I traded a glance. What now? I stepped forward. "Has any young woman been to the house in recent days, to see anyone? To visit one of your maids, perhaps?"

"There was a young Portuguese girl here on Friday last, with her brother, delivering flowers for Mrs. Morgan's tea soiree."

I shook my head. That would have been several days ago. Lillian died in the hours right before we discovered her in the water. And Lillian certainly hadn't been of Portuguese descent, nor did she have a brother. Still, "Can you describe this girl?"

"Certainly." She spoke as if I had suggested she had been careless in making note of who came and went at Beacon Rock. "Dark hair and eyes, pretty in that southern European way, petite."

Definitely not Lillian Fahey. Just to be thorough, I asked, "Have any other deliveries been brought by women?"

The housekeeper shook her head. "No. Most of our deliveries are brought by men. I'd remember any other females. Now, if that's all, I must return to my duties."

"Yes, of course," Lucy Carnegie said. "Thank you, Mrs. Gage. If you do remember any other female visitors who came in the past day or so, or if any of your staff mentions one, please let me know."

The woman nodded, curtseyed, and went on her way. Mrs. Carnegie and I turned to each other. She said, "That doesn't mean Lillian Fahey wasn't here, does it?"

"No. It means if she was here, she came by stealth, and left the same way."

We made our way back outside and onto the main drive-way, and from there to the service drive. It was used to access the lower gardens beneath the bridge, and to bring deliveries to the service entrance. It also led to the stable block. We made our way down and walked along it. I strolled with my head down, my gaze sweeping the ground, searching for any evidence of Lillian Fahey. But what could there be?

"Her purse," I mused aloud.

"I'm sorry?"

"Her purse, Mrs. Carnegie. It was not on her person when we found her. If only we could find it."

"Probably washed out to sea or at the bottom of the bay."

"Yes, probably." But I continued to search. I guided us toward the edge of the promontory that overlooked the boathouse and the waters of Brenton Cove. "Someone could certainly fall to their death from here. Or be pushed." After we searched through the shrubbery and hung as far over the edge as we dared to see if Miss Fahey's handbag perhaps clung to the cliff face, I straightened and turned about. "We should speak to the gatekeeper. He might know something."

But the gatekeeper had nothing to add. He had seen no one come through the gates, female or otherwise, who had not been accounted for on the Morgans' guest list or the housekeeper's expected deliveries.

"She could have come by boat," I said as we made our way back up the drive. "That would actually be likeliest, wouldn't it, that she and Mr. Rayburn met down at the dock rather than anywhere near the house. She would probably have sent a message ahead first."

"Or perhaps it was his idea to meet at the dock," Mrs. Carnegie said after a moment's reflection. "Especially if he wished to dispatch her quickly and easily."

I couldn't help grinning. When Mrs. Carnegie inquired as to what was so funny, I said, "For someone who doesn't wish to incriminate anyone, you certainly have a way with words."

We both turned serious as we returned to the stairs leading down to the dock. "You needn't walk me down, Miss Cross." She gazed out at the lowering afternoon sun, a fiery reflection in the bay to the west of us. To the east, the sky was just beginning to turn that shade of lavender that hails the coming of evening. "I'm sure you're eager to be home."

"I wish to have another look around the *Bessie Rogers*, so yes, I'll walk down with you."

Mrs. Carnegie's oarsman sat beside the boathouse, looking as content as if he sat comfortably in his own parlor. He spared us nary a glance at our approach, but did take up the oars from the deck of the little craft and slip them into the rowlocks. Mrs. Carnegie held up a hand to indicate she wasn't quite ready to leave and followed me onto the *Bessie Rogers*.

Several minutes later, I leaned against the main mast. "Nothing unusual," I admitted with a sigh. Perhaps, after all, Lillian Fahey fell from the ferry, and no foul play had been involved.

"Perhaps the boathouse," Mrs. Carnegie suggested, and started in that direction. I hurried to catch up to her.

"I hope it isn't kept locked."

"No, they never lock it. There's nothing to steal, really, and the Morgans wish their friends to know they're always welcome to stop here. There's a telephone that rings up at the main house."

"Is there?" My mind began to race. "Perhaps Miss Fahey arrived and rang up to the house to let Mr. Rayburn know she was here. That could account for no one having seen her arrival, or their rendezvous, for that matter." Another thought doused that theory. "But then someone would have spoken to her."

"Perhaps Mr. Rayburn himself answered the call. He and the other crewmen *are* staying in the servants' quarters. Or perhaps one of his mates answered."

"I do wish they were at hand."

The main interior of the boathouse held a large sofa and several easy chairs, all in hunter green leather and accessorized with dark-stained federal tables featuring the ball and claw feet so prevalent in Newport's furniture making. A small fireplace surprised me, as I hadn't noticed a chimney outside. Then I realized it was only for show. The estate being used only in the summer months, there would never be a need for a warming fire. Above a solid oak mantel, a painting displayed a bright scene of yachts at sea. I recognized the *Corsair* and even the *Dungeness*. Several other craft surrounded them. I didn't recognize the artist's name and supposed the Morgans wouldn't wish to put one of their treasures in an unlocked boathouse. Still, the work was of good quality and showed off the artist's considerable skill.

I allowed myself only a few moments to study the images

before turning my attention to the rest of the room. It was obviously cleaned on a regular basis, as not a speck of dust marred any surface. I opened the door to a storage room, filled with boating supplies such as extra lines and ropes. Folded sails occupied an entire case of shelving. I discovered lanterns and flares in a cabinet. The dim light of only one small window broke the monotony of the pine board walls. A pair of wide double doors led back outside, daylight slipping in through the minute gap where the doors met. The tide slapped against them, and I surmised this must give access to the slip where the Morgans kept a small boat they used to shuttle back and forth to their anchored yacht.

Finding no evidence of there having been a scuffle in this room, nor a reason Lillian Fahey would have entered in the first place, I returned to the main room. Three large windows flooded the space with late afternoon light, gilding Mrs. Carnegie's silhouette as she walked here and there, stopping to study the items on a tabletop, a lamp on a sideboard, the volumes that filled a bookcase.

"I wish I knew what it was we were looking for," she said with her back to me. She bent lower over the bottom shelves of a corner piece.

So did I. I thought again about Lillian's missing handbag, which could very well be in the water, forever lost. Her hat as well, now that I thought about it. The photograph had adhered itself to the wet lining of her pocket and thus stayed in place. What else might she have had on her that could have come loose in a struggle?

A hat pin; a brooch, bracelet, or necklace; a bit of ribbon—but no, her outfit had had braided velvet trim, but no sign of ribbon that I had noticed. Her shirt, either. Her gloves had remained on her hands. It seemed hopeless, finding whatever traces Lillian Fahey might have left behind. That was, of course, if she had ever been here at all.

*   *   *

I stood on the dock, waving to Mrs. Carnegie as she made her way back to the *Dungeness*. A sense of fruitlessness engulfed me. Our searching had turned up nothing to refute the notion of Lillian Fahey having taken her own life. Nothing—except my adamant belief to the contrary based on her father's description of her character and the fact that she had come to Newport donned in the latest menswear fashion, which to me suggested an independent-minded and assertive woman.

Was that enough to erase the blemish of suicide? I was determined that it would be.

The sun nearly touched the horizon over Jamestown, and soon the long blue shadows would be swallowed by darkness. I knew Ocean Avenue as well as my own reflection in a mirror, but even I didn't relish the thought of maneuvering the sinuous road at night. And Nanny, my housekeeper, friend, and surrogate grandmother, would begin to worry if I didn't make an appearance soon.

Those thoughts sent me to the steps, but as I set my foot on the bottom one, someone hailed from the water.

"Ahoy!"

I turned to see a single-masted cutter, perhaps fifty feet in length, drifting toward the pier. A man stood at the bow, waving his hat at me, while the three-man crew steered her in. Moments later the craft drifted close to the *Bessie Rogers*, and the man jumped from one deck to the other. He wore gray pinstriped trousers and a dark blue coat with white piping along the lapels. He carried his straw boater as he took the barque in two long strides and leaped onto the dock.

"Hallo there, Miss Cross."

With the sunset behind him and his face in shadow, it took me a moment to recognize Tyrone Kerr, the youngest member of the previous evening's get together, Derrick and me aside. "How do you do today, Mr. Kerr?"

"I'm well, thanks." He gestured to the sailboat, which had turned about and was making its way back to the harbor. "Fine vessel, wouldn't you say? I'm thinking of buying her. Not up to the America's Cup standards, but she's perfect for the gentlemen's racing circuit here and across the pond. I intend to pilot her myself."

"I see. She's a handsome cutter."

"I see you know your boats, Miss Cross, despite not being a sailor." His grin let me know he was teasing and not holding my lack of sea legs against me.

"One of our pastimes as children was sitting on the piers along the harbor and identifying each boat that passed us by. But if you were to quiz me on more than basic shapes, I'm afraid I wouldn't do very well," I added with a rueful chuckle.

"I wouldn't dream of quizzing you, Miss Cross." He slid a cigarette case from his inner coat pocket and flipped it open. He held it out to me, but I declined with a shake of my head. He selected a cigarette for himself and struck a match on the side of the case to light it. "That was an awful thing, last night. Terrible way to end the evening." A stream of smoke accompanied the words. "Poor Elizabeth and Edwin."

Poor Lillian Fahey, I thought, but kept it to myself. The Four Hundred were typically so caught up in the minutiae of their own lives, they often didn't extend much empathy to those outside their circles. Still, I wondered . . .

"Have you an acquaintance with Eben Fahey, Mr. Kerr?"

"Eben Fahey? The engineer?"

"Then you at least know of him. But are you acquainted with him?"

"Yes, we've met in New York, at the yacht club headquarters, a time or two. But otherwise, no, I can't claim to know him well. Why?"

"Because it was his daughter we found in the water last night."

"Good grief, it can't be!"

I nodded. "Her name was Lillian."

He blew out a breath and wiped a coat sleeve across his forehead. Almost absently, he set his boater on his head and took a long drag from his cigarette. "I can't believe it. That's awfully coincidental, isn't it? I mean, here we are discussing the cup races, and the daughter of one of the very men whose innovations make it possible for us to win . . ." He trailed off, his features contorting with shocked disbelief. He turned and began walking until he reached one of the benches on either side of the boathouse door. He sank onto it. I followed and sat beside him. On this side of the dock, facing away from the bay, the shadows were fast deepening.

"Yes, it *is* frightfully coincidental, Mr. Kerr. It makes me question the conclusion that her death was an accident—or the suicide the police have come to believe."

"A suicide? No, surely not. Here, in Newport? Why no, I'd never believe it." He spoke as if nothing unfortunate or tragic could ever occur here, in Rhode Island's beautiful City by the Sea. Yet I knew better. Though suicide might not be as common an occurrence, murder was another matter altogether.

"I don't believe it either," I told him. "Not suicide. Tell me, had you ever met her?"

"No," he said without pause. "She never accompanied her father to the yacht club when I was there."

I let the silence stretch for several moments, allowing Mr. Kerr his private thoughts, before asking, "How well do you know Wallace Rayburn?"

"Rayburn?" The question apparently startled him. "Why?"

"Because we've reason to believe he and Lillian Fahey had been acquainted. Would you know anything about that?"

"I'm afraid not. But I'm not the right person to ask, Miss Cross. He and I aren't in the same circle, you see. He's more of a . . ." Again, he trailed off, leaving the thought unfinished. He raised his cigarette to his lips.

I surmised he meant that Wallace Rayburn, as a member of the *Columbia*'s crew, was more of a servant than an acquaintance of the men who were financing the next Cup challenge. But I supplied a different term. "More of an employee?"

"Yes, that." He nodded his agreement. "And Rayburn is a quiet type. Keeps to himself, for the most part. But if he did know this woman, Lillian Fahey, what then?"

"It raises certain questions, doesn't it?" I watched the smoke from his cigarette spiral in gray curls against the sky. "Such as, why did he show no recognition when he helped take her out of the water? How did he remain so emotionless?"

"Perhaps he didn't know her, then."

"Perhaps."

He turned a little toward me. "What makes you think he did?"

"The evidence found on her person pointed to a man with the initials *WR*. The police believe, and I concur, that she came to Newport to see this man, and that she died as a result."

He studied me a moment. "But you don't agree with much else the police have concluded, do you?"

"No, Mr. Kerr, I don't. I don't think Lillian Fahey killed herself over a failed relationship."

"And you believe Rayburn is involved."

MURDER AT BEACON ROCK   65

"I don't know. That's why I'd like to speak with him, see what he has to say."

A frown formed beneath the brim of his hat. "Why? What's it to you, Miss Cross? Why not let the police handle it?"

"I told you. They believe it was a suicide, and I don't. Not without further proof one way or the other. Perhaps it's my reporter's instincts that won't let the matter drop. Perhaps it's a kinship all women share, prompting us to do right by one another when the proper channels fail us."

"It's that important to you." He made this pronouncement quietly, in a tone that suggested he respected my determination, even if he didn't wholly agree with it.

"It is. So can you tell me anything about Wallace Rayburn? Had he been acting strangely lately? Especially yesterday."

"No, not that I noticed. We were aboard the *Columbia* in the morning, though we didn't take her out."

"What about later in the day? Was he at Beacon Rock? Or did he leave the premises?"

"Are you asking if I can provide him with an alibi?"

I nodded.

"I'm afraid I can't, Miss Cross. Since the *Columbia* stayed moored all day, the crew had free time in the afternoon. I couldn't tell you what he did or where he went between that morning and when he came running onto this dock and jumped in to retrieve that girl's body."

I came to my feet. "I've kept you long enough. I'm sure the Morgans will begin to wonder what has become of their guest. Good evening, Mr. Kerr."

"Wait, I'll escort you up." He stood and offered me his arm. We climbed the steps in silence, me in the lead, pausing a time or two to catch our breath from the steep ascent. At the top, he walked me to my carriage, still waiting for me on the circular drive. "If you like, I'll arrange for you to speak with Rayburn. How's tomorrow?"

"Tomorrow will do nicely, Mr. Kerr. How will you manage it?"

"It won't be difficult. I'll send you a message about where to meet us."

"I have a telephone. Just ask the operator to connect you with Gull Manor."

Chapter 6

Tyrone Kerr telephoned early the next morning to tell me of his plan. After a quick breakfast, I enlisted Nanny's help in preparing for an outing. She secured my hair in a tight braid, which she then coiled at the back of my head. I didn't bother with jewelry of any sort, and picked out a pair of low-heeled boots to ensure my feet would be steady.

"It's as casual as can be, but I've always liked this frock on you, Emma." Nanny turned away from the wardrobe with the dress draped over her arm. It was something I'd gotten from my cousin, Gertrude Vanderbilt, a few years ago. All right, it was a castoff, if the truth be told, as were many of my gowns. Though Gertrude was several inches taller and larger boned than I was, I could always count on Nanny's seamstress skills to make any garment look like it was designed especially for me. "The proportions are perfect on your little figure and the colors suit you."

She approached me where I stood in front of the tall mirror in chemise, stockings, petticoats, and corset. Cloth-covered buttons traveled down the back of the dress to below the waist, so rather than risk mussing my hair, Nanny helped me step into it. Of airy off-white linen with a squared collar of coral lawn, matching cuffs, and trim near the hem, the dress had been meant for the tennis court, but it would be suitable for today's outing.

Gertrude had begun gifting me with her hand-me-downs many years ago, when she perceived my need for them. I had inherited my house, a New England shingle-style on the edge of the Atlantic Ocean, from my great-aunt Sadie, along with a modest annuity that had helped keep the place running. Evening gowns and sporting attire had not been among those necessities and I had been willing, happily enough, to go without. Gertrude wouldn't have it, however, and insisted she supplement my wardrobe.

My Vanderbilt cousins, several times removed, had always been generous toward me. From frequent invitations to visit them at The Breakers during the summer months, to the telephone Uncle Cornelius had had installed in the alcove beneath my staircase, to the little gifts that had made life easier and more enjoyable, they had shown no lack of kindness toward me. Oh, at times it had come with a price to be sure, but nothing more onerous than Aunt Alice's numerous attempts to find me a suitable husband. She had finally given up trying, but I knew she would rejoice in my engagement to Derrick Andrews as soon as she learned of it, which would be soon.

When Uncle Cornelius passed away last September, his largesse had once again been extended to me, in a way that had left me breathless. Though pennies compared to the family's many millions, ten thousand dollars in funds and an additional ten thousand in railroad stock had left me, by my standards, extraordinarily wealthy. Never again would Gull Manor go without repairs. I could replace my shabby furnishings. Food—and treats—we would have in abundance.

Though fashionable gowns from the House of Worth remained beyond my means, I could nonetheless order smart ensembles from fashion houses from New York to Boston, if I wished.

And yet . . .

I had done precious few of those things. Yes, we were comfortable and more secure than ever before. At first, I had found it difficult to discuss my inheritance, though I hadn't known why. The reason had dawned on me slowly, but it was based on what I had long known: that, however much I esteemed my Vanderbilt relatives, no matter what private affection I felt for them, I could not escape the fact that their fortune had been gotten on the backs of the less fortunate. People with far less than I had ever had, who worked harder than I could ever conceive. I wished I could believe Uncle Cornelius had always been fair and generous with his employees, but I knew that he, and most industrialists like him, had depended on cheap labor and had manipulated the courts and the labor unions to keep it so. How then, could I use the money gotten by such means for fripperies and luxuries?

Nanny continued fussing over me, straightening here, smoothing there, before finally setting my straw boater with its grosgrain band on my head and securing it with hat pins in two places. She stepped back and surveyed me. Her eyes narrowed in speculation behind their half-moon spectacles. "Katie should go with you."

"It's not necessary, I assure you."

"It wouldn't be unusual for an unmarried woman to have her maid with her."

"And it won't be untoward not to have her with me. We'll be out on deck, in plain view, the entire time."

"But what if . . ." Nanny's bottom lip disappeared between her teeth. "What if this Rayburn fellow *did* murder

Miss Fahey? And what if he takes it into his head to murder *you*, and in the same way? Right over the side of the boat."

"Mr. Kerr won't let that happen." I turned back toward the mirror, lifting my chin as I straightened the tie that hung sailor-like from the center of the dress's collar.

Nanny placed her forefinger beneath my chin and turned my face back in her direction. "What if *Mr. Kerr* murdered Miss Fahey?"

"Well, then, Mr. Rayburn will protect me."

"Perhaps they were in on it together." Her eyes sparked with alarm, as if this scenario only just occurred to her and it frightened her to no end. "Call Derrick. Have him come along."

I grasped her shoulders. "Nanny, dearest, I'll be fine." I kissed her cheeks for good measure, then hurried out of the room.

My spaniel mix, Patch, met me at the bottom of the stairs and followed me out to the front yard. His tail wagging, he bounded across the grass to the corner of the house, apparently hoping we would walk around to the boulder-strewn edge of the property that jutted into the ocean. Then he doubled back, leaping and running, to hurry me along.

When I didn't follow, but rather walked to the north border of my property, he seemed rather put out. He cocked his ears quizzically, then changed course and followed me. With my furry escort, whose exuberance had yet to diminish though he was no longer a puppy, I traipsed across an empty parcel of land and to the home of my nearest neighbors, the Ansons. I waved at Mrs. Anson, hanging out the wash, and turned not toward the house but to their pier.

Soon, the same cutter Tyrone Kerr had arrived in yesterday reappeared from around Brenton Point. Its sails flashed golden in the morning sunlight as she headed straight toward me, as Mr. Kerr and I had agreed upon the day before.

This time, only two individuals manned the vessel: Mr. Kerr himself and, though I could not quite make out his features, Wallace Rayburn.

They put in gently beside the pier, and Mr. Kerr handed me carefully onto the craft. As soon as I felt steady on the deck, I said to Patch, "Home now, boy. I'll see you later."

He stood his ground and *woofed*.

I shook my head. "Not this time. Go home and be a good boy for Nanny and Katie. I'll be home later."

At mention of Katie, he had already turned to go. They say animals are incapable of learning language, but I fully believed my canine friend had come to associate my maid's name with clandestine treats slipped to him from countertops and beneath tables. Nanny and I knew; we just never said anything.

Mr. Kerr, who had removed his boater in greeting, set it back on his head as he laughed at Patch's eagerness to be gone. "Ready for a brisk sail, Miss Cross?"

We sailed around the southern tip of the island before turning north. We were now following the Cliff Walk and could see the backs of the great cottages high above us, including those belonging to my Vanderbilt relatives: Rough Point, Marble House, Beaulieu, The Breakers. Sadly, only Beaulieu continued to be a Vanderbilt summer home, rented each year by my cousin Neily and his wife Grace from John Jacob Astor. Both The Breakers and Marble House stood empty. I think Aunt Alice couldn't bear to return to Newport without Uncle Cornelius, and since Aunt Alva's marriage to Oliver Belmont five years ago, they had resided at his cottage, Belcourt. As for Rough Point, Uncle Frederick and his wife, Louise, had decided one year that they no longer cared for Newport society and began summering at their estate in Hyde Park.

I sat comfortably in the stern while Mr. Kerr and Mr. Rayburn did the work of sailing the vessel. The seas were calm and the winds fair, so I entertained no worries about sudden squalls, but instead relaxed and enjoyed the caress of the breeze across my face. In my lap I held a notebook and pencil ready for when Mr. Kerr called out explanations about how and why the craft maneuvered the way it did, how the design differed from, say, a sloop or a ketch. He also outlined his experience on the racing circuit. I knew I would have the workings of a fine article on sailing by the time our excursion ended.

We sailed past Easton's Beach, with its boardwalk, pavilion, and many gaily striped awnings shielding bathers from the sun. A few of them waved at us from where they stood splashing in the water. We kept going, rounding the island farther still, passing Purgatory Chasm and eventually sailing into Sachuest Bay. The beach, typically called Second Beach by the locals, stretched in a long, white arch that embraced the water's edge. There were far fewer bathers here than at Easton's Beach.

Here Mr. Kerr and Wallace Rayburn came about and gently brought the boat to a standstill. Mr. Rayburn looked puzzled, but trimmed the mainsail without question. His puzzlement increased when Mr. Kerr bade him join us in the stern. The boat drifted gently with the currents.

"So, what do you think of her, Miss Cross?" Mr. Kerr asked, propping his foot on the bench seat on which I perched.

"My opinion of her hasn't changed from when I saw you put into Brenton Cove yesterday, Mr. Kerr. She cuts through the waves neatly and cleanly, like a knife through butter."

"That she does." Mr. Kerr opened his coat and loosened his cravat a fraction to allow the breeze to cool him down. "Then you think I should buy her?"

"I wouldn't dare influence you one way or the other, Mr. Kerr. It's your decision. Do you own other vessels?"

He went on to describe not only the boats currently in his possession, but ones he had owned over the years. He also seemed to delight in telling me about the Cleveland Runabout automobile he had purchased earlier this year, and the St. Louis Motor Carriage he had on order. Next came an account of his stable of racehorses.

"I am a sportsman through and through, Miss Cross. If something moves fast, I want it."

"And when you aren't engaged in such endeavors, Mr. Kerr, what is it you do?" I held my pencil above my notebook, ready to scribble down more information. The reading public would be fascinated with this inside look at one of Newport's most eligible bachelors. It wasn't my usual field of interest, but when I returned to the *Messenger* I'd hand over my notes to our society reporter, Ethan Merriman, for a full write-up.

"Do?" He looked thoroughly mystified.

"Do you work, Mr. Kerr? What is your business?"

"Oh. Ah. My family is in timber and paper products. I'm a major stockholder, but I let my older brothers handle the day-to-day nonsense."

"I see." I did see, more than he probably understood. His use of the word *nonsense* was telling. My own cousins, Neily and his brother, Alfred—Cornelius's primary heir—were hard workers. But their younger brother, Reggie, rarely deigned to visit the offices of the New York Central Railroad and held no significant position there. He, too, loved his sailing vessels, automobiles, and racehorses. In fact, he was currently scouting land in Portsmouth, on the other end of Aquidneck Island, to establish a stud farm. But Reggie, in his idleness, had also developed a passion for drink, and even at the young age of twenty, the liquor was taking its toll.

I glanced over at Wallace Rayburn, perched against the gunwale and looking uncertain. He was a nice-looking young man, with brown hair streaked golden by the sun and a smattering of freckles across his nose, chin, and forehead. "And you, Mr. Rayburn? Are you otherwise employed when not racing? What does a crewman do on the off season?"

He mumbled something about being permanently in the Morgans' employ and there being plenty of upkeep on their various yachts throughout the year. When they traveled the world on their steamers, he and the other crewmen accompanied them.

"That can't leave much time for a young man to socialize," I commented.

His puzzlement returned, the tips of his ears turning red. Tyrone Kerr chuckled. "I'm sure our Mr. Rayburn finds a way."

I treated the younger man to a beaming smile and tried to sound as naive as I could. "Do you have a sweetheart, Mr. Rayburn?"

"N-no, Miss Cross, I don't."

"Oh, that's too bad. No one to toss a flower to as you sail for parts unknown? No one eagerly awaiting your return?"

He shook his head. "No. No one."

Mr. Kerr reached over and swatted the younger man's shoulder. "Oh, I'll bet old Rayburn has a sweetheart in every port."

Mr. Rayburn's color heightened, obscuring his freckles, and he again shook his head, more vehemently this time. "Mr. Kerr, it's not right to talk that way in front of a lady."

"It's quite all right, Mr. Rayburn," I assured him. "I was only teasing. And I shouldn't. You were very heroic the other night when you jumped in the water to keep that woman from drifting away. Did you know her father is part of the yacht racing industry?"

I watched him carefully, looking for another rise in his color, a twitch of his lips, a tightening around his eyes. He held himself steady, however, merely continuing to frown. "I didn't know that. Who is he?"

"Eben Fahey, the engineer."

His eyebrows shot up and he gave a little gasp. "What?"

"Yes. It seems his daughter came up to Newport without telling her father or their housekeeper where she was going, as if her errand here were some great secret. It's very strange. Did you know her, Mr. Rayburn?"

"Actually, I met her once." His admission surprised me. "Mr. Fahey came to take a look at the *Columbia* earlier this year, and his daughter came with him. They introduced themselves to the crew and asked us questions about how she was handling." He glanced over at Mr. Kerr and surprised me further. "You remember, don't you, Mr. Kerr?"

Tyrone Kerr hesitated so briefly I might have imagined it. "I'm afraid I've no recollection of her being there."

"You commented on her red and blue dress, about how patriotic she looked," Wallace Rayburn persisted.

Mr. Kerr appeared baffled a moment, before his expression cleared. "Was that Miss Fahey?"

Young Mr. Rayburn nodded. "A pretty girl, too. What an awful thing, her drowning like that, especially given her background. But what was she doing in Newport?"

"That's what a lot of people would like to know," I said. "You weren't aware she had arrived?"

"No. Why would I be?"

"Then you didn't know her?" I asked him calmly.

His gaze sharpened. "I just said I'd only met her the one time, Miss Cross."

"Oh, yes. Yes, you did." I made a mark in my notebook,

merely to let Mr. Rayburn believe I'd found something significant in his statement, that perhaps I didn't wholly trust his word. Color once more flooded his face.

"Now, see here." He left off, obviously at a loss as to what to say next.

"Yes, Mr. Rayburn?" I treated him to an innocent expression. "I'm terribly sorry if I've upset you."

"You've done no such thing," he insisted, then gave a forced laugh. "I've no reason to be upset, have I?"

His posing it as a question, rather than a statement, gave me pause. I saw my puzzlement mirrored in Tyrone Kerr's own features. "Of course not," I said with a soft laugh.

"Well, it's just that I suddenly felt as if you wished to catch me up in . . . I don't know . . . in a lie or something."

"Not at all." I put my notebook and pencil aside. "I was hoping you might have been acquainted with Miss Fahey. As I said, many people are hoping to find out what brought her to Newport. The police, her father, her friends and acquaintances at home. And when you said you knew her—"

"Met her once," he corrected me.

I paused long enough to see if my mention of the people who knew Miss Fahey back home would have any effect on him. Surely, if she'd had a beau, someone must have known about it. Even if Miss Fahey kept it from becoming common knowledge, she must have confided in at least one intimate friend. Was Mr. Rayburn worried that friend might name him?

But already his complexion had returned to its natural coloring, indicating to me that, while I might have made him feel the victim of undue scrutiny, he wasn't thinking beyond that initial insult. I decided to test him one more time. "And you didn't recognize her at all the other night? She didn't seem the least bit familiar?"

"Not in the least," he replied. "It was dark, and she'd been in the water for a good three hours by then. When I met her aboard the *Columbia*, she'd been impeccably groomed, not drenched with her hair in a wet, tangled mess."

Yes, that could certainly account for anyone not recognizing her in death. And Mr. Rayburn had admitted to having met her, when he could easily have denied it, and later, if he'd been challenged, simply said he'd forgotten—as Mr. Kerr had claimed.

Only one detail prevented me from completely believing Mr. Rayburn's story: the accuracy with which he'd known how long she had been in the water. It seemed he had followed the story closely, noticing the police believed she had jumped from the evening's last ferry. Perhaps Mr. Rayburn was more astute than he seemed, or perhaps there was another, more sinister reason he knew how long she had drifted with the tide.

That evening, Nanny, Katie, Derrick, and I gathered around the dining room table. Nanny had roasted a pheasant, which she served with summer squash and a potato soufflé, a recipe she had won from the cook's assistant at Chateau-sur-Mer in a game of cribbage. As we ate, the tart fragrance of a rhubarb pie drifted down the hallway from the kitchen to tempt us to hurry through our meal.

It was after Katie and I brought in tea and dessert that I decided to discuss my interview with Tyrone Kerr and Wallace Rayburn. Nanny and Katie and I often sifted through the details of the news stories I worked on, as I found each provided her own unique insight. They both understood the workings of Newport's servants—how they thought, what mattered most to them, what concerned them. Added to that, the servants of this town knew everything about the families they worked for. Nanny belonged to that extensive network, which put her in a unique position to gather endless amounts of information.

Katie, who came to this country from Ireland in her midteens, also understood what it was to be falsely accused, to be bullied by her employer, and to be frightened and alone and desperate. She had pounded on my door one night after being thrown out of my own relatives' cottage, The Breakers, not only accused of stealing, but in the family way. My relatives had failed her by not better protecting her from men—in this case a very young man—who would take advantage of her. She had been a shy, timid creature in those days, but several years here at Gull Manor had taught her not only that she needn't fear being bodily harmed, but also needn't fear having opinions, nor expressing them.

After I recounted my sail around the southern portion of the island earlier, Katie said, "Why would this Wallace Rayburn admit to meeting Miss Fahey if he had something to hide?"

"Because there were others onboard who could contradict him," Nanny pointed out. She dipped the point of a carving knife into the center of the pie and cut a straight line to the edge. "One of his crewmates could easily remember her being aboard the *Columbia*, and then Mr. Rayburn would be made out to be a liar."

"Yes, contradicted," Derrick mused, watching Nanny cut slices and set them neatly on each plate. "I'm more interested in why Tyrone denied having met her."

"I wondered about that, too." I took a plate from Nanny and passed it down the table to Derrick. "It might simply have slipped his mind. For a boy like Wallace Rayburn—and he *is* a boy, really—Miss Fahey's appearance on the *Columbia* might have seemed something of an event. As he said, a pretty girl treading where usually only men tend to be. But for Mr. Kerr, who keeps company with some of the most polished young ladies of the Four Hundred, it would have been much more trivial, beneath his notice, really."

"Yes, perhaps." With each of us served a generous slice of pie, Derrick tucked into his. "Ah, Mrs. O'Neal, you've quite done it again." She attempted to suppress a feline grin at the praise. He set down his fork and said to me, "So, either of them might have been lying, or neither of them. But you have established that both of them *did* know Miss Fahey."

"I'll wager it's Wallace Rayburn who's lying," Katie said. Once, making such a statement in front of company, and especially male company, would have turned her a mortified shade of scarlet, a color that thoroughly clashed with her copper-colored hair. I smiled at her, even though I wasn't sure I agreed with her. "There's the name Wally on the photograph, and the *R* on Miss Fahey's ring. Doesn't that fairly well cinch it?"

"The problem is," I said, "Wallace Rayburn doesn't strike me as the sort of young man Lillian Fahey would have become attached to."

"How could you be sure of the kind of man Miss Fahey would fancy?" Nanny reached for the teapot, which Katie hefted and passed to her.

"It's a hunch, to be sure," I admitted, "but based on the same reasons I don't believe she would have taken her own life over a man. Her father described her as intelligent and knowledgeable in the sciences. The fashions she favored showed her to be a woman of the twentieth century. I believe she would have been too sophisticated for someone like Wallace Rayburn."

I saw that I had Derrick's full attention as he asked, "What kind of man is he?"

"An awkward one." I thought back to my encounter with him on the cutter. "One who seems out of his element discussing anything other than sails and rigging and water currents. Even the slightest reference to a personal life turned him several shades of red."

"Well, then, perhaps he does have something to hide," Derrick reasoned. "Perhaps your talk of Miss Fahey made him nervous because he's guilty."

"Perhaps." I took another bite of pie, letting the buttery crust and the sweet-tangy filling melt over my tongue before washing them down with a sip of honey-sweetened tea. "And as Katie said, there *is* his name on the photograph and his initial on the ring."

"And you detest coincidences," he reminded me with a slightly smug smile.

"That's because they reek like a mudflat at low tide," I joked.

His expression turned serious. "I don't suppose we can persuade you to back away from this one? Especially now that Rayburn knows you're watching him. You might have tipped your hand too far this morning."

"I might have, and I'll be careful, but I'm not going to leave it alone. Not unless I can persuade the police to keep investigating."

"Ha. Good luck with that." Derrick finished his last fork-ful of pie and used the implement to scrape the remnants from the plate. Nanny sliced another piece and pushed the platter in his direction. He accepted the offering with a grateful nod and a long reach. We had long since dispensed with ceremony at Gull Manor.

"No one can persuade this one of anything, if she hasn't a mind to listen," Nanny told him, then turned her attention to me. "You are as stubborn as a barnacle on the side of an old boat."

"Why, thank you, Nanny. I'm flattered." And in a way, I was. What Nanny termed *stubborn* I thought of as tenacity, a trait that had seen me through more than my share of conundrums and perilous situations. "I do have a plan, I'll have you all know. First, I'm going down to the waterfront to see if anyone remembers Lillian Fahey arriving in Newport."

"And second?" Derrick asked with a decided lack of enthusiasm.

"I'm going to Long Island. It might be the only place where answers can be found."

Chapter 7

In the morning, I hurried through some edits I needed to make to some of the previous day's news items and dropped them on Stanley Sheppard's desk in the front office on my way out the door.

"Leaving again, Miss Cross?"

I was adjusting the pin in my straw boater as I shouldered the door open. "I'll be back soon," I lied, for I had no idea how long my errand might take.

He fingered the pipe on its stand on the corner of his desk. "Still the Fahey story?"

"Still. I'm going down to Long Wharf to see what I can learn."

He nodded and waved a hand in the air, symbolically shooing me out.

I hopped onto the Spring Street trolley and rode it as far as Washington Square, where I alighted and turned west toward Long Wharf. Soon, the bustle of Newport's largest commercial pier surrounded me. Dust churned up by wagons and carts made me cough. The sharp odors of fish and rotting bait made me wrinkle my nose, as did many of the dockhands and sailors who veered too close as they passed me by. The trains putting in just south of the wharf belched coal smoke that stung my eyes and made them tear. One would think all of this might make me wish to flee, but to a Newporter born and raised just minutes from here, these were simply the characteristics of the place I called home.

A line of coaches and wagons waited in a snaking queue along the wharf's edge to take arriving passengers to other parts of the island. Starting with the head of the line, I made my way down, stopping to describe Lillian Fahey to each driver and ask if she had hired his services two days ago. Although a few of them had read the story about Lillian in various newspapers, none of them remembered having seen her the day she died.

At the main ferry landing, I approached the ticket house window and waited for the man inside to look up from the schedule open in his hands. "Yes?" He looked at me more directly and smiled. "Oh, Emma, it's you. Going off island today, are you?"

"No, Mr. Grimsley, I'm looking for information." Jessep Grimsley was a Point resident who lived with his wife on the next street over from Walnut Street, where I had grown up. They'd raised a brood of children they had somehow fit into their small saltbox home, some of whom I had played with. My brother, Brady, had gotten into mischief with the two oldest boys. "I'm hoping you might remember something about a young woman who arrived in Newport two days ago. . . ." I went on to describe Lillian Fahey. "She most likely purchased a return ticket for the evening ferry."

"The missus and I read your article about her in the *Messenger*. The problem is, Emma, so many people come and go this way every day. I sell them tickets, but I'm sorry to admit I don't pay much attention to them, unless they're townspeople I know."

"I understand, Mr. Grimsley. I was just so hoping there might be something you could tell me."

"Your article didn't say so, but I've heard from others that the police reckon she jumped from the last ferry. Is that so?"

"That's what I'm trying to find out." I thanked him for his time and wandered farther along the wharf, stepping around spilled fish guts outside the bait shops, steaming piles of horse manure, or pools of goodness knew what outside the pubs. Then I had a thought that sent me farther still, to the slips where the smallest boats at Long Wharf were moored. For the most part, these boatmen rowed people back and forth to their steamers anchored in the harbor. If Lillian Fahey had visited Beacon Rock before she died, but hadn't come by land, there was only one other way she could have gotten there.

I repeated my queries twice more, and was once again moving on when a muscular hand, soiled in the creases and beneath the nails, wrapped around my upper arm. I jumped in alarm and nearly swung my fist as I turned to behold, not a roughneck about to accost me, but another childhood friend of my brother's.

"Angus, you almost became the recipient of a bloodied nose!" I relaxed my hand and grinned as I spoke, glad to see his friendly face. Though about the same age as Brady, Angus appeared at least a decade older, with sharp crow's feet beside his eyes and deep brackets scoring the corners of his mouth. Fiery freckles matched the blazing color of his hair, beginning to dull with the influx of gray and receding at the temples.

"Getting into fresh trouble, Emma? I can't think of any other reason you'd be down here this time of day."

"I suppose I am, Angus. You won't write to Brady in New York and tell him, will you?" We both knew he wouldn't, and we shared a laugh. "But let me tell you why I'm here."

Once again, I described Miss Fahey, and Angus's blue eyes, the only part of him that retained the vibrance of youth, sparked. "*That's* the woman they're saying jumped from the evening ferry?"

I nodded, suddenly hopeful and anxious to hear more. "Do you remember her?"

"Of course. I rowed her across the harbor and back."

"She hired you?" My surprise couldn't have been greater, yet Angus surprised me yet more when he shook his head.

"No, I *rescued* her." His chest puffed out slightly. "I was sitting on the dock by the skiff, minding my own business, when I hear a voice. A woman's. And any fool could hear she was mad, Emma. And frightened. So I looked about until I spotted her. She looked like quality, but the man she was ordering to leave her alone was anything but. He looked like a ruffian, a right mean little fellow. Slightly familiar, too." He frowned a moment, as if trying to recall. "Like I'd seen him around here before. But her—not at all."

"You say this fellow looked slightly familiar. Can you describe him? Is he someone you've seen many times before, or only once or twice?"

"I wish I could say, Emma." Angus swept thick shafts of hair back from his face. "I can't place him, only that I *had* seen him before, which means he isn't a townie. Could be from one of the scrod or lobster boats, or somehow attached to the summer set. But he looks like every other dock-worker, fisherman, or troublemaker carousing on Long Wharf."

I nodded in understanding. "What were they saying?"

"I couldn't make it out, but I could see how upset she was, so I walked on over and told her her transport was ready to go."

"And she just went with you?"

"She hesitated a little, but then she nodded and followed me to my skiff. When we got in, I told her if she wanted, I'd row her a little ways along and let her off at the next wharf. Wouldn't charge her, either."

"That was splendid of you, Angus." I grinned and patted his forearm. "You're a worthy gentleman." That raised a blush beneath his freckles. "What time did all this happen?"

"Time? Hmm . . ." He rubbed his chin and then scratched his left shoulder with his right hand. "Not sure. Afternoon, sometime. After lunch. Maybe two, two thirty?"

I wished he could be more precise, but Angus had never been one to live by timetables. At any rate, the notion of Lillian arriving in Newport around midafternoon made sense if she had traveled up from New York. "What happened next? Where did you take her?"

"Well, once she settled in the skiff and we set off, she insisted on paying me. Not to take her to the next wharf, but to Brenton Cove."

The skiff rocked in the wake of larger vessels as Angus rowed us south between Goat Island and the shore, taking us toward Brenton Cove. We passed Newport's many other wharves along Thames Street, bustling with the activity of the shops, warehouses, and industries housed on each one. So much of that effort served the great houses—food and drink, coal, furnishings and other luxuries brought in solely for the benefit of people like the Vanderbilts, the Astors, the Delafields, Goelets. . . . If those families should one day stop summering here, what would happen to Newport? Could we survive without them?

Yes. My mind defiantly shouted the word. Our little city had survived the Revolutionary War and the devastation of British occupation; had emerged from the loss of the wealthy Southerners who had summered here before the Civil War, never to return. Storms, fires, epidemics . . . Newport had weathered them all. The people of this island were nothing if not resilient; nothing if not too stubborn to ever admit defeat.

If only Lillian Fahey had proved as resilient.

I asked Angus, "Did she talk much along the way?"

"Not at all, really. She thanked me, we settled on a fare, and that was it."

"And did you pull in by the boathouse at Beacon Rock? Did she get out?"

He shook his head. "We didn't go near the boathouse. We hardly put into the cove at all. I brought us to a standstill and held her steady"—he jutted his chin to indicate he had held the skiff steady, and not Miss Fahey—"while the lady just sat and stared a while."

"Stared at what?"

"I didn't ask."

No, of course he hadn't. And why should Miss Fahey have confided in a boatman hired to row her across the harbor?

We entered Brenton Cove, presided over by the promontory upon which Beacon Rock perched like a king on his throne. The yachts bobbed and swayed gently, the riggings slapping against their masts like hollow drumbeats echoing across the water. It looked very much as it did the other night, only this time from the perspective of the water and with the sun shining on the gleaming hulls and sparkling along the polished woodwork.

What had Lillian Fahey seen here? What had she learned, and where had she gone next in response? Had she returned here later, perhaps to confront Wallace Rayburn? Had they met in town? And who was this roughneck who had appeared to threaten her? As these questions raced through my mind, Angus sat quietly, letting me look my fill, just as he had done for Lillian. What had she seen?

Suddenly, a sensation crawled into my brain. Something was different from the night of the Morgans' dinner party. I stared harder, adding the shade of my hand to that of my hat brim, craning forward on the rough plank seat at the back of Angus's skiff. I realized the spacing between the boats had changed. The *Columbia* still sat where it had been, in its spot of honor closest to the Morgans' pier. Lucy Carnegie's *Dungeness* hadn't moved either. John and Fanny Morgan's *May* had indeed moved, but wherever it had gone, it was back. But one of the vessels I'd viewed from the cliffs was no longer there—I was certain of it.

"Has one of the guests left Beacon Rock?" I wondered aloud.

"What's that?"

I regarded Angus's mildly curious features and shrugged. "Nothing. Let's get back, shall we? And please do something for me. In the next days, keep an eye out for that ruffian who accosted Lillian Fahey. Let me know if you see him again."

Upon my return to town, I detoured to the police station to relate this latest development concerning Lillian Fahey's last hours of life. Jesse was as disappointed as I that Angus couldn't more accurately describe the man in question. But Angus had been right. This individual sounded like countless others coming and going from Newport's waterfront. Even if Angus had noticed a scar or tattoo, he would still be describing scores of men. Jesse said he would have the uniformed officers who patrolled the wharf area keep an eye out for troublemakers, especially ones they weren't familiar with. And he would ask them to check in with Angus regularly, in case he spotted the man again.

The missing vessel continued to bother me, and I longed to return to Beacon Rock to see if any of the guests had left. First, I returned to the *Messenger*, where I organized my notes on everything Angus had told me and added my own thoughts and suspicions. Then Ethan and I worked on the article about Tyrone Kerr. I granted Ethan the byline, something I thought he deserved, but which he balked at.

"You did the interview, Miss Cross."

"For ulterior motives. I truly wasn't all that interested in Mr. Kerr's yachting experiences as much as I wished to question Wallace Rayburn. Besides, you'll do a better job of it. You're a much better society journalist than I ever was."

"Only because your heart was never in it," he pointed out.

"And yours is, which is why you'll write a better article and why you should have the byline."

"Stop arguing, you two." Derrick strolled through the doorway, grinning. "Ethan, the article is yours. Emma won't have time to get it written up before we leave tomorrow."

I tucked a sheaf of papers into a drawer and stood up from my desk. "And where is it we're going?"

"To Long Island, to find out more about Miss Fahey. And we'll be traveling in style. We'll go on the *Polaris*."

Elizabeth Morgan would not be glad to see me again. That much I knew. Yet the gatekeeper allowed me entrance through the gates and across the bridge, so at least she hadn't specifically banned me from the property. Rather than approach the house, I followed the walkway leading to the staircase down to the boathouse. As I stood at the top, the world seemed to open up before me, miles and miles of sea, land, and sky, their colors so sharp and vivid my eyes began to tear.

My gaze lowered to the water. Had I only imagined a missing vessel? It wasn't as though I had counted them initially. There were several of them rolling gently on the waves, turning the cove into a miniature harbor to mirror the much larger one to my north. As earlier, the *Columbia* still occupied its place closest to the pier.

"Miss Cross, what are you doing here?" The amiable male

voice pulled me from my thoughts, and I turned to see hand-some Bernard Delafield strolling in my direction. A cigarette extended from the fingers of his right hand, while the other occupied a pocket in his trousers. His coat was unbuttoned to reveal the striped vest beneath, and his necktie, loosely knotted, fluttered lightly in the breeze.

"Good afternoon, Mr. Delafield. I hope this isn't consid-ered trespassing," I joked, though I knew very well I was.

"Goodness no, Miss Cross. Not as far as I'm concerned." He came to stand at my side, so close he had to tuck his chin to look down at me. The heated interest in his gaze, which bored into me, made me want to step away, but I held my ground.

"Are you going for a sail, Mr. Delafield?"

"Call me Bernard. May I call you Emma?"

I ignored this. "Which of them belongs to you and Mrs. Delafield?" I emphasized my reference to his wife as I ges-tured down at the yachts.

"That one." He also pointed, his long arm extending in a way that made me feel crowded, as if against a wall. He indi-cated one of the smaller craft, but still impressive to my eyes. "The *Cassiopeia*."

"The Vain Queen," I interpreted.

He inclined his head. "Very good, Miss Cross. Can you guess for whom I named her?"

I certainly didn't wish to play that game with him, felt no desire to help him disparage his wife. "I wouldn't presume."

That made him turn more toward me. After a pause, he replied, "No, I shouldn't think you would." His smile re-turned, producing dimples. "Care to join me for a swing 'round the harbor?"

That prompted a shrewd smile of my own. "No, thank you, Mr. Delafield."

"Bernard. We sailors needn't stand on ceremony." He continued to stand too close for my comfort. I prompted him to ease away a fraction by pretending to swat at imaginary insects. It was either move or be struck.

"You forget, though, that I'm not a sailor."

"Ah, yes. A thing the rest of us are determined to remedy. If you're to be Andrews's wife, you must share his interests."

"It's never stood between us before." I spared him a glance and shrugged. "Truly, I don't believe Derrick is quite as enamored of sailing as the rest of you. He enjoys a hearty challenge, though, which is what I believe explains his participation in the Cup Races." Before he could respond to that, I once again pointed toward the water. "Is it me, or has one of the yachts left the cove?"

A voice called out from behind us, "That would be mine, Miss Cross." Tyrone Kerr joined us at the top of the staircase. "I sent it up the bay to Warwick for maintenance. Why do you ask?"

"Good afternoon, Mr. Kerr." I shook his hand. Apparently, though a vessel had left port, its owner hadn't—indeed, no one seemed to have "fled" Beacon Rock as I had initially feared. "No reason in particular. I just noticed there appeared to be one fewer at anchorage today."

"What sharp perception you have, Miss Cross." Mr. Kerr turned his attention to Bernard Delafield. "It's no use attempting to fool this one, Delafield. If you've got a secret, she'll find you out."

"And plaster it all over the front page of the *Messenger*," I teased, playing along.

Mr. Kerr slapped a hand over his heart. "Heaven forbid. I surrender, Miss Cross. I'll confess all my secrets if you'll only spare me the infamy of such a downfall."

"I suppose I owe you, after that splendid sail yesterday. You'll find the *Messenger*'s article on your sporting experiences quite to your liking, I believe."

This produced a sullen expression in Mr. Delafield. His

dimples vanished. "You sailed with Kerr but won't sail with me? Should I be insulted?"

"Not at all," I replied. "My sail with Mr. Kerr was a professional endeavor in pursuit of an exclusive for the *Messenger*. A day in the life of a sportsman, that sort of thing. We were accompanied by one of the *Columbia*'s crewmen," I added, to drive home the point that I was not in the habit of socializing with men I barely knew, single or otherwise.

Mr. Delafield looked only slightly mollified. "I see. Well, if you'd like another exclusive, let me know."

"Thank you." I smiled sweetly. "I shall, should we need another article nearly identical to the one we are going to run in tomorrow's edition."

Chapter 8

It was after the *Polaris* skirted Block Island that I began to doubt my sea legs. The glorious summer skies under which we left Newport hours ago had gradually darkened, at first so imperceptibly none of us noticed—not Derrick or me or even the steamer's crew. Then the seas began to heave, making me feel as though I stood at the center of a seesaw, one foot on either side of the pivot. Soon after spotting Block Island in the distance, I noticed a ridge growing beside Derrick's right eyebrow, a sign of his increasing concern.

He said nothing, but I felt his frequent glances darting in my direction, and that, more than the lead-lined clouds and frothing seas, raised my alarm. I held off until the first, fat raindrops began splattering the deck before asking, "Will it be very bad, do you think? Should we put into the nearest port?" I tried to envision where that might be. If we were north and just west of Block Island, perhaps New London?

My question spawned a tender smile as Derrick ducked beneath my umbrella and grasped my shoulders. "No, not as bad as all that. Small though she is in comparison to some of the others, the *Polaris* is capable of transatlantic travel, and she's seen her share of storms. No, it's you I'm worried about. How will you weather the wind and waves if the weather should deteriorate in earnest? Perhaps the train would have been the better choice after all."

"Nonsense." My courage had rallied in the wake of his re-assurances. "I've been fine so far and will continue to be so."

Oh, such brave words. And how untrue they proved.

The rain soon came in driving sheets, the sudden force prompting Derrick to send me into one of the staterooms, one apparently once used by the previous owner's daughter. I went willingly, knowing that tucking myself safely away would relieve Derrick and the others of having to worry about me. The wind whipped across the deck and slammed rain against the windows. The waves tossed us about like old driftwood. And, oh, how my stomach roiled. Though I started out sitting upright on a sofa built into the wall, I soon lay prone across the bed, face down, my very being swamped in a pool of misery.

Although, I was happy later to realize, not literally. Some-how, all I had consumed for breakfast and in the hours since remained where it was supposed to be, so that I needn't add the ignominy of leaning my face over the edge of some poor hapless basin.

Still, in my wretchedness, dismal thoughts crowded in on my consciousness. Was this a sign? Bad enough I didn't share Derrick's or, indeed, the entire Four Hundred's, inter-est in sailing. I felt as if I'd failed him—failed yet another test set before me. Did my present state prove he and I weren't compatible, that our social stations and lifestyles were too different for us to find common ground within our mar-riage? Oh, sailing might seem a trivial enough thing. Let my husband sail when he wished, and I would stay home. But his being able to ride out the storm on deck while I languished here, tangled in the bedcovers, seemed too symbolic to ignore.

As I said, I wallowed in misery, in queasy wretchedness. It was no time to analyze my relationship or anything else, yet with each creak of the vessel, each howl of the wind, another disheartening thought wormed its way into my psyche.

The sudden opening of the stateroom door startled me, and for a moment I feared the wind had blown its way inside. Never mind that the door opened outward. Derrick stepped inside and tugged the door closed behind him. In one hand he balanced a tray, which he set on the table beside the bed. "We're sailing out of the storm, and things will be calming down shortly. I've brought you some ginger and chamomile tea, and some oyster crackers. That should set you right."

Yes, in my distress, I hadn't noticed, but the rocking of the vessel had lessened. I pushed up onto one hand, my head sagging between my shoulders. With my other hand I pressed my forehead. There was no concealing how I felt. "Thank you. How did you know?"

"You were just beginning to turn a bit green when I sent you inside." He leaned closer, brushing my hair with his palm. "Emma, I'm sorry. This is my fault. I never stopped to consider sailing might have this effect on you."

"I'm sure most women of your acquaintance could have ridden out this storm at the bow of the ship, face to the wind." My attempt at humor produced a groan.

Derrick brought the teacup beneath my lips and bade me drink. I wrapped my hands around the warm porcelain and sipped. Immediately, I felt better—fractionally, but still better. I sipped some more, and then reached for the crackers.

"I'm sorry I left you alone in here," he said. "I should have come sooner."

"No, there was nothing you could have done. Better you were out there being of use than in here holding my hand."

As I set down the cup, he took my hand. "I can't think of a better use of my time."

With that, he kissed me, climbed onto the bed beside me, and wrapped me in his arms.

I cupped his cheek, enjoying the feel of his afternoon growth of beard against my palm. "This is hardly what one would consider proper," I teased. "Aunt Alice would be scandalized beyond recovery."

"I won't tell her if you won't. Besides, as your future husband, I'm merely ensuring *your* recovery."

Whatever demons had invaded my being during the voyage, by the time we anchored in Manhasset Bay the next morning and I set my feet on solid ground, my courage and my optimism had returned. So much so I laughed inwardly at my foolishness. Derrick and I had been through so much together, had faced so many obstacles over the past few years, that the thought of a bout of seasickness coming between us or in any way being symbolic was ludicrous.

We made our way by hired carriage to the village of Great Neck, where Lillian Fahey had made her home with her father. Surrounded mostly by rolling farmland dotted with cattle and horses, small, recently built neighborhoods radiated out from the main rail line that connected this part of Long Island with New York City. I supposed the train was what made it possible for Eben Fahey to live this far from Manhattan and still do business there, while at the same time being accessible to the wealthy who sailed their yachts on Long Island Sound. Having spent a year among the skyscrapers, traffic, and crowds of New York City, I certainly understood his desire to live in quieter, more peaceful surroundings.

Before leaving Newport, Derrick and I had visited Mr. Fahey at his boardinghouse on Kay Street. He had supplied us with a few names of his daughter's closest friends, and today we hoped to learn more about Lillian's activities, as well as her state of mind, before she had set out for Newport. Odd, but he had seemed nervous about our making the voyage. Had he somehow known the weather would turn foul? I doubted it. At the last minute, he had even offered to accompany us, and I had found myself dissuading him of the notion by reminding him he should remain in Newport in case the police—Jesse in particular—discovered something new.

What had raised his jitters, then?

"Did you notice it?" I asked Derrick as our carriage approached the first address on our list. "Mr. Fahey seemed as if he didn't wish us to come here."

He knocked on the ceiling of the cab and told the driver to pull over. "I think the man is simply distraught over his daughter's death."

"Then you don't think he's trying to hide something?"

"I think he's desperate to know the truth of what happened."

"Then why discourage us from coming?" I replaced my hat in preparation of exiting the vehicle.

"Don't forget, with the stance the police have taken, he sees us as his only allies. Us and Jesse. Our leaving must leave him feeling slightly abandoned."

"Perhaps."

My arm in his, I tried to dismiss my qualms. In one sense, I had enjoyed the carriage ride into Great Neck. Feeling quite myself again, I had relaxed despite the bumpy road jostling us about. That jostling had landed my shoulder against Derrick's, and he had taken my hand to steady me. No, on second thought, he had not held my hand to steady me. He had entwined his fingers with mine because, within the dim interior of the cab, we had all the privacy in the world. There were none to raise eyebrows or tell tales or, even with the best of intentions, attempt to make plans for us. I had held off telling Aunt Alice and the rest of the family about our engagement, convincing myself it wasn't right to flaunt my happiness so soon after Uncle Cornelius's death last September.

But if I acknowledged the truth, I also dreaded Aunt Alice's interference. Would she wish to take over the plans for the wedding? Make it a grand affair, sparing no expense? She would mean well, but her idea of a wedding and mine were vastly different.

I put such thoughts aside as we walked along the sidewalk in a modest neighborhood of two-story brick houses with neat front yards. Colorful roses and other summer blooms vied with the bright greens of June, and rows of oak trees planted along each side of the street provided cooling shade. The scene was one of peaceful domesticity, suggesting the inhabitants led orderly and productive lives.

"Number twenty-nine," I said, citing the numbers beside the front door. "This should be Lillian's friend Merrilee Williamson's house."

We knocked at the front door, which was opened by a housemaid. When we inquired after Miss Williamson, the maid looked us up and down, apparently came to a decision, and admitted us to the foyer. "I'll see if Miss Williamson is receiving," she said with a curtsey, and climbed the staircase to one side of the central hall. Judging by the home's moderate dimensions, I guessed her to be the family's main servant, with perhaps a cook and possibly a man-of-all-work as well.

A parlor and dining room sat to either side of us, the furnishings solid and respectable. The hall narrowed past the staircase and extended to the rear of the house, ending at a back door that overlooked a patio. A quietness pervaded the place, but for a melodic chirping coming from the parlor. I moved to the doorway and peeked in to see a generously proportioned cage suspended from its hook on a pole, with a pair of bright yellow canaries inside.

"Good morning. I'm Merrilee Williamson." The voice startled me and I turned about, feeling somehow guilty, as if I'd been spying. A pretty woman in pale blue muslin stood at the bottom of the staircase, her auburn hair secured with a ribbon that matched her dress and falling in soft waves down her back. She looked very young and regarded us with a curious but calm expression that spoke of an intelligent mind. "I'm sorry, but have we met before?"

"No, we haven't met, Miss Williamson." I approached her with my hand extended. She shook it politely. "I'm Emma Cross and this is Derrick Andrews. We've come from Newport."

Before I could say anything more Miss Williamson gasped. "Then you're here about Lillian."

"Yes, we are."

"I don't believe she killed herself." Her eyes blazed and she shook her head as she spoke. "I never shall believe it."

I hadn't included the police's theory in my article, but apparently other newspapers had. It took me aback that such news had traveled so quickly, and I remained speechless for several moments.

"We don't believe it, either, Miss Williamson," Derrick said gently, taking over while I collected myself. "That's why we've come."

"Is there somewhere we could talk?" I asked her, prompting her to walk past us, gesturing for us to follow as she went.

She brought us into the parlor, where we took seats at the end of the room farthest from the doorway. Again, the furnishings suggested modest, middle-class prosperity—respectable, comfortable, but certainly not extravagant.

"Miss Williamson," I began once we'd settled, "what can you tell us about Lillian Fahey? Her father mentioned you and she had been friends since girlhood."

She frowned, light ridges forming between her eyes. "First, what can you tell me about how she died? I only know what the newspapers have reported. It's terrible, her dying so far from home. I feel I should have been there. Perhaps I might have prevented it. Or, if nothing else, I should be there now, so that she isn't so alone in death." Her voice caught, and she tugged a handkerchief out from the sleeve of her dress.

"I don't believe there is anything you could have done," I said to soothe her, but in fact I wondered. If Lillian hadn't gone alone to Newport, if she'd had a companion to keep her in check and prevent her from falling prey to whomever she had followed there, would she still be alive? Or had her killer been determined to see her in her grave? "But yes, I understand your desire to know more. We'll tell you as much as we know."

"You found her, didn't you?" Tears glittered on Miss Williamson's lashes. I nodded in reply to her question. "If not for that, we would never have known, would we? Oh, if only I hadn't let her go alone."

Derrick and I shared a frown over that declaration. I said, "You were aware ahead of time of her trip north?"

"No, in truth I was not." She dabbed her handkerchief at her eyes. "But something was wrong. That much I knew. I simply didn't know what."

"Did you ask Miss Fahey about it?"

She had turned her eyes toward her lap. Now she glanced up with a fervent look. "Of course I asked her. What kind of friend do you think I am? I asked over and over what was wrong. I begged her to confide in me. But each time, she tried to pretend nothing was amiss."

"What led you to suspect something was wrong?" Derrick asked.

"Oh, nothing specific." She fluttered the handkerchief in the air in a gesture of futility. "Only years of knowing Lillian, of being so familiar with her humors and mannerisms that I could detect when something wasn't right. When something vexed her. And something did. Of that I was certain."

"Can you be more specific?" When Miss Williamson scowled, I entreated, "Please, it could help in discovering the truth. Was there, do you think, someone else involved?"

Miss Williamson sat back against her armchair and released a breath. "I don't know. At first I thought perhaps she had argued with her father."

"Did they argue often?" I put in before she could go on.

She shook her head. "Rarely. Never, really, not over anything serious. Lillian and her father were as close as could be. She had no mother, you know."

Derrick and I nodded.

"And they respected each other. But it was also so uncharacteristic of Lillian to be out of sorts that my first thought was that it had to do with Mr. Fahey. But no, I don't think it was."

"You say you believed something vexed her," I said. "How did she behave to make you feel that way?"

"Distracted. And, of course, evasive whenever I asked her what was wrong. No matter what she told me, though, she could never reassure me or set my mind at rest. And I thought . . ." She sighed. "She seemed plagued by guilt."

"Guilt," Derrick repeated. We exchanged a glance. Had Lillian done something she regretted, so much so she couldn't confide in her closest friend?

"Yes," Merrilee Williamson said firmly. "I believe Lillian had a secret that was eating away at her."

Frustration mounted inside me that we had come all this

way and might yet learn little about Lillian Fahey. "You've no idea what that secret could have pertained to?"

"No, Miss Cross, I'm afraid I don't—to my deepest regret and sorrow."

We spent most of the afternoon visiting the other friends on Mr. Fahey's list. There were four in all, including Merrilee Williamson, though none of the others seemed to be as intimate with Lillian as Miss Williamson. They had all attended school together, went to the same church, and lived within a couple of miles of one another.

"Church," I said aloud, after we drew away from the last house on our list.

"You're feeling a need for worship?" Derrick asked seriously enough.

"No, silly. I'm wondering if her pastor might know something."

"Possible, but unlikely. If Lillian couldn't confide in her closest friend, I doubt very much she would have found the courage to bring the matter to anyone else, even her minister. Especially her minister."

"You have a good point there," I conceded. "Yes, both women and girls go first to their friends before anyone else. At least that's been my experience."

Derrick threaded his fingers through mine. "One aspect of Miss Fahey seems consistent among her friends, and that is her intelligence and good sense. Her steady temperament and quiet resolve."

I nodded in agreement. "And it supports my view that Lillian would never have considered a boy like Wallace Rayburn a suitable beau."

Derrick turned to me more fully, his face half in shadow and half illuminated by the sun streaming in the carriage window. One eyebrow listed quizzically. "Your cousin Consuelo."

The reminder brought back the events of the summer of '95, when my intervention had saved not only Consuelo's reputation, but her very life. I shook my head. "That was very different."

"Consuelo was the same age then as Lillian was now."

"I realize that, but Consuelo had been completely sheltered all her life, and her relationship with her mother had been contentious for years. Though she has always been intelligent, I would not have described her then as being of steady temperament or quiet resolve. Her forced engagement to the Duke of Marlborough made her distraught, and she behaved recklessly as a result."

"Perhaps you're right about Lillian, then."

"I believe I am, although the smallest smidgeon of doubt does linger in my mind. We need to be sure."

He nodded. "It's time to go to the Faheys' home and see what we can learn there. Perhaps Lillian kept a photograph of this *Wally dearest* somewhere in her bedroom."

I agreed, and Derrick gave our driver the directions. Ten minutes later we alighted in front of a house of similar proportions and design to the Williamsons'. Our knock at the front door brought, not a maid this time, but an older woman dressed in the simple but dignified black serge of a housekeeper. Derrick introduced us, and, like Merrilee Williamson, the woman recognized my name from the newspapers. Like Miss Williamson, she produced a handkerchief, this time from a pocket in her dress, and dabbed at the corners of her eyes.

"Oh, my Lillian. Dearest, dearest Lillian."

"We're sorry to upset you, ma'am." I reached out and touched my fingertips to her wrist. "But we're trying to learn more about her so we can discover exactly what happened to her."

"Never was there a more kindhearted girl. Such a lovely, generous, caring young lady, our Lillian was." Blinking rapidly, she shook her head as if to clear it. "Do forgive me. I'm Hester Portman. I've worked for the Faheys since before Mrs. Fahey passed."

"Will you speak with us, Mrs. Portman?" I used as gentle a tone as I could. "We shouldn't take much of your time."

"Oh, that doesn't much matter. My time is my own with no one else here." She bit back a sob. She glanced around at our surroundings, a center hall similar to that at the Williamson house, with the two formal rooms on either side. "Would you mind coming back to the kitchen? I realize you're guests, but it simply doesn't feel proper for me to make free with this part of the house."

She led the way to a spacious kitchen. A variety of copper pots and pans hung above the stove and center worktable, beyond which sat a rectangular oak table and chairs. "Will you take tea?" Mrs. Portman asked us as we settled in.

"No, thank you." I placed my handbag on the table and folded my hands before it. "You've already told us Lillian was generous and caring. What else can you tell us about her?"

"I don't mind saying I often thought of her as my own daughter, or as near as she could have been."

"Was there any relation between you?" I asked, knowing oftentimes a distant cousin or maiden aunt went to live in the home of a widower with children to raise.

"No, I'm just an employee. Or was. I don't know if Mr. Fahey will keep me on now that Lillian is gone." She raised the handkerchief to her eyes. "But she and I were close, I'll tell you truly. Why, in the afternoons, we would have tea together at this very table. You'll probably think it unseemly, that kind of familiarity between a servant and the daughter of her employer."

"I don't find that unseemly at all. My housekeeper is more like a grandmother to me, and most days she and our maid-of-all-work take our meals together, either in the morning room or the kitchen, at a table very much like this, except ours is round."

She regarded me with a tilt of her head, her handkerchief hovering close to her eyes. "Hmm . . . Perhaps you're rather like my Lillian, then."

"Mrs. Portman, can you tell us if Lillian had a special gentleman friend?" Derrick asked, leaning slightly across the table toward her to invite her confidence.

"A suitor? Why, no. I shouldn't think so. She would have said as much, wouldn't she?"

"Are you sure?" I found it increasingly frustrating that while Lillian clearly had had a beau, not one person in her life had any inkling of it. "Perhaps it was a new development and she wasn't ready to discuss it yet."

"Lillian did not keep secrets." The woman blinked several times, her nose becoming pinched. "Not from her father and not from me."

"I'm sorry. Please, tell us more about her," I urged, duly chastised and seeing the necessity of allowing Mrs. Portman to speak her mind uninterrupted.

"Well . . . she has—had—a very inquisitive mind, that one." The housekeeper relaxed somewhat, settling back in her chair. She gazed down at her hands. "From a very young age she took an interest in her father's work. Why, how that child could work sums in her head, and later, as she got older, work out formulas I'd never comprehend if I lived to be a hundred."

"We understand she assisted her father in his work," Derrick prompted.

"That she did. A proper assistant, she became in time." Her fondness for the young woman rang in her voice. "Oh, but she never tried to take credit—never made it out to be anything but her father's work. There's some, well, who would have wanted the recognition, but for Lillian the joy was in the doing. And knowing she was such a help to her father, especially in these latter years. Why, the poor man . . ."

She trailed off, but my mind had already jumped to the alert. *Had* Lillian Fahey been so unassuming when it came to the work she did? Had she been as modest as all that, or had contention existed between her and her father, a sense of resentment that Lillian, a woman, would gain no respect for her achievements? Did she blame her father for that?

A glance at Derrick confirmed that he shared similar speculations. Then there was what Mrs. Portman had said last: *Why, the poor man . . .*

"Poor," I said, before she could move on to another topic. "Is he ill?"

"Noooo," she said, drawing out the word. "Not ill, not exactly. But he's not a young man anymore, is he? And as people grow older, well, they tend to forget things from time to time, don't they?"

"And Lillian reminded him of things he needed to do, yes?" Derrick suggested. "Perhaps kept his schedule for him?"

"Yes, that's it exactly," the woman said. "And also . . . she . . ." Here she stopped again and compressed her lips as if to prevent the words from escaping. She pushed to her feet. "I've said too much. Perhaps you should go."

Derrick and I came to our feet as well. I said, "Please, Mrs. Portman, do remember we're only trying to find justice for Lillian. To learn what really happened to her."

"She didn't kill herself, that much I can tell you," she all but shouted. She grabbed a small pot off a hook and slammed it down onto the worktable. "She did not take her own life."

"We believe she was murdered," I said evenly to Mrs. Portman's back. Would that send her running from the room in tears or would she order us out?

She turned around slowly, still gripping the handle of the pot. I braced for the possibility that she would come at us with it, but her hand drifted to her side. "Who would want to murder our darling Lillian? Why?"

"That's what we are going to find out," I assured her in a resolute voice. "With your help," I added just as firmly.

Derrick held out his hand to her. "Would you allow us to see Lillian's bedroom and the study where she and her father did their work?"

She turned away long enough to set the copper pot down, then came forward and placed her trembling hand in Derrick's. "Come with me."

Chapter 9

Hester Portman clutched Derrick's hand all the way up the stairs, as if she feared falling. And perhaps she would have. It was clear Lillian's death had left a deep laceration on the woman's heart.

At the top landing, the housekeeper turned left and passed two doors before opening a third. We entered a room furnished in painted wood furniture, a canopied bed, and soothing shades of green. A glass-fronted cabinet displaying an array of dolls symbolized the girl becoming a woman, as did the dressing table with its perfume bottles and mother-of-pearl comb and brush set sharing space with a container of hair ribbons.

At first glance, this was a typical young woman's bedroom. I moved first to the bedside cabinet and opened the drawer on top, raising a protest from Mrs. Portman.

"I cannot allow you to disturb her things. It isn't right."

I turned to face her. "I understand your feelings, but Lillian will not be back. She can't be offended by an invasion of privacy. Whatever secrets she might have kept no longer matter to her, but may matter very much in discovering how and why she died."

The woman hesitated a long moment before releasing a breath. "Yes, of course you're right." She gestured for me to continue.

I returned to searching through the drawer, and then opened the cabinet door beneath. A well-loved and tattered bunny, obviously hand stitched and wearing a pink frock and matching hat, peeked out at me. I reached in.

"Oh, that's Mrs. Lovebunny," Mrs. Portman said behind me with a trace of a chuckle. "Lillian's great-aunt made it. It was Lillian's favorite toy as a young child. And even nowadays, she would on occasion take her out and snuggle with her. Mostly when she was feeling sad, I suppose."

After running my hand over one floppy velvet ear, I carefully placed the creature back in her hiding place. I turned again. "Was Lillian often sad?"

"Not unusually so. But there were times I know she wished her mother were here to confide in, or give her advice. Even with me here, sometimes a girl needs her mother."

Yes, I knew that to be true. Though my mother was very much alive, she and my father had been living in France for more than five years now, and there were times I yearned for her presence, for an encouraging word or a sympathetic hand to hold.

Derrick had remained in the doorway with Mrs. Portman, and I understood why. A young lady's room was simply not his purview. As it was, he looked awkward and out of place. I continued my search alone until the housekeeper ventured farther into the room.

"Just what exactly are you looking for?"

"Photographs, letters, perhaps even a memento or two, particularly one you don't recognize."

"Ah, I see." She went to the dressing table and opened the jewelry box sitting in one corner. After gazing down at it a moment, she brought it to the bed and dumped the contents onto the counterpane. Necklaces, bracelets, and brooches clinked as she fingered through them. I continued my search, moving to the bureau. Finally, at my request, Derrick looked behind paintings, under furniture, beneath the mattress. This wasn't the first time I'd searched someone's room, and contrary to what I'd said to Mrs. Portman, I did feel twinges of guilt, as though I were intruding on someone's privacy.

It didn't matter; in the end, we found nothing. Either Lillian's ties with *Wally darling* were wholly encompassed in the photograph and the ring she wore, or she had hidden other mementos so well they might never be found.

"What about Mr. Fahey's study," Derrick suggested, and once again, Mrs. Portman led the way, opening a door to the attic steps.

The room at the top of the house had ample lighting through dormer windows, and the interior had been decorated in the deep, rich tones of a man's private sanctuary. Besides a large oak desk, there stood two long worktables, each with its own sturdy chair, and a faded sofa. On the walls, where they weren't sloping beneath the eaves, hung photographs of various vessels.

Derrick went to stand in front of one. "This is the *Columbia*," he said. He pointed to another. "And this, your uncle William's *Defender*. There are private yachts in the mix, too."

"Yes," Mrs. Portman said with obvious pride, "Mr. Fahey does a lively business with the wealthy set. He and Lillian are—were—quite comfortable here." She seemed about to say something more when a frown creased her brow. "Now, that's a strange thing. . . ."

She crossed the room, putting herself between me and whatever had caught her notice. Derrick and I exchanged a glance and waited. I heard the creak of a door and saw that she had opened a closet.

"This door is always kept locked. If it's not locked, you see, it tends to open on its own." She stepped inside, and Derrick and I crossed to her. She stood inside a large closet with shelves on three walls, most of them neatly lined with carboard boxes, each with its own lid. One box sat open on the floor, its cover tossed aside, and the contents strewn over the oak boards. "Mr. Fahey would never leave his work in such disarray. Never."

"What do you think this signifies?" I asked her.

"I don't know. . . ." She crouched and gathered the papers into a pile.

"Will you allow me to go over them?" Without waiting for an answer, Derrick crouched beside her, helped neaten the stack, and assisted Mrs. Portman to her feet. "This could give us some hint about why Lillian went to Newport."

"I don't see how." The woman gazed into his eyes with an almost childlike trust.

"I won't know until I look through." He lifted the box and brought it out to set on one of the tables.

While he sifted through, I continued to question the housekeeper. "You say Mr. Fahey would never have left his files in such a state?"

"Never. He is always most particular about keeping his things in order. And as I said, he always kept the door locked."

"What if he had been going through that box when he learned of his daughter's fate?" I suggested. "Don't you think he might have been in such a hurry to set out to Newport, he simply left things as we found them?"

She shook her head adamantly. "No. When the telegram came, he had just returned home from the City, after meeting with a client the previous afternoon. He'd left home shortly after Lillian left, just as calmly as you please."

"He left right after Lillian did?" I wished to make absolutely certain I'd heard correctly.

"Yes, and I'm quite sure he'd have tidied up first before leaving the house."

"And you say he returned the next day?"

"Early the next morning. He often spends the night in the City after his meetings. The telegram came shortly after he arrived." Emotion filled her face, and her chin dropped. "As soon as he read it he rushed off, back to the City, where he could catch the first train north. So you see, he hadn't had time to come up here and fuss with his files."

I glanced over my shoulder at Derrick, diligently scanning every page. I believed I already knew the answer, but I asked, gesturing at the box of papers, "Then who could have done this?"

She pursed her lips, then compressed them. "I . . . I don't know."

"It wasn't you," I said.

"Goodness, no!"

I believed her. "Had you gone out at all after Mr. Fahey left for the City that first day?"

"No. Not even to go to market. I didn't need anything."

"And no one came to the house, say to visit Lillian?"

"Not to my knowledge. No one knocked at the door."

I thought a moment, before asking, "And the morning she left, what do you remember about her mood? Her demeanor? Was she jittery? Or withdrawn?"

"Well . . . now that you mention it, she *was* a bit quiet that morning. When I asked her if anything was wrong, she said she was pondering one of her father's formulas. I didn't bother her after that."

"Did she say where she was going when she left the house?"

"Yes, to her friend Merrilee's. She lives over—"

"Yes, we've met Miss Williamson. She hadn't seen Lillian." So Lillian had lied to cover her tracks, to give her more time before anyone noticed her missing.

Suddenly, the most likely explanation for the unlocked closet door and the open box of files seemed obvious. To Derrick, I said, "It won't matter what is in *those* pages. The clue is in which ones might be missing, and whether Lillian took them."

Derrick let the couple of pages he had been perusing fall to the tabletop. "The answer, then, is in why she might have taken them, and to whom she gave them."

"Oh, no, Miss Cross, Mr. Andrews. You're quite wrong. Lillian would never . . ." The housekeeper trailed off, her doubts etched deeply into her features.

"He never mentioned anything missing from his study," I said to Derrick as we set out in the carriage for our last stop here in Great Neck—the photography studio where Lillian had her last photo taken. "And something tells me whatever it was, he did know about it before he left the house that day. Why would Mr. Fahey keep such a secret unless he suspected his daughter had taken the documents?"

"I hate to think it of her." With a soft laugh, he paused. "Funny, isn't it, that we never knew her, yet I find myself wanting to champion Lillian. I don't want to find flaws in her character."

"Nor do I. But if we're to suspect her of the theft, we must also suspect her father of . . ." I found myself unable to say it out loud. But since we'd left the Fahey home, one thought kept throbbing through my brain, creating an ache in my temples. Had Eben Fahey, in a fit of rage over his daughter's betrayal, followed her to Newport and murdered her?

I glanced up to catch Derrick's intense scrutiny on me. "You think he did it?"

I shook my head. "I don't *think* it, exactly, but I acknowledge it must be considered."

He blew out a breath. "Yes, you're right." He made a fist and brought it down, albeit softly, beside him on the leather seat. "So here we are, with both Lillian and Eben under suspicion. What a horrible thought, that father and daughter did this to themselves."

"Perhaps we're about to find out whether she was alone or accompanied when she had her photo taken," I said as the carriage rolled to a stop. Outside, small shops lined the street. We alighted in front of one, its front window filled with enlargements of individual portraits and larger groups. Gold lettering proclaimed: EDWARD GORMAN PHOTOGRAPHY.

"There doesn't appear to be any customers inside," I commented, gazing in through the window. "In fact, the place looks empty."

Derrick tried the door, which opened outward. Inside, all was dark and silent. An ominous sensation gathered in the pit of my stomach. "I don't like this," Derrick said, echoing my exact thoughts. "Perhaps you should wait outside."

"Don't be ridiculous," I said with more courage than I felt. However, a smidgeon of fear had never sent me running before. Situated around the studio, several backdrops and lighting equipment stood ready to capture the images of customers, but each possessed an abandoned air, as if awaiting the arrival of ghosts. Was Lillian's among them?

"Hello," Derrick called out. "Is anyone here? I suppose he could be in his darkroom," he added more quietly. "Let's see if we can find it."

We walked through the shop proper into a rear area. One doorway led into what appeared to be a small kitchen. The other, the door partially but not quite closed, into pitch darkness. A chemical odor emanated from inside.

"His darkroom?" I surmised. "Hello? Mr. Gorman?" Upon receiving no reply, the tension that had gripped me upon entering the studio began to drain away. "He must have run out. We should wait in the main room."

Derrick shook his head, pushed the door wider, and stepped across the threshold. I followed close behind him, feeling suddenly on the alert again. A secondary odor swirled among that of the sulfur dioxide and formaldehyde used in developing the pictures. It was a smell I'd become all too familiar with in recent years.

He tripped, and I ran into him from behind, nearly causing us both to fall. He turned and put his arms around me to steady us both. A soft finger of light from beyond the doorway found its way in, and a pair of legs, bent at awkward angles, took shape before us.

Derrick fell into a crouch, and I beside him. A man lay face down, his arms and legs sprawling. "Mr. Gorman, I presume," Derrick whispered.

No blood had pooled around the body. Had Edward Gorman been strangled? I wished to know, but knew better than to disturb the scene. Although we both believed the culprit had long since vacated Mr. Gorman's studio, neither of us wished to remain inside while the other went to summon the police. We left together and within a block found a uniformed officer walking his beat. While he went to alert his superiors at the local station, we returned to the shop.

Quickly we switched on the electric lights in the main room of the studio, and then slipped behind the counter. The cash register drawer was closed and appeared not to have been tampered with, ruling out a random robbery. And given that Edward Gorman had been struck down in his darkroom, or perhaps the rear hallway and then dragged into the darkroom, and there appeared to have been no ransacking of the place, we could not but conclude this had been an intended murder rather than a burglary.

After searching behind the counter, I found the appointment book on the top shelf of a cabinet. Our time alone here would be limited. I quickly opened the book and riffled through the pages until I found the entries for June, a month ago, when Lillian had had her picture taken. Using my finger, I scanned each page. Mr. Gorman had been a busy man; he must have made a good living, for every slot had been filled. Here and there notations caught my eye, such as *Milton Wedding, Rogers Graduation, Bradford Christening*.

Then my finger landed on it: *Fahey Portrait*, followed by the details: Lillian Fahey, two o'clock, Thursday, June the seventh. Right below her name, something else had been written smaller, in a cramped hand, as if added in later. *Raleigh Portrait*. And then the details: *Walter Raleigh, two o'clock, Thursday, June the seventh.*

"Good heavens, Derrick. Come here." He had been combing the room, looking for anything out of the ordinary. He came quickly to my side.

"What have you got there?"

I poked the page with my finger. "Lillian didn't come alone. Someone else had his portrait done at the same time. Look at this name."

He looked, and then frowned. "Is this a joke?"

"I don't know. But certainly *Wally darling* had accompanied Lillian here that day."

The front door opened with a sudden tramping of feet, and a man in plainclothes followed by two uniformed officers hurried in. The plainclothes man scowled at us and announced, "Detective Johnston. You two found the body?"

"Yes, we did," Derrick said calmly.

"You shouldn't have come back inside." A gesture from him sent the two officers into the back rooms. "What are you doing there? Come out from behind that counter."

"Sir," I said as I complied with his order, "we've come from Newport and are trying to find out more about a young lady who had her picture taken here a month ago. Lillian Fahey."

"The dead girl," he said indelicately. "Yes, we know all about her. But neither of you look like cops to me. So what are you doing here?"

"Exactly what Miss Cross just said." Appearing undaunted, Derrick approached the man with his hand extended. "I'm Derrick Andrews of the *Providence Sun* and the *Newport Messenger*."

"Reporters, eh? Just what we need."

"If we hadn't come looking for answers about Lillian, there's no telling how long it might have been before someone discovered Mr. Gorman in his darkroom." Though Derrick's goal was obviously to placate the detective, he nonetheless used the tone of authority all men of his class learned as early on as adolescence. Would it work with Detective Johnston?

Apparently not. "Great," he said with no small amount of sarcasm. "We thank you. You may go now."

I strode toward him, one hand on my hip. "Don't you wish to question us?"

"Did you kill him?"

"No, Detective." I bridled. "Of course we didn't kill him."

"Did you see who killed him?"

I let out a huff. "No, we did not."

The man shrugged. "Then why would we need to question you?"

From the corner of my eye I could see Derrick's jaw had gone square and tight, and an angry muscle pulsed in his cheek. When he spoke, it was with shredded patience. "Perhaps you might wish to know what Miss Cross discovered just before you and your men came stumbling in."

The detective's scowl returned severalfold. His eyes narrowed, but Derrick spoke again before he could utter a word.

"Lillian Fahey had a portrait taken here a month ago. The photo was found on her person when she turned up drowned in Newport. Upon looking through Mr. Gorman's register entries from a month ago, it became apparent that Miss Fahey came here with a man who used the name Walter Raleigh. Are you familiar with that name?"

"I'm not entirely daft." The scowl melted into puzzlement. "You mean as in *Sir* Walter Raleigh?"

"One could assume it had been a joke between them," I said, "but it might mean something important. We don't believe Lillian drowned by accident. We believe someone murdered her, and perhaps the same person showed up here and murdered Mr. Gorman, the only other person who might be able to identify this Walter Raleigh."

"Well, I'll be." The detective dragged his hat from his head, something he had neglected to do upon entering the studio. "You might actually have something there. But how are we supposed to track down a man using the name of an explorer who died—what? Some three hundred years ago? And why Raleigh?"

"Again, it could mean something significant." I chewed my bottom lip as I tried to think of possibilities. "And one way to track him down would be to search for the negatives.

One would assume Mr. Gorman would have stored them in folders or envelopes marked with the customer's name."

Derrick began shaking his head as soon as I spoke the word *negatives*. "I'm afraid even if Mr. Gorman *had* stored the negatives, they're likely gone now. Walter Raleigh would have taken them after dispensing with the poor man."

I felt deflated. "You're right. Now what?"

"We'll search anyway," Detective Johnston said. He wrote down our names and how we might be reached if he had further questions for us. With a sense of defeat, Derrick and I left soon after. He paid the carriage driver and released him. We continued on foot through the village toward the train station.

"The name Walter Raleigh certainly corresponds easily with Wallace Rayburn," Derrick said as we walked. "Both are seafaring men. But from your description of Wallace and from what I know of him myself, the similarity ends there. Rayburn, for the most part, is an inexperienced youth whose talents lay entirely within the domain of yachting, while Raleigh had been a politician, writer, explorer, and adventurer. He explored Virginia prior to the English establishing their settlements there and traveled to South America to search for the mythical city of El Dorado. Not that he found it."

"Yes," I agreed, "beyond their maritime experience, the two couldn't be more dissimilar." I slipped my arm through Derrick's, walking close at his side, once again enjoying being in a place where no one knew us and couldn't go telling tales. "Could it be as simple as Wallace Rayburn admiring Raleigh, perhaps wishing he could be more like him? Does the quiet young man who blushes at mere mention of having a sweetheart idolize the audacious Raleigh, or perhaps even see him as an alter ego?"

"It's entirely possible. But then where does Lillian fit in?"

"Perhaps with her, he could become that alter ego," I replied, "become a modern-day Raleigh, at least in demeanor if not in his actions. A bit of a swashbuckler might have appealed to her, a young woman experiencing her first romantic interlude, one she felt compelled to keep secret from her father and friends."

"If the same person who murdered Lillian also killed Mr. Gorman, one has to wonder how he got to Great Neck and to the shop before we did. And where is he now?"

"Presumably on his way back to Newport." Then I considered the first question. "We were delayed by the storm. Could someone have gotten here faster by train?"

"Hardly likely. The trains skirt the coast of Connecticut before turning south, whereas we took a diagonal course that cut out miles."

"Well then, could it have been possible to sail around the storm, thus making better time than we did?"

"Yes, but there's another possibility." He turned a grim face toward me. "That after killing Lillian, the murderer headed straight for Great Neck to take care of Mr. Gorman."

"Yes!" The notion drew a gasp from me. "Because of the *carte de visite* found on her. The murderer knew right away the photographer would need to be silenced. Oh, Derrick, if only we'd moved faster, or sent the man a warning."

"We had no way of knowing then that Lillian hadn't visited the studio on her own."

My stomach sank. "In which case, he'd already be back in Newport by now, and his absence might not even have been noticed. Perhaps we should get back."

Derrick laughed. "You're not getting out of this next errand so easily. No, let's keep to our plan. But we'll detour long enough to send Jesse a wire."

After stopping at the post office to send a telegram, we

continued on to the train station, built within the past few years to bring this part of Long Island closer, in terms of travel, to New York City. We stopped at the ticket booth, purchased round-trip tickets, and stepped around to wait on the platform. Speaking of secrets and mysteries, it was time I divulged mine to Aunt Alice.

Chapter 10

When the carriage that had taken us from Grand Central Station arrived at West Fifty-Seventh Street and Fifth Avenue, a wave of uncertainty concerning the wisdom of this visit came over me.

"She isn't going to be at all happy with us," I told Derrick, gazing out the window at the chateau-style mansion that took up the entire frontage of the avenue between Fifty-Seventh and Fifty-Eighth Streets. With its towers and turrets, peaks and dormers, and its liberal use of granite trim, the house conveyed an enduring message: Cornelius and Alice Vanderbilt will not be outdone.

But Uncle Cornelius *had* been outdone—by life itself—and only Alice lived there now, alone but for her youngest daughter, Gladys, the servants, and her memories of happier times.

"Perhaps not," Derrick replied with his typical calm, "but we have no choice after admitting to our engagement to Edwin and Elizabeth and their guests. You've put this off long enough, my dear. Alice might already have heard by now."

"That's what I'm afraid of. We never should have told anyone before her." I worried the fringe hanging from the bottom of my handbag. "What a foolish and unthinking thing to have done."

"What choice did we have at the time?" Like me, Derrick leaned closer to the window, hovering over my shoulder to gaze up at the mammoth edifice of brick and stone filling our view. "It's become increasingly obvious to society that you and I have reached an understanding. We're seen too often together for any other explanation, even that of working to-gether at the *Messenger*."

When I said nothing, nervously combing the braided satin fringe through my fingers, he grasped my shoulder and turned me toward him. "Emma, my darling, it's been a year."

"Not quite. Uncle Cornelius died in September."

"Yes, but in society, the beginning of a new summer Sea-son constitutes the beginning of a new year."

He had a point. Society revolved around these summer months, for it was now that the families of the Four Hun-dred renewed their ties with one another and forged new al-liances, particularly through the marriages of their grown children.

"Besides," he continued, "even if she's unhappy now, she'll get over it and be delighted for us."

"Also what I'm afraid of," I mumbled.

"What on earth does that mean?"

"It means"—I gathered my skirts in preparation of step-ping down to the sidewalk—"that once she's reconciled to our engagement, it won't be our wedding in the planning, it'll be *hers*."

He laughed. "Give your aunt Alice some credit. She'll want you to be happy."

I shrugged and didn't correct him. Aunt Alice would want me to be happy, to be sure. The problem was in the form that happiness should take. Aunt Alice always believed her way was the best way, and she didn't often stop to listen to the desires of the person she was trying to help.

Hence the reason I had put off this moment for so long.

Derrick seemed to sense the turn my thoughts had taken, for he said, "I, for one, have grown tired of all the secrecy. I might almost think you were ashamed of the choice you made."

That snapped me out of my worries and brought on new ones; with my hesitancy over the past several months, I might have hurt Derrick's feelings, made him doubt my love for him. "Don't be ridiculous. I could never be ashamed of marrying you."

His gaze bore into me. "Really?"

"Derrick, I—" The slight twitch of his lips sent relief coursing through me. I swatted his arm and laughed. "You! Don't do that. I'm enough of a jittery mess as it is."

He pressed the door latch with one hand and offered me the other. "Let's go get this over with. Whatever wrath Aunt Alice heaps down upon our heads, we'll endure it together."

Once again, his mock seriousness made me laugh and did wonders for my courage. He was right. Aunt Alice might be momentarily annoyed with us, but soon enough her anger would abate.

"I just realized something," I said as we climbed the steps to the front door. Derrick raised the knocker.

"What's that?"

"I haven't yet told my parents about us. So if nothing else, Aunt Alice can have the satisfaction of knowing before they do."

Right before he let the knocker fall, he ducked beneath my hat brim and kissed me on the nose.

Mr. Mason, who usually at this time of year presided as butler at The Breakers in Newport, opened the door to us.

Equal to Derrick in height and a handsome man even in middle age, he looked more than pleased to see us.

"Miss Cross. Mr. Andrews. What a surprise." He opened the door wider and stepped aside to let us enter. "Mrs. Vanderbilt will be delighted. I trust you are both well?"

I realized he probably hadn't heard about Lillian Fahey or how Lucy Carnegie and I had discovered her body in Brenton Cove. I decided not to enlighten him, at least not then. Mr. Mason and I had been fast friends since the days when, as a little girl, I would visit my cousins at The Breakers in the summertime. Then, in the summer of '95, there had been a murder and theft at The Breakers, and Mason had fallen under suspicion. He had been fired from his position, but I had helped clear his name and reputation and restored him to the household.

"Is Aunt Alice in?" I asked, relinquishing my hat and gloves to his care. Derrick did the same.

"Oh, she is indeed. She has just sat down for tea in the Watercolor Room. Yes, she's taken to having her afternoon tea in the Watercolor Room ever since Mr. Vanderbilt passed. I believe she finds the colors of the paintings lining its walls soothing."

"I'm glad they bring her comfort," I said, privately acknowledging that the Watercolor Room was one of my favorites here, too.

From the vestibule, we moved into the entrance hall, a two-story space dominated by a spiral staircase carved from purest white Caen marble. It was the centerpiece of this house and a feat of artistry, but the structure had always unsettled me. While I understood society's penchant for dramatic staircases, the winding of this one had always seemed to conceal something sinister, as if a monster or cutthroat might jump out of the shadows at every turn.

"Follow me, please," Mason said after storing our hats and gloves. "I don't believe there is any need to announce you."

We passed into the shockingly ornate expanse of the ballroom, which opened onto nearly every other room on the first floor. In the back right corner, we passed through a pair of glass and filigreed iron doors into a vaulted room set up like a gallery, with colonnaded arches framing the artwork as well as the floor-to-ceiling windows peering out onto a veranda opposite them. Alice Vanderbilt sat at a small table before one of the windows, working her way through a tiered assortment of tiny sandwiches and petit fours. As had been the case since Uncle Cornelius's passing, she wore head-to-toe black and little jewelry, other than a rope of jet beads looped twice around her neck in place of the pearls she usually sported, and, of course, her wedding ring. She looked up as we came in and sprang to her feet.

"Emmaline! Mr. Andrews!" But instantaneously, her expression fell and the excitement faded from her still-lovely blue eyes. "What am I saying? I'm not talking to you two."

Blast. Aunt Alice had apparently heard of our engagement.

I decided to try ignoring her pique. "It's wonderful to see you, Aunt Alice. You're looking quite well."

"You needn't flatter me, Emmaline. I'm highly peeved with you." Speaking in the disapproving tones of the Sunday School teacher she had once been, she folded her arms across her chest. Her gaze shifted briefly to Derrick. "You too, Mr. Andrews." She sighed deeply and dramatically, but as she did so, the ice in her demeanor melted a fraction. "Well, you might as well show me."

I understood what she meant, and a portion of my trepidation lifted. With a barely restrained grin, I removed a glove and held out my left hand, presenting the engagement ring Derrick had given me last September but which I'd only recently begun to wear. If Aunt Alice was demanding to see it, she couldn't be all that upset with me.

After a brief hesitation, she swept closer and grabbed my hand. *"Hmph."* She examined the three diamonds, one large round one flanked by two smaller baguettes, set on a filigreed platinum band. "Respectable. Remarkable, really. I'm surprised you accepted it, Emmaline. It isn't too much of a show of wealth for you?"

Well, she hadn't *quite* thawed yet—not entirely. But neither had she dropped my hand. Hopeful, and with a fond look at Derrick, I said, "The workmanship on the band is extraordinary. It shows great artistry. And to me, the two smaller stones represent Derrick and me, with the larger one being the life we will make together."

"Hmph," she repeated, though her expression softened again. "A sentimental notion. All right, then, come and sit."

As if they had been listening by the doorway, a pair of footmen entered from the dining room. Aunt Alice resumed her seat and rearranged her tea things to make room for us. The footmen placed extra dishes, cups, and saucers on the table, as well as two chairs they brought from the side of the room.

Aunt Alice busied herself pouring tea into our cups. "Did you just arrive from Newport?"

I started to correct her, to tell her we had taken the train from Great Neck, when Derrick jumped in with, "Yes, we did. We realized it was high time we came and told you our news. Emma wished to do it sooner, but business kept me north, as well as neither of us wishing to flaunt our happiness in light of Mr. Vanderbilt's passing."

"Bah." Aunt Alice offered me the sugar bowl and creamer even as she continued scolding us. "That didn't stop you from flaunting your happiness with the Morgans. Did you think I wouldn't hear?"

Good heavens, no, I *hadn't* thought she would hear so soon. Had Elizabeth or Fanny Morgan telegrammed her the next morning?

"Aunt Alice, we're very sorry. But we're here now, aren't we? And all we want is for you to give us your blessing and be happy for us. You *are* happy, aren't you?"

She narrowed her eyes at me. "Does Alva know?"

Aunt Alice and her former sister-in-law had always carried on a vehement competition, each wishing to outdo the other in a quest to be considered *The* Mrs. Vanderbilt by society. With Alva and William's divorce, Aunt Alice had won that round, but apparently the acrimony still existed between them. Eagerly and happily, I replied, "Aunt Alva has no idea, and neither do my parents, yet."

She pursed her lips and continued to hold me in her gaze as though I were a bug under a field glass. Then she sighed again, this time less theatrically. "In that case, yes, Emma-line, I'm very happy for you both. I've wanted to see you married these many years, and I had begun to think it might never happen. You can be so stubborn, young lady. You get that from your father, you do."

Yes. My father had frustrated not only his parents but the entire extended family by insisting on pursuing the life of an artist rather than going into business with his distant Vanderbilt cousins. Thus far, he had not made his fortune, but I believed he and my mother, living as expatriates in Paris, were happy with the decisions they had made. As was I with my decisions, and I had my stubbornness to thank for it.

I grasped Aunt Alice's hand and leaned to kiss her cheek. That brought the first true smile to her lips since we'd entered the room.

"Well then," she said briskly, rubbing her palms together. "We'll need to plan, won't we? What about a Christmas wedding? We'll order you a Worth gown, of course. You could be married in St. Bartholomew's and hold the reception here. . . ."

My stomach curled in on itself. The battlelines were drawn. Somehow, I managed to smile and nod and make no promises, nor commit to anything. Aunt Alice didn't seem to notice.

At Aunt Alice's fervent request, we spent the night in the City. That evening we enjoyed a quiet family dinner with her, my cousin Gertrude and her husband, Harry Whitney, my youngest cousin, Gladys, and my half brother, Brady, who had been working for the New York Central for several years now. Some time ago, Uncle Cornelius had despaired of Brady ever being more than a wastrel, but with time and effort on Brady's part, our patriarch had come to see his worth. Brady had made him proud, and me as well.

Gertrude and Harry left around ten o'clock, though they hadn't far to go as their mansion stood directly across Fifth Avenue. On the way up to our rooms, Derrick and I stole a few kisses in the spiral of the staircase, and I decided perhaps the structure wasn't so ominous after all. On the second-floor landing, he took me in his arms and kissed me again, and whispered against my brow how happy he was that we could begin planning our wedding.

I entered my bedroom smiling, but before I could close the door behind me, Brady pushed his way in. "I hope you don't think Alice is the only one peeved with you, Em. Why didn't you tell me? *Me*, Em. Your own brother."

At the genuine hurt in his eyes, I gave him a brief hug. Then I blew out a breath and drifted to the dressing table, where I sat and regarded him through the mirror. I began fishing for the hairpins at the back of my head. "I would have, you know, had you been in Newport more often."

"That's no excuse. I saw you at Christmas, didn't I? And at Easter, and a few times in between."

"You saw me briefly each time you came," I reminded him. As my hair fell around my shoulders, I leaned on my elbows on the tabletop. "Most of your time was spent with Hannah, if I remember correctly." I wiggled my eyebrows at him. "Anything to report on that front?"

"Don't change the subject." Shoving sandy blond hair back from his brow, he loosened his necktie and perched near the corner of the bed. "But yes . . . and no. Seems Hannah is a woman after your own heart, Em."

Hannah Hanson was another of our childhood friends who grew up in the Point neighborhood beside Newport Harbor. After finishing our high school studies, Hannah had gone away to Providence to study to become a nurse. Now she was back in Newport working at our local hospital, as much a dedicated working woman as I. Something in my brother's expression told me he wasn't quite as happy about matters as he could be.

I rose from the dressing table and went to sit beside Brady. "By that do you mean she isn't ready to drop her nursing career and come running down to New York to be with you?"

He shrugged, but I knew from long years of experience that that meant yes.

"By the same token, you could drop your career here at the New York Central and go home to Newport to be with her."

"That's not the same at all," he grumbled.

"Oh, isn't it?" I leaned away, grinning. "How is it different? No, let me guess. You're a man, and she's a woman, so therefore your employment takes precedence over hers."

"Are you going to keep working once you and Derrick are married?" He spoke with defiance, as if the answer was already decided.

"Yes, I am, Brady. I have no intention of leaving the *Messenger*. And you shouldn't need me to tell you that."

"But is that realistic? What about children?"

I took his hand and gave it a squeeze. "God willing, Derrick and I will have children. And they will be my priority. Of course. But that doesn't mean I won't find the time to pursue the occupation I love. I've worked too hard to simply let it all go."

"Hannah could work here, in the City," he said, beginning to sound like a sulking little boy.

"Don't pout," I told him, and chucked his chin. For all that Brady had several years on me, it had been I who had often taken on the role of surrogate parent in our relationship. "But what you're saying is true. Hannah could have an outstanding career at a hospital here. Have you talked about it?" His silence was telling. "You haven't. Why not? Are you waiting for her to read your mind?"

His silence continued. I poked his ribs with my elbow. He finally admitted, "Well, yes. Shouldn't it be obvious?"

I tossed my head back and laughed, then sobered when he continued to look baffled. "No, Brady, what goes on in your mind is rarely obvious. I think I understand what the problem is. Have you asked her to marry you?"

"No, not yet. If she's not willing to come to the City, how would we live? I couldn't make the salary I'm getting at the New York Central in Newport."

"And she isn't about to up and move to New York without a commitment from you." I shook my head at him. "Really, Brady, the two of you need to talk. Come to Newport as soon as you can and tell Hannah how you feel. Although . . ." I sighed. "I've already lost your company, for most of the year. I'll be sad to lose hers, too."

"Move the *Messenger* to the City," he suggested brightly.

We both knew that would never happen. I was too much of a Newport girl, through and through.

The return voyage to Newport was peaceful, with not so much as a raindrop on the horizon. My stomach rejoiced. I rejoiced yet again after disembarking and finding a note at the *Messenger* from Angus, asking me to come and see him at Long Wharf. It didn't matter that I'd just come from there upon leaving the *Polaris.* I knew if he wished to see me it must be important.

Thanks to Derrick, my baggage had already been sent on to Gull Manor. He had remained onboard to receive a report from his captain on any repairs that might be needed and to approve the purchase of supplies that must be reordered. I checked my correspondence, looked over some articles that had come over the Associated Press wire, and made my way back out to the front office.

Mr. Sheppard eyed me with a shake of his head. "Leaving so soon? You've only just arrived."

I grinned at the sarcasm in his tone. "I might have a scoop from Angus MacPhearson."

"Ah, the boatman with the wild red hair," he said in an almost singsong voice, "and a permanent drunken swagger."

"Angus isn't a drunkard." My eyebrows went up in righteous indignation. I didn't like it when people spoke ill of my fellow Newporters, not even when it held some truth. "Not all the time, anyway."

"If you say so."

"I do. He has something to tell me, and for him to have come all this way from either Long Wharf or his home on the Point, it must be important."

"The Fahey story?"

"It could only be."

"What are you waiting for, then? Get going." Mr. Sheppard waved me out of the building.

On my way to the wharf, I wondered how I hadn't seen Angus upon leaving the *Polaris*. Perhaps he'd been hired to shuttle someone out into the harbor, but what if he had been in one of Long Wharf's numerous taverns? Mr. Sheppard hadn't been far off, if the truth be told. Angus was a good soul and an honest man, but not always the most dependable.

I found him sitting in his skiff. No, *slumped* was the more accurate term. And snoring. I must have missed him by minutes earlier, and yes, he must have been imbibing at one of those taverns. I carefully stepped down into the skiff, sat opposite him, and shook his shoulder.

"Angus, wake up."

"Mmm . . ."

"Angus MacPhearson, you asked to see me. Here I am. Now wake up."

"Wha—? Go away."

The fumes from the beer he'd consumed nearly knocked me into the water. I shook him again, then quickly leaned away. "Angus, it's Emma. You asked me to come as soon as I got back to Newport. I'm here, so you had better wake up."

He opened one bright blue eye, but only halfway. "Emma? That you?"

I gazed around for a bucket or anything that might hold water—enough to douse him with—but there was nothing at hand. I supposed I would have more luck if I came back later, or tomorrow, but after Derrick's and my failure to learn much of significance on Long Island, the thought of waiting even another minute seemed interminable.

"Angus," I shouted to seize his attention. He reluctantly opened both eyes, groaning as he did so. He squinted and shaded his eyes from the sun. "Does what you have to tell me have to do with Lillian Fahey?"

"Who?"

I experienced a moment's uneasiness. The last time Angus had something important to tell me, it had been about Brady, and how he had turned onto a self-destructive path after several years of sobriety. But no, it couldn't be about Brady this time. He was in New York. Derrick and I had just seen him and he had been well—and entirely sober.

I nudged again. "Lillian Fahey, the woman who drowned, you dullard." I didn't mean the insult, but I knew it would penetrate the haze of alcohol. Even drunk, Angus had as much self-respect as the next man.

"Oh, her. Yeah." He struggled to sit up straighter and nearly fell over.

I grabbed his arm to help steady him. "What about her? What have you discovered?"

He scratched his head. "Coarse hair."

"What?"

"That's where he is."

"Who? Angus, you're not making sense."

He shook his head, the strands the wind had blown loose from the leather queue at his nape falling into his face. He swiped them away from his eyes. Yes, he did have coarse hair, but what did that have to do with anything?

"The hooligan who threatened the girl. He's aboard the coarse hair."

It was my turn to shake my head, until his meaning suddenly dawned on me. "The *Corsair*? John Morgan's yacht?"

Angus nodded, his chin nearly striking his chest. "That's it. That's what I said. He's a gob, I think."

A sailor of the lowest order, one who did the dirtiest jobs on a vessel. I sat up straight, leaning away from Angus. My thoughts raced. Once again, we were back at Beacon Rock, or at least, Brenton Cove. Could John Morgan have any-thing to do with Lillian's death? And who was this gob?

"How do you know this, Angus?"

"Followed him in my skiff." He lovingly patted the side of the little boat. "Tracked 'im down first at the Rambler's Inn. Been going there a lot, I hear."

I knew the place. Even among the unruliest dockworkers, it was considered a rough establishment. Men typically went there looking for a fight, and more often than not, they found one.

This suggested our hooligan was a man to fear.

Chapter 11

I knew better than to go alone. The man Angus had described to me might work on the yacht of one of the most famous men in America, and that yacht might be crowded with servants and crewmen, but a vessel the size of the *Corsair* nonetheless provided countless opportunities to corner someone, not to mention easily dispose of the body.

Together Derrick and I traveled to Beacon Rock. Angus being in the condition he was in, I pressed a few coins into his hand and told him to sleep it off. When Derrick met me at the wharf, we hired another boat and set out. The afternoon shadows were darkening by then, although Brenton Cove, on the west side of the island, would be bathed in burnished hues of marigold and amber.

Angus had even provided me a name, which he had overheard at the Rambler's Inn. Cob Hendricks. It shouldn't prove too difficult to find him on the *Corsair*, provided his fellow crewmen were willing to speak up.

"They might not be," Derrick murmured to me as our boatman took us south. "As soon as the pair of us, dressed as we are, mention his name, his mates will more than likely shrug and walk away."

"They might be persuaded." I touched my handbag. When I gained my inheritance from Uncle Cornelius, I had vowed not to use the money for frivolous reasons. Finding a killer was far from frivolous. "Or we might get lucky and come upon this Cob on our own. He'll have no idea we're coming and won't be on his guard."

"That's *if* your friend gave you an apt description. We could climb aboard and find ourselves surrounded by a score of men all fitting the same description." Derrick spoke without sarcasm or disdain. He was right to be skeptical of Angus while in his cups, and ordinarily I would have agreed with him. However, Angus had never steered me wrong before, and besides, he hadn't been drinking when he first found Cob at the Rambler's Inn and then followed him to the *Corsair*.

At least, I didn't think he had been.

We entered Brenton Cove and pulled up to the *Corsair* just as the sun sank behind a deep blue mound of clouds hovering over Conanicut Island across the bay. We were welcomed aboard by the steward on duty, but when we asked about the man named Cob and described him, he became hesitant.

"The Morgans aren't here at present," he told us with an embarrassed half smile. "They're attending a function at the golf club."

"We needn't bother Mr. and Mrs. Morgan with this," I countered. "We only need to ask the man a question or two."

The steward took on a stern look. "May I ask what this is about?"

"It . . ." I sighed. I hadn't wanted to explain our errand,

not in any great detail. "It has to do with the woman who was found in the water by the Morgans' boathouse."

"And you think—"

"We only wish to speak with the man," Derrick said. He had taken that tone again, the one that tended to persuade people to do as he asked.

A sheen of perspiration broke out across the steward's forehead. A corner of his lip ducked between his teeth for an instant. A bit farther along the deck, a door closed with a thud. Brisk footsteps sounded from somewhere inside the cabins, moving away from us until they faded. The steward noticed, too, as evidenced by the stiffening of his posture and the darting of his gaze.

He cleared his throat and said, "I'm sorry. I can't allow you below deck without permission from Mr. Morgan, and he and Mrs. Morgan won't be back for hours yet."

"You needn't allow us below deck, then." I smiled my most ingenuous smile. "Just ask the man named Cob to come up here."

"That would be highly irregular, miss."

"Look," Derrick began, no longer with authority, but simmering with anger. I subtly moved my hand until it came in contact with his. He fell silent.

"Can you at least tell us if any of the crew went missing the day after the woman was found?" Perhaps we might gain a clue as to who had murdered Edward Gorman.

"Missing?" The steward gave a shrug. "Quite a number of our people were given time off that day. Mrs. Morgan's idea."

"And do you know where most of them spent the hours?" I remained optimistic we might learn something. "Were any of them late getting back?"

"Once they're off the ship, it's none of my business where any of our people go." He raised his voice slightly, as though hoping his reply might be heard by someone other than Derrick and me. "Even if I did know, I don't think I'd divulge the information without first consulting with Mr. Morgan."

"Fair enough." I sighed, wishing I could shake the information out of him. By Derrick's expression, he shared my frustration. "We'll come back when the Morgans are here. Thank you for your time."

Soon we were back in the little sailboat, heading to town to retrieve Derrick's carriage. I felt his gaze burning into me, his expression filled with puzzlement. "Why did you give up so easily?"

"I persisted as far as I thought prudent," I replied wearily. The wind picked up, and I held on to my hat brim despite the pin holding it fast. "The steward is afraid of that man, of Cob." I whispered the name, not wanting our boatman to overhear.

"Yes, I had the same impression. Still."

"And someone was listening in on us. I think he might have allowed us to go below deck—perhaps pretend we'd slipped down on our own—except for that door opening and closing nearby. Did you notice?"

"Not particularly, no." His brow furrowed as he considered. "I suppose I merely thought it was someone going about their business, but now that you mention it—"

"He or she hurried away," I finished for him. "Possibly to let our man know we were looking for him. I'm afraid we might have tipped our hand."

"Blast, you're probably right about that." As the breeze ushered in cooler night air, he put his arm around my shoulders. I felt a moment's hesitation, an instinct to pull away. We were home, after all, and no longer on Long Island where no one knew us. Yet, glancing down, I saw the slight bulge beneath my left-hand glove, where my engagement ring encircled my ring finger. Once news of our impending marriage became widely known, society would no longer frown on such stolen intimacies between us. No, instead they would frown on Derrick's lack of wisdom in tying himself to a woman of my stature.

We were silent for most of the remaining trip, waiting until reaching Long Wharf and the privacy of Derrick's carriage before discussing the matter further. Although I offered to take a hired carriage home, he insisted on driving me out to Ocean Avenue. The fiery sunset had yielded to a brooding purple sky.

"If this Cob is involved, I'm thinking he acted on behalf of someone else," I said. "What would a lowly seaman do with scientific calculations designed to make yachts go faster?"

"Sell them, of course. To the highest bidder. And he's in a position to find them."

"Is he, though?" I thought about it and shook my head. "Someone like John Morgan wouldn't even know his name, for all Cob works on the *Corsair.* Not that John Morgan would stoop to stealing the secrets of another man's livelihood. A person who might be more in a position to sell such secrets is . . ."

Derrick took his eyes off the pitted and winding road—growing ever more dangerous as the last of the daylight faded—to glance over at me. "Who? Or need I even ask?"

"Wallace Rayburn," I said with a nod. "He's close enough to the sort of people who would pay for such information, while his own lack of wealth might prompt him to do so."

"And there remains the compelling and damning evidence of *Wally darling*, Walter Raleigh, and Rayburn's matching initials."

"It's too easy," I brooded. "And you'll never convince me Lillian could ever be in love with Wallace Rayburn. And no matter what else, I do believe she loved her *Wally darling.*"

Derrick stayed for dinner—Nanny insisted—and when I walked him outside to his carriage, he took my face in his hands. "I love you, Emma. Perhaps . . ." He inhaled deeply and released it slowly, his breath feathering against my cheek. "Perhaps we should let this one go."

I blinked in surprise. "That's not at all what I expected you to say. Why?"

"I don't know. This feels . . . too dangerous. Too twisted. It's likely to lead us—lead *you*—into a coil too tangled to escape. Let's visit Jesse tomorrow, tell him everything we've learned, let him take over."

"He's been ordered not to. Again." It sat like soured dough in the pit of my stomach, the number of times he'd been ordered to step away from a case involving members of the Four Hundred. Oh, thieves, murderers, extortionists—he had solved countless crimes and sent the culprits to prison. But always in society matters, the police were cut off at the knees, their authority superseded by the number of dollars this or that industrialist had sunk into a politician's career.

Had I grown cynical? No, I had grown into a realist.

Derrick watched me, the night shadows turning his handsome face into a series of strong planes and angles. "What are you thinking now?" Did I hear a faint sardonic note in his question?

I chose to ignore it, and ran my palm down the neck of one of the Cleveland bays. "Perhaps *Wally darling* is merely incidental to what happened, or perhaps he urged Lillian to make a terrible mistake. But I can't dismiss the possibility that Eben didn't go to New York for his meeting, but followed Lillian. Traced her to Newport. Found her here and . . ."

"Killed his own daughter. Emma . . ." He reached out and caught my hand, the one that had not suddenly stilled on the horse's mane. "I agree it's possible, but I don't think so. He was distraught, clearly grieving when he learned of her death."

"Remorse?"

"I don't know. What about the photographer? If Fahey was in Newport at the time of Gorman's death . . ."

"It's not impossible for Fahey to have gotten to Long Island and back in the time it took us to do so. Quicker, in fact, since we spent a night in the City. I wish to speak with him. Tomorrow. I need to hear his explanations from his own lips, while looking him in the eye. And then we'll go to Jesse and tell him what we know."

"Is that a promise?"

In lieu of an answer, I wrapped both arms around his neck and rose on tiptoe to kiss him.

Mr. Fahey had no objections to meeting Derrick and me in town the following morning. In fact, the note he sent to the *Messenger* in response to our invitation to meet us at the little café several doors down sounded more than accommodating, but downright eager. One might assume he wished to know what we had learned in New York concerning his daughter's death, but I suspected it wasn't as simple as that. Rather, I believed he wanted to know if we had learned his secret.

Derrick and I arrived a few minutes early, ordered coffee, and settled in to wait for the older man. There were a few other patrons, their conversation a steady but quiet murmur.

"Perhaps we should have had Jesse here for this," Derrick said with a glance out the window onto busy Spring Street.

"I can remember a time when you avoided involving Jesse at all costs," I gently teased him.

That brought his gaze back to me. His hand drifted across the table to mine, and he smiled as he fingered the ring I wore. "Things were different then, weren't they?"

"Oh, I suppose. Jesse has moved on, hasn't he?"

"That's not what I mean." Derrick lifted my hand to his lips, then released me when the bell above the door tinkled. Mr. Fahey doffed his bowler hat as he made his way over to us.

Short spirals of coarse silver hair stood up on end, as if he hadn't taken the time to tame them with pomade earlier before setting his hat on his head. He pulled out a chair and sat, then used his forefinger to push his spectacles higher. "Good morning. I assume you learned something on Long Island, yes?"

An air of trepidation accompanied the question. Seeing as he had gotten straight to the point, I saw no reason not to myself. "Mr. Fahey, why did you not tell us about the stolen engineering formulations?"

The man paled. His eyes, slightly rheumy, darted between Derrick and me. He let out a sigh.

"Then you did know," Derrick said evenly.

"How could I not?" He made another adjustment to his spectacles and ran a hand over the side of his hair. "My closet door was open, a file box gone through. . . ."

"According to your housekeeper," I began slowly, thinking back, "you were home when Lillian left for Newport, but left shortly after her. Had you discovered the theft, suspected your daughter, and gone after her?"

"No!" The man turned scarlet before the color once again drained from his face. "You're accusing me of murdering my own daughter. Good God, how could you?"

"Did you murder Lillian, Mr. Fahey?" I spoke so quietly, he leaned forward, neck craned, to hear me.

He began shaking his head. His fingers shook, too. "I did not murder my daughter, Miss Cross. I didn't discover the theft until the next day, when I'd returned from my meetings in the City. Even then, I didn't suspect Lillian. Why should I? She was as dedicated to my work as I was."

Dedicated to my work. I couldn't help repeating the

phrase in my head. It had been *his* work, not Lillian's, however much she might have assisted him; however much some of those formulations might have been hers. Had she finally decided it was time to strike out on her own?

"Your housekeeper seemed to think you hadn't had time to go up to your office that morning, that the telegram came and you hurried off to Newport." Derrick raised an eyebrow as if sighting prey through a rifle scope.

"Mrs. Portman was wrong. I went directly upstairs when I got home. I always do." He focused on pouring himself a cup of coffee from the pot that sat on the table. When he raised the cup, it shook in his grasp.

"And until the telegram arrived, you had no idea where Lilian had gone?" I pressed.

"No, none at all." He removed his spectacles, wiped a coat sleeve across his brow, and set them back on his nose.

"And what did you think when you noticed your work had been gone through?" Derrick asked. Our questions were coming rapidly, giving Mr. Fahey little time to think. We had planned it that way, in hopes his replies would be sincere and not artifice.

"I didn't know what to think." He passed a hand over his hair again. "I didn't know what to do about it."

I wrapped my hands around my coffee cup, the liquid inside having grown cool and no longer radiating warmth through the porcelain. "Why didn't you tell us of the apparent theft? Why didn't you tell Detective Whyte? Or did you?"

Gaze on the tabletop, he shook his head. "I did not. Can't you see? I didn't wish to. Lillian was my daughter. My beloved child and the only family left to me." His gaze rose, meeting first mine and then Derrick's. "I didn't wish to sully her name, even in death. I wished to leave her reputation as a good girl, an honest girl, intact."

"Do you believe she stole the formulations?" I asked him.

"No, I do not."

"Then who do you think did?"

He took a long time in answering, staring into his coffee. Finally, he braved lifting the cup and taking a sip. Only after he had set it down again did he say, "I believe there might have been a man."

"As I suggested when we first spoke?" I raised a rather accusing eyebrow at him.

He nodded. "Yes, someone who deceived her into believing he loved her." He went silent, his gaze turning fierce behind the magnified glint of his spectacles. "He killed her. He must have."

It was my turn to shake my head. "Why did you deny that Lillian had a beau?"

"Her reputation." The reply held a note of pleading, of anguish.

"You would let a killer go free to save your daughter's reputation?" I couldn't conceal my disdain. To think a father could hold his daughter's reputation in higher regard than her very life. The notion made me loathe the man in front of me, if only for the briefest of instants.

"Oh, what does it matter now?" he said, still pleading. "She is dead. I want her killer brought to justice, Miss Cross, Mr. Andrews. Find the person who did this to her."

"We can only do that if you are honest with us, Mr. Fahey. If you stop hiding the truth." Derrick spoke bluntly, even harshly. "Lillian's actions matter. What she did prior to coming to Newport matters. Her intentions matter. Very much. So stop trying to preserve your daughter as you wanted her to be and come to terms with who she really was, for good or ill."

Tears formed in the man's eyes. "You are asking me to betray her memory," he whispered.

"No." I reached across the table and pressed my hand to his wrist. "We're asking you to *honor* her memory by acknowledging her as she was and working to find who murdered her. I believe Lillian to have been the intelligent, even brilliant young woman you first described to us. I believe she was a good daughter to you. A good person. But one who perhaps took a wrong turn. She was human, as are we all. We are all susceptible to making mistakes, Mr. Fahey."

"I think, perhaps, I never knew her at all," he whispered, and hid his face in his hands.

After helping Nanny and Katie with the dishes that evening, I stepped out the kitchen door into our rear garden and strolled past the laundry yard and our small barn, where my carriage horses, youthful Maestro and elderly, retired Barney, slumbered comfortably in the warmth of hay and the heat of their own bodies. Patch streaked out the door beside me and I let him go. He had the awakening night noises to investigate, smells to explore, and, of course, his own business to conduct. I walked on alone to where the property narrowed, where the ocean surrounded me on three sides.

It wasn't quite Beacon Rock. The perspective was much lower, only a few feet above the waterline. But where Beacon Rock gazed out over the harbor, Fort Adams and Jamestown in the distance, from where I stood I saw only the endless ocean, miles upon miles of the one power on earth so great it could never be tamed or even tempered by man.

Indeed, the Atlantic was restless tonight, slapping hard against the boulders that bordered my small peninsula. The spray nearly reached me, and the forceful heaving imparted a sense of restlessness in me, too. I felt the water's tug within me, and the oppressiveness of the day's heat that had yet to lift. Felt the closeness of a nearly starless sky hovering just above my head. But where Patch could run, jump, circle, and leap, I merely stood, letting the winds skimming off the water encircle me, blow my hair out of place, sweep my skirts around my legs.

Thoughts of Lillian swirled in my mind like the eddies caught between the boulders. Who had she been? Beloved daughter? Trusted friend? Smart but ingenuous, naive enough to have been taken in by a calculating man?

Or had she been the calculating one? I sighed. In the end, it didn't matter which. I believed she had been murdered, and whoever she had been, she hadn't deserved to have her life cut short. And now, she deserved justice.

Before leaving Mr. Fahey earlier I had asked him one last question: where was he yesterday and the evening before? He'd seemed utterly puzzled by my query, hesitating only an instant before replying that he'd been in Newport, had been since first arriving the day after Lillian's death. What nagged at me was his inability to prove it. He had spent much of his time in his room at the inn where he was staying. Yes, he had gone out, purchased his meals, and ate them back in his room. He'd spoken to no one, given no one a reason to remember him. I wished to believe he'd been telling the truth, wished to absolve him of all suspicion.

My speculations scattered on a sudden turning of the breeze. Even above the push of the waves and the wind singing in my ears, I heard a sound behind me. Not Patch— not a joyous, bounding run, nor a snuffling, digging, or scratching, but a very human step, the creak of a twig breaking underfoot. In the instant my senses came alert, my first thought was that Derrick had come, unannounced, to surprise me. But just as instantly, I realized he would not sneak up on me like that in the dark, especially with a potential killer on the loose.

I whirled about and beheld a woman, her outlines bathed

in darkness. She wore a plain calico dress, its light color glowing slightly against the gloom, and a straw hat with a narrow brim tied beneath her chin. Her expression melted into the darkness, unreadable.

Initially, no sense of panic struck me. She would not be the first woman to show up at Gull Manor under cover of night seeking help. My great-aunt Sadie, the house's owner before me, had opened her door to any woman who needed a place to stay—or to hide—and I had followed suit, inviting in the helpless, the hurt, the abused, who hurried up my drive over the years. Was this woman one of them?

Suddenly, I didn't think so. She shifted closer and a pale snippet of moonlight caught her features. Her expression sent a ripple of fear through me. "Who are you? What do you want?"

She raised a hand, and with a shock I saw the wooden baton she gripped, like a policeman's truncheon. "Leave him alone. Don't meddle in things that haven't to do with you."

My thoughts went to Patch, and I wondered where he was. There were empty lands adjoining mine, and he could have wandered to one side or the other, too far to have heard this woman come up the drive. Otherwise, he would have come running and barking his greetings. I hoped he had found enough of interest elsewhere to keep him occupied, lest he try to protect me and be injured for his pains.

"I have no idea what or whom you're talking about," I said, attempting to cover my fear with bravado. "And I think you should leave." Yet, a memory struck me, that of a door opening and closing, and footsteps receding through the staterooms aboard J.P. Morgan's yacht. "Who are you?" I asked—no, demanded—again.

"My name doesn't matter." Her voice came out coarse and guttural, and I couldn't decide if it was her habitual tone or if she was trying to frighten me more than I already was. She struck the baton at the air in front of me, punctuating each angry syllable like a conductor leading the storm in the third movement of Vivaldi's *Summer*. My instincts urged me to duck and run. Unfortunately, she stood between me and the house. "You're to leave well enough alone, do you hear? No more questions."

A scratching in the undergrowth along the edge of my property drew my attention. My unwelcome guest heard it, too, and turned her head perhaps with that same sort of instinct that had urged me to run. Nothing happened for a second or two. The night air became oppressive, seeming to hold me pinned, scarce able to draw a breath. Then the scratching continued, drawing closer, and finally, barking announced Patch's return. I silently willed him away, but in the same moment my intruder turned again. Patch darted out from the hedges, and without another thought I sprang forward.

Chapter 12

I hurled myself into the woman with the full force of my weight. We both went down, she onto her back and me on top of her. In the confusion, I grabbed the baton. I pinned her shoulder with one hand, drew my knee up onto her thigh, while with the other hand I tossed the baton as hard as I could. Patch reached us and jumped into the fray. His wagging tail indicated he hadn't yet realized the danger and thought this a brilliant game. When the woman might have overpowered me—I could feel her superior strength while my own began to wane—Patch's antics kept her from achieving any semblance of balance to pull herself up. Between his barking, my calls for help, and the woman's shouted curses, the kitchen door opened. Nanny and Katie came running out.

Each had brought a makeshift weapon: Nanny a copper frying pan and Katie the stiff broom she used to tidy up the steps and path out to the laundry yard. They reached us in seconds, and each stood over us with chest heaving and weapon raised.

"If you make another move," Nanny said in her sternest governess's voice, "you shall find yourself sorrier than you have ever been."

"Not to mention a lot more sore than you've ever been," Katie added, with a shake of her broom for good measure.

I slowly eased off the woman but I didn't go far, ready to tackle her again if need be. "Who are you? And how dare you disturb the peace of our home?"

She didn't speak at first, but stared up at me and gasped for breath. Her eyes narrowed to slits, and her lips jutted around unspoken oaths. Then she charged, "You disturbed the peace of mine first."

This unexpected reply took me aback, and I sat back on my heels to study her. Finally, I offered her a hand to help her sit up. "Slowly," I warned, and she heeded my word. When she faced me levelly, I said, "I have done no such thing. Never disturbed your peace."

"You have," she insisted. "And you'll get me and my Cob fired."

Cob.

I pushed to my feet. Patch came trotting to my side, a stick protruding from either side of his snout. No, not a simple stick. He had the baton. He'd assumed I threw it as part of the game and had run off to retrieve it. I accepted it gratefully from him and ignored his disappointed whine when I failed to toss it again. I held it tight in my right hand and once again offered the other to help the woman to her feet.

"Let's go inside," I said, "and you can explain yourself."

"Miss Emma, are you sure?" Katie's broom poked the air toward the woman. "A she-demon, this one."

"It's all right, Katie. I believe the moment for violence has passed, if it ever existed." Though in truth, I was more hopeful of that than positive.

Nanny took a step back to allow the woman and me to

precede her to the house, but her grip on the frying pan remained tight, and she walked close behind us. Katie, too, her stiff-bristle broom aloft and ready.

"Sit," I ordered when we reached the kitchen. I pointed to the nearest chair at our pine table. She sat, removed her hat, and stared up at me with wide, dark eyes. Here, in the light, I saw she was young, about my age perhaps, though a tightness to her features suggested a harsher life than I had led. So did the coarseness of her hair, pulled back into a coiled braid—where it hadn't fallen out in frizzed strands during our struggle. I realized I must look equally disheveled and swept loose hairs back from my face.

Without a word Nanny went to the stove and put the kettle on. Katie began getting out cups and saucers. When she reached for plates, she hesitated and gazed at me in question. I turned to the woman.

"Are you hungry?"

She shook her head. Katie left the plates on their shelf. Little was said until the tea had been poured, cream and sugar added. Nanny's frying pan and Katie's broom remained within reach. Patch, having sensed the tension once we all had stepped inside, sat upright on his haunches beside me, his inquisitive gaze pinned on our guest.

I said, "You're Cob Hendricks's wife, yes?"

She nodded, sipped her tea, sighed.

"You both work on the *Corsair*," I went on. After another nod, I continued, "And you were listening in—eavesdropping—that day my associate and I went to ask your husband some questions."

Nanny's gaze had darted to me when I referred to Derrick as *my associate*. There had been two reasons for it. One, I had grown so used to secrecy that I still hesitated to announce our status to the world. And two, this woman didn't need to know my business. That I had come with the owner of the newspaper I worked for sufficed for now.

"I heard you talking through the open windows," she said in a hoarse voice. Was it that way naturally, I wondered again, or a result of our tussle? "Of course I listened in once I heard my husband's name mentioned. What wife wouldn't?"

"Fair enough," I conceded. Yes, perhaps I would have done the same. If I thought some harm might befall Derrick—yes, I'd listen in, take up arms, do anything and everything I could to forestall such ill fortune. "I assume you're a maid?"

"Head chambermaid."

"And your husband?"

"Works in the boiler room, mostly shoveling coal, but other things as he's told to do. It's hard work. Dirty and dangerous. And you'll get him fired with your questions, and me along with him. I came because it isn't fair, it isn't what we deserve. Just leave us alone and let us get on with our work and our lives."

This speech astonished me—Nanny and Katie, too, by their expressions. Tea went forgotten in the ensuring moments, until Nanny snatched hers from its saucer. Before she raised the cup to her lips, she scowled. "I'd watch it, making demands of Miss Cross after coming here with a wooden stick to threaten her like you did. Crazy as a bat, you must be. It's a wonder she hasn't telephoned for the police. She still might, mightn't you, Emma?"

Katie added her consensus with rapid shakes of her head and an eager light in her eyes.

I let Nanny's question go unanswered, my gaze never leaving the woman. "Tell me your name."

Her lips pursed in tight reluctance. Then she murmured, "Polly."

I studied my hand, the tips of my fingernails. "And how much do you really know about your husband, Polly?"

"What's that supposed to mean? I know my husband as well as any wife knows her man."

"Where does he go in his spare time?"

An angry frown erupted between her brows. "He hasn't spare time. He works always."

"No, he doesn't," I contradicted her with a shake of my head. "Here, while the *Corsair* is anchored, there is no coal needing to be shoveled. Not much, anyway. And I happen to know Cob was seen in town on numerous occasions, frequenting the taverns on and near Long Wharf."

That raised a shrug. "A man's got the right to amuse himself, hasn't he? He's got the right to enjoy a pint now and again."

"I agree," I calmly replied. "But he doesn't have the right to threaten women—nor do you, for that matter."

"What women?" The question came sharply, like the sting of a whip.

"One in particular, named Lillian Fahey." I held her gaze again, relentlessly. "Do you know of her?"

Cautiously, slowly, she said, "Heard tell of her. She drowned. Fell from the night ferry."

"Maybe. Maybe not." I watched a tremor pass through her before adding, "Cob was seen threatening her the afternoon before she died, on Long Wharf."

"Whoever said that lied." Polly gripped the edges of the table and leaned forward. "Maybe you're lying."

Nanny struck the table with the flat of her hand. "Don't you ever accuse Miss Cross of lying."

"Miss Emma would never—*never*!" Katie turned feverishly pink. I resisted the urge to smile and thank them for their loyalty.

A long breath escaping her, Polly sat back. Her bluster wilted from her shoulders and drained from her features. "It's not his fault," she whispered. "He only does what he's told."

"Told by whom?" I asked first, though other questions had immediately come to mind.

"I don't know."

"Surely you can do better than that," Nanny murmured.

"If he does anything wrong," Polly retorted, "it's at the bidding of his superiors. What's folks like us supposed to do?"

"Have you ever been asked to do something you knew was wrong?" I asked her. "Spy on the Morgans' guests aboard the yacht? Take something from one of the staterooms?"

Her mouth turned down with indignation. "No, never. And I wouldn't anyways."

"Then why should your husband?" I countered.

"It's different for him. No one thinks a woman can do anything important. I'm expected to clean and tidy, that's all."

I sat back, thinking, my arms crossed over my chest. I didn't like the possibilities churning in my mind. Still, I asked, "Has Mr. Morgan ever sent Cob on a questionable errand?"

When she shook her head, I believed her. It was unlikely that any difficulty, legal or otherwise, would prompt a man like J.P. Morgan to engage the services of a ruffian like Cob Hendricks, at least according to Angus's description of him. I had yet to see the man for myself.

"There is one thing . . ." Polly hesitated, chewing her lip. "I shouldn't . . . it could get Cob in trouble."

I gently reminded her, "He's already done the deed that could get him into trouble."

"He had nothing to do with that woman's death!" she snapped back.

I waited for her ire to settle. "Perhaps not, but remember, he *was* seen threatening her on the very day she died. Now, it might help your husband if we knew who, if anyone, instructed him to do so."

She bought herself some time by raising her teacup, but after a tiny sip she lowered it and made a face. "It's grown cold."

"So has our patience." Nanny nonetheless pressed to her feet, refilled the kettle, and brewed a fresh pot. It took some minutes, but I didn't press Polly in the meanwhile, not until Nanny poured out more tea for all of us. "There, it's hot. Drink. And then talk."

I merely raised my eyebrows at Polly, but even that small gesture confirmed Nanny's statement about our patience.

"There was one night, a couple of nights before that woman died, when Cob took one of the small boats and rowed over to the boathouse. The one at the bottom of the cliff."

I nodded my familiarity with the Morgans' boathouse.

"Well, there was someone waiting for him. I know that because when Cob got close—which I could see by the lantern he took with him—another lantern moved to the end of the pier. Then the two lights stayed where they were, like Cob and whoever it was were talking. It didn't look like Cob got out of the boat."

I folded my hands on the table and leaned toward her, eager for more. "But you couldn't see this individual's face?"

"It was too far away, wasn't it? And it was dark. No, I could only see the lights, but I knew one was Cob's because I'd watched as soon as I saw him setting off. I almost called down to him, asked him what he was about." Her chin dropped. "I knew he wouldn't like that, that there would have been hell to pay later, once he got back."

A chill traveled my spine, and I darted glances at Katie and Nanny. Nanny looked angry, and a pained memory flitted across Katie's face. I turned back to Polly. "He hits you sometimes, does he?"

She shrugged. "He's a man. I'm his wife. Sometimes I forget my place."

"Polly . . ." I wished to offer comfort as much as I wanted to dissuade her of such a notion, but she cut me off.

"Anyways, I had work to do, didn't I? So I stopped watching and got on with it."

I had another question for her, one I was sure she wasn't going to like. But would she answer? "Has your husband been away from the *Corsair* longer than usual in the past couple of days? Overnight, perhaps?"

"No, he hasn't."

"Are there witnesses to corroborate that? Other than yourself?"

"If you won't take my word for it, you'll have to ask his mates, won't you. But I'll warn you now, they're a rough bunch and don't take kindly to anyone making accusations against one of their own." She drained her teacup and stood. "I've got to go."

"Wait." I came to my feet as well. "How did you get here?"

"Came in with one of the chef's assistants earlier when she came to shop. She'll be long gone by now. I'll have to make my own way back."

"Did you walk all the way out here from town?" Katie asked, incredulous.

Polly gave another shrug. "Once I found out where you lived, I hitched a ride on a baker's delivery cart. Let me off about a half mile down this twisty road of yours. I suppose I'm walking back. And finding someone to row me out to the cove."

"Katie." I appealed to my maid-of-all-work with an apologetic look. It was dark and getting on toward bedtime, but I couldn't let Polly Hendricks walk all the way back into town, only to run the risk of not finding a boatman willing to take her back down the shoreline to Brenton Cove.

Katie didn't need any explanation, but followed me out to the barn, where we roused a sleepy Maestro and hitched him to my carriage. I had no intention of driving all the way into town, however, not when I knew where we could borrow a dingy much closer. Some twenty minutes after setting out, Polly and I arrived at Beacon Rock.

I was not completely proud of the fact that returning Polly to the *Corsair* provided me with another opportunity, which did, in part, inspire my eagerness to see her safely home. Before leaving Gull Manor, I asked Nanny to telephone Derrick and request that he meet me at Beacon Rock's pier. On the drive there, I worried that Nanny might not be able to reach him, but either way, I intended to row Polly out to her employer's yacht and ask her to find her husband for me.

But Derrick was there, not down at the pier, but waiting for me at the gate, where we had no trouble entering. He kissed me openly in greeting, something I had yet to become used to, and although the evening shadows provided some concealment, my face heated in response.

Derrick manned the oars of the Morgans' dingy and soon enough we reached the *Corsair*. Polly, who had spoken not at all after returning Derrick's greeting with a terse "Sir," looked not only puzzled, but alarmed when we followed her out of the craft and onto the steps that spanned the side of the yacht.

"We need you to let your husband know we're here to see him," I told her, and braced for her protestations.

They were not long in coming. "I can't. He'll know I interfered. It won't go well for me."

This was different from her earlier fears of being dismissed from their jobs. This indicated bodily harm to herself, something for which I would not be responsible if I could help it. "Does he know you've left the vessel tonight?"

"I don't think so. I left after we'd had our supper in the lower galley. He'd have been dicing and playing cards ever since."

"Then go ahead in," I told her. "We'll wait a few minutes, and appeal to the steward. Your name will never come into it."

She nodded and resumed her climb, while Derrick and I waited. I hoped our little scheme would work, and that no one was even then observing us. The one benefit of being where we were, in the sheltered confines of Brenton Cove beneath the watchful eye of Beacon Rock, was that yacht owners and crew alike felt at ease and security was lax.

Derrick consulted his pocket watch. "Ready?"

I nodded and proceeded him up the steps. He stayed close behind me, as if to catch me should my foot slip. It both warmed my heart and irritated me no end, since I had believed he had learned to trust my abilities to take care of myself. Then again, did I want him to completely trust me where that was concerned, or did I rather like him in the role of protector?

It was a question I would contemplate later, in the quiet of my home. Now, we reached the main deck and opened the gate to step aboard. We were almost immediately intercepted by yet another steward, and I couldn't decide if that was fortunate or not, as we were compelled to explain our business all over again.

The man removed his cap, scratched his head, and spoke to Derrick despite my having made the entreaty to see Cob Hendricks. "I'm not sure I can accommodate that request, sir."

I frowned at what I perceived as a slight due to my sex, but didn't interrupt when Derrick asked, "Are the Morgans here tonight?"

"Out, sir, till later. Much later."

"The Belmonts' ball," I remembered. My aunt Alva and her husband, Oliver Belmont, were having an affair at Belcourt tonight. I had been invited but had respectfully declined. Aunt Alva's parties always left me exhausted. The steward made no comment, neither to confirm nor deny his employers' whereabouts.

Instead, he sat his cap back on his head and asked, "This Cob. Has he done anything we should know about?"

"No, we have a couple of questions for him." Only I would have been able to detect Derrick's growing impatience.

Silence ensued as the steward apparently thought it over. Finally, he gave a nod. "I don't see the harm in it. Just that, if there is something we should know, you'll tell me or Mr. Morgan, or someone, yes, sir? Oh, and I will have to inform Mr. Morgan of your . . . visit."

"Fair enough, yes." Despite Derrick's amiable answer, his tone held an edge that prompted the other man to escort us into the aft parlor and bid us make ourselves comfortable while we waited.

Derrick and I sat together on a settee done in azure brocade embroidered with gold and silver dragons. As on Lucy Carnegie's *Dungeness*, this parlor might have graced any grand house with its rich carvings, gilded accents, and silk upholsteries. I took it all in and marveled at the expense.

The steward returned with Cob Hendricks in tow. The man had obviously changed out of work clothes, exchanging them for a collared shirt, vest, and coat, ill-fitting though it was. He had not, apparently, had time for a shave, not before coming up to the parlor or, indeed, even that morning. He had, however, scrubbed the coal dust and grime of the boiler room from his face and hands.

Cob made no move to sit. Indeed, a man of his ilk would never dare do so anywhere but in quarters reserved for workers and crewmen. He stood at awkward attention, with a simmering resentment just below the surface of his placid expression. The steward hovered behind him until Derrick shot a gaze in his direction and raised an eyebrow.

"I'll be right outside," the man said, as if matters might deteriorate to the point that we would need rescuing. He backed his way out the door.

The necessary part Derrick had played having concluded, he now looked to me. "Emma?"

With a nod, I said, "Mr. Hendricks, we're here about Lillian Fahey."

"Who?"

"Lillian Fahey," I enunciated. "The woman you were seen threatening on Long Wharf the day she died."

"No idea what you're talking about."

"We believe you know all about it, Mr. Hendricks." I let my gaze roam his length before making eye contact again. "Why did you approach Lillian on Long Wharf? What did you say to her? And were you acting under someone else's orders?"

"I told you, I have no idea what you're talking about. I've got work to do. I'd best get on with it."

"At this time of night?" Derrick tsked. "I doubt very much you're needed anywhere at the moment. My guess is we took you away from your mates and a good bottle of . . . what is it you prefer, Mr. Hendricks? Rum? Whiskey? Gin? What brings you to the Long Wharf taverns in the evenings?"

Cob Hendricks shoved his hands in his trouser pockets. "Doesn't much matter, does it? One's as good as another."

"Liquid courage, eh?" Derrick spoke as if to a mate of his own. "Tell me, did you need a drink before accosting Miss Fahey on the wharf?"

"No, I—" He broke off, but he had said enough to assure us that Angus had been right about what and whom he had seen that day.

"Mr. Hendricks, if you were told to frighten Lillian Fahey, you'd do best to come clean about it," I said. "I assure you, your name will be given to the police, and you'll *have* to answer their questions, even if you continue to evade ours. Now, I don't believe you personally had any argument with Miss Fahey. Someone sent you to her, didn't they? And probably paid you well for your services."

How I wished I could persuade him to tell the truth by revealing that he had been observed rowing to the Morgans' pier one night for a private conversation with whoever had awaited his arrival. He wouldn't necessarily know that observer had been his wife, but he could render a guess and make her suffer for it. It was too big a risk to take. Yes, Polly Hendricks had accosted me in my own backyard, had threatened to cudgel me and might have done so if I hadn't overpowered her. Did she deserve my protection?

Yes, she did. If she chose to break the law, then the law should set matters to rights, not an irate husband.

A mean smile spread across his face. "Give my name to the cops, go ahead. I'll wager any witnesses at Long Wharf were half pickled anyway and their word wouldn't hold up in court."

Derrick stood and shoved his face close to Cob's. "You'd risk your own freedom to protect someone else's?"

"How are you so sure I'm someone's lackey?" Cob's eyes narrowed, cold and snakelike.

Because Cob Hendricks could not have had access to Eben Fahey's workroom, not to mention he could not have gone far with the stolen formulas. For one, he simply didn't have access to the kind of men who could profit from those formulas and were willing to pay for them. Which meant whoever had paid Cob to threaten Lillian was something of a go-between in society.

A man like Wallace Rayburn—not too lowly, and just high enough to be able to approach the right people with Mr. Fahey's formulations. But then again, Cob's eagerness to protect the individual suggested someone able to instill a certain amount of fear in him. I simply couldn't see Wallace Rayburn as that sort of man.

"Where were you yesterday and the night before that, Mr. Hendricks?" My sudden change in subject startled him. His eyes widened, but then the snakelike coolness returned.

"Here. Or in town. I don't know. I come and go, and I do what I'm told."

Yes, Polly had said as much. It seemed we could neither coax nor frighten Cob Hendricks into cooperating. He didn't wait to be dismissed, but suddenly turned on his heel—again with that snide little smile—and left us. The steward wasted no time in returning.

"Finished?"

"We are." Derrick offered me his arm and we made our way, under the steward's diligent supervision, to the vessel's outer steps.

Chapter 13

"You shouldn't have gone to speak with that man," Lucy Carnegie warned me the next day aboard the *Dungeness*. She was holding a small luncheon for the backers of the *Columbia*, and while my presence there obviously ruffled a couple of feathers—namely those of Elizabeth Morgan and Ruth Delafield—Mrs. Carnegie had insisted I accompany Derrick when I'd offered to stay away.

"It's not as if I went alone," I said in my defense. She and I stood to one side beneath the overhang that shaded the deck outside the fore saloon. The others mingled close by, their hands occupied with champagne cocktails and hors d'oeuvres. The two ladies in question were giving me a wide berth; clearly they had not forgiven me for my insinuations concerning why the police had hurried to close the investigation of Lillian Fahey's death. Another reason to shun me, perhaps, stemmed from my having come straight from the offices of the *Messenger*: I hadn't bothered to change out of my workaday clothes of dark blue walking suit and starched white shirtwaist. I stood in stark contrast to their airy muslin and lawn.

"Even with Derrick along, you took an awful chance." She moved closer and lowered her voice, but not the vehemence it carried. "Men like this Cob Hendricks, a member of a ship's maintenance crew, are typically of the roughest sort, often merely a step or two above criminals. They're known for drinking and fighting in their spare time."

"Yes, Mrs. Carnegie, I realize this but—"

"They have precious few ties to anyone. Many of them are released from their positions at the end of the sailing season, and thus have little loyalty to anyone but themselves."

"Mr. Hendricks *is* married," I reminded her.

"To a woman who waved a club at you on your own property."

Yes. I had told her everything that had happened. I hadn't meant to, really, but something about her easygoing camaraderie and forthright candidness invited my confidences. Much like the blunt Mamie Fish, with whom I had once solved a crime, or formidable Aunt Alva, although without the complication of Aunt Alva having been a Vanderbilt, no longer being so, but still having much to prove to the family and the rest of the world.

I didn't know if Lucy Carnegie and I were truly friends, but I hoped so. I enjoyed her company and usually found her advice sound. Even now, I knew she was right.

"It wasn't exactly a club," I persisted, nonetheless. "It wasn't quite that substantial."

"Perhaps not, but a knock on the head would still have raised a darned good bump."

I couldn't argue there. She moved off to mingle with her other guests, and I did the same. While Mrs. Morgan and Mrs. Delafield might not have been happy to have me there, I was still Mrs. Carnegie's guest and they didn't dare openly avoid me. Fanny Morgan, John Morgan's wife, didn't appear to share their distaste, and she and I fell to discussing the season's upcoming charity luncheons. It gave me an opportunity to bring up St. Nicholas Orphanage in Providence, to which I had been donating for years. At first my contributions had been rather negligible, but since gaining my inheritance from Cornelius Vanderbilt, I had increased the dollar amounts manyfold.

While we talked, I kept an eye out for Derrick, and wondered where he had gotten to. None of the other men were absent; no one, in fact, but him. Just as Mrs. Carnegie announced luncheon served in the dining room, he came sauntering up from below deck, a puzzled look on his face. No one else noticed the look, or his absence, and the afternoon proceeded routinely enough.

It wasn't until we were in his carriage heading back to town and the *Messenger* that he turned to me and said, "The *Dungeness* has seen the hand of Eben Fahey."

While I had expected some explanation of why he had wandered off, I hadn't expected this. "What do you mean?"

"I won't get technical because, your not being a sailor, the finer details will be lost on you."

I took no offense; when it came to watercraft, he was correct. Instead, I waited for him to continue.

"I began noticing design elements, modern ones, on the *Dungeness* that I'd seen elsewhere. Namely, the *Columbia*, and the *Corsair*. Things first caught my attention on deck, so after poking around a bit I went below to ask some friendly questions about the engine and the propulsion system, you know, sailor to sailor. Now, especially with the *Dungeness* and the *Corsair*, these elements would have been recent improvements, because when they were built these particulars wouldn't have been in use yet."

He waited for the implication to dawn on me, which it quickly did. "Would Eben Fahey be responsible for these changes?"

"He most certainly would."

One revelation led to another. "Mrs. Carnegie never mentioned knowing him at all. Not even in a business sense. Nothing. As if she barely ever heard of him."

"Exactly."

"Even when we learned Lillian's identity, she didn't bat an eyelash." I sat back against the carriage seat, staring at the road ahead but not seeing it. "She lied then." I shook my head as disappointment swept through me. "Why would she lie?"

Derrick made no reply, his attention on the pair of bays pulling the carriage.

"Perhaps there's a good explanation." There had to be. I *wanted* there to be. "How long has she had the *Dungeness*? Perhaps a former owner . . . ?"

"She commissioned the building of the vessel," he said with a sigh. "She would have commissioned any later improvements to it as well."

"Oh, Derrick, I don't want to suspect her."

"Neither do I."

"What on earth could a woman of Lucy Carnegie's age, social position, and wealth have had against a girl like Lillian Fahey?" I watched as we passed rolling hillsides on either side of the road, before turning toward town and the bay. Derrick stayed silent, knowing I was attempting to work it out. "Surely they could not have fought over a man, this Walter Raleigh. That wouldn't make sense at all. And I'm reasonably certain Mrs. Carnegie couldn't have had trouble paying Eben Fahey for his services."

"No," he agreed. "Her husband left her with enormous wealth."

"But if she wasn't happy with his work, she might have refused to pay him. And Lillian might have come here demanding compensation for her father. . . ." That reasoning sounded hollow even to my ears, and Derrick's skepticism showed in his expression. "No," I concluded, "it isn't that either."

"It could simply be that she didn't think to mention knowing Eben Fahey." The carriage listed as we rounded the bend onto Thames Street. "She warned me to stay away from Cob Hendricks."

"Sound advice."

"Perhaps. But what if she did so to protect her accomplice?"

Derrick glanced over at me. "Do you really believe that?"

I shook my head. "No, but that doesn't mean it isn't possible."

At the *Messenger,* we discovered Ethan Merriman, the reporter with whom I shared office space, had left to attend several events that afternoon, one after another. The summer Season was like that, what with charity functions, garden parties, sporting events, not to mention nighttime activities such as theater, private musicales, and balls. A society journalist found him- or herself in high demand, not only because readers lapped up the details of such affairs, but also because the Four Hundred themselves reveled in showing off their wealth in print.

Ethan's absence suited our purposes as Derrick and I, and a few minutes later, Jesse, crowded into the tiny office. We began by informing Jesse of our talk with Cob Hendricks, to which he shrugged and expressed his relief that I hadn't gone alone. Then Derrick explained what he believed to be a clear link between Eben Fahey and Lucy Carnegie, though she had never given the slightest hint of knowing him—nothing beyond having heard of him by reputation.

When we had finished, Jesse asked, "And you feel this adds her to the list of suspects in Miss Fahey's death?"

"Don't you?" I asked in return. "It *is* suspicious, don't you think? Not that I readily believe in Mrs. Carnegie's guilt, mind you, but we can't completely discount her, can we?"

"I suppose not." Jesse, sitting at Ethan's desk, slumped lower in a corner of the wooden rolling chair and draped an arm across its back. "But to be honest, I'd much prefer our culprit to be this Cob Hendricks than a member of the Four Hundred." He held up a hand to forestall the protest that had, indeed, risen to my lips. "Before you get your dander up, you know how hard it is to bring charges against one of *his* set." Derision marked those last two words as he jerked his chin at Derrick.

"I'm from Providence, not New York, so technically I'm not a member of the Four Hundred." Derrick's own chin jutted in indignation. Not that either of them was sincere in disparaging the other. They had years ago developed a rivalry—over me—which, though now amicably settled, continued as a source of amusement between them.

"You might as well be," Jesse retorted. He played with the brim of his derby, sitting on the desk in front of him. "The point is, charging one of your wealthy brethren with a crime is a colossal headache for the police and prosecutors alike. Not that I enjoy seeing a member of my own class saddled with crimes they didn't commit. But this Cob Hendricks sounds like a nasty piece of work and it wouldn't pain me any if he turned out to be the culprit. And, of our suspects, he was the last to see Miss Fahey alive."

"As far as we know, that is." I shook my head as doubts once again reared up. "No, I think if Cob murdered Lillian, it was at the behest of someone else."

"Then there's his wife," Derrick added, "another piece of work."

Having been hovering near him, I leaned over the desk and swatted his arm. I didn't wish to believe the worst of Polly for no better reason than that she had obviously lived a harsh life, and such women tugged at my heartstrings. But I had to admit he had a point.

"Tell me about this Polly Hendricks," Jesse said in that policeman's analytical tone I'd come to know well.

I recounted how she had turned up in my yard ready to beat me with her wooden baton if I didn't agree to leave her husband alone. I also described how she had defended him, despite implying that he sometimes became violent with her.

"A brute of a husband," Jesse mused. "And an angry wife. Could Cob and this Lillian have been carrying on?" When I again started to protest, Jesse cut me off. "It wouldn't be the first time a roughneck of his sort turned the head of a well-born young lady. I don't understand it, but there it is."

Derrick nodded. "We've considered that, too."

"And fairly well dismissed it," I put in. "It's hard enough to picture Lillian with Wallace Rayburn, never mind a man like Cob Hendricks. Yes, I know you're thinking of my cousin Consuelo."

Jesse held out a hand, palm up, and echoed Derrick's words from the other day. "Lillian was the same age as your cousin was then."

"But a vastly different kind of girl," I insisted. "By all accounts, Lillian was steadier and more mature than Consuelo at the same age. You know how it is with the daughters of the Four Hundred. They're practically kept under lock and key—in fact, for a time Consuelo was. And they're told nothing about life until they absolutely need to know. It wasn't like that for Lillian. She had friends, could come and go as she pleased, for the most part. She helped her father in his work and it appeared he trusted and respected her."

"At least, according to him," Jesse reminded me.

"And her housekeeper." I'd begun pacing the narrow expanse of the office. Now I perched at the edge of my desk, behind which Derrick sat. "Then we have Eben Fahey him-

self, and when exactly he discovered his formulations missing. Did he believe Lillian to be at her friend's house until the
telegram from Newport arrived? Or did he discover Lillian
had taken the plans and come after her?"

"It's difficult to envision a man killing his own daughter."
Derrick turned the swiveling chair side to side, facing me,
then Jesse, and back again. "It's too heinous to consider."

"But it does happen," Jesse murmured. "One question is
if Lillian obviously had a beau, why didn't her father know
about it? Why the secrecy?"

I thought that over. My own parents had left Newport
shortly after I turned eighteen. They'd moved to Paris,
where my father could paint and study with the artists who
had flocked there over the past couple of decades. Essen-
tially, I had been left to my own devices, although even as a
child I had realized, on some level, that I came in second
with them, behind art and the art world. My great-aunt
Sadie had swiftly swooped in and offered me a home at Gull
Manor, making it lovingly clear that, since she had no children of her own, she wished me to be her heir. But what this
all amounted to was my having navigated the unfamiliar waters of young adulthood without the influence of a father.

What kinds of things did fathers object to when it came to
their daughter's potential beaus? Instead of looking to my
own family, I looked to Derrick's, and why his parents objected to me. "Perhaps Lillian feared her father wouldn't
think her choice was good enough for her. Perhaps not a
good enough provider. That would hold true whether it was
Cob Hendricks or Wallace Rayburn."

"There might have been some black mark against this fellow or his family," Jesse suggested.

"Or the man is a professional rival," Derrick said, "which
fits with the formulations being stolen. In which case, Eben
Fahey would have been justified in his objections."

"Or it could simply be that Mr. Fahey considered his daughter too young for an attachment, or he enjoyed having her home and didn't wish her to leave yet." I slid off the desk and continued pacing. "Wallace Rayburn," I said, ticking off another of our suspects. "If Cob can fall under suspicion of having won Lillian's affections in order to steal her father's work, Mr. Rayburn certainly can. He's still not the sort of man I could picture Lillian setting her cap for, but he's a good deal closer to her world than Cob is and can more easily move within it."

"Walter Raleigh." Derrick tented his fingers beneath his chin. "Who is he most likely to be? Rayburn? Perhaps, but perhaps not."

"There's the coincidence of having the same initials," I mused aloud. "And being a sportsman, part of a racing crew, and living an adventurous life. He could easily identify with someone like Sir Walter Raleigh."

"But you hate coincidences." Derrick showed me an ironic smile.

"Just so. And this one is altogether too easy." I crossed my arms over my chest.

"You yourself pointed out that Rayburn is no genius," Jesse said. "Just a basic young man with an aptitude for sailing. Is it that much of a coincidence that as a boy, he noticed the similarity between his name and that of an adventurer and decided to make a game of it?"

"Perhaps not." But I shook my head, still unconvinced. "I'm all but certain the person who murdered Lillian can be found at Beacon Rock." I turned to face Derrick and Jesse. "There are Tyrone Kerr and the Delafields."

Derrick's gaze narrowed as he considered. "Tyrone might have run through his inheritance by now and needed those formulations to raise some cash. Lord knows, he's got little enough interest in the family holdings. He's much more dedicated to proving himself a dashing bachelor."

"That rather makes him a Raleigh type, doesn't it?" Jesse placed the flats of his hands on the desktop and leaned forward. "What about the Delafields? What kind of money do they have?"

"The Delafield family hasn't much money of their own anymore," Derrick supplied, "though their pedigree is good. They were heavily invested in agriculture, namely wheat exports, and lost a bundle back in the panic of '93. They're not destitute, mind you, but he certainly couldn't keep *Mrs.* Delafield in the style to which she is accustomed without digging into her considerable dowry."

"She wants a divorce," I blurted. Then, more sedately, I added, "He has refused, by what I've heard."

"So we can't discount him either." Jesse threaded his fingers together. "He might not like living off his wife's money and wants more of his own. And being married certainly doesn't rule him out, especially if there are problems between him and his wife."

"Exactly," I agreed. "He's no stranger to flirtation, I can tell you that."

Derrick nearly came out of his chair. "What does that mean?"

"Nothing I couldn't handle." I raised both hands in a gesture that urged him to relax. "It wouldn't surprise me if he toyed with Lillian, used her, got his hands on those formulations, and . . ." I trailed off, having been about to conclude with, "disposed of her." But flirtation was one thing, murder another. Did I want Bernard Delafield to be guilty simply because I didn't like him?

Both men were watching me closely, subtly nodding, and I realized I hadn't needed to complete the thought, as they had followed my logic anyway.

"He may have done all of that," Derrick said, "yet not gone so far as to murder Lillian. Perhaps he even cared for her. But if Ruth discovered her husband's indiscretion, she might have taken care of Lillian herself. How easy would it be for anyone, woman or man, to push someone off Beacon Rock?"

"We're getting nowhere. No closer to discovering which of them caused Lillian to drown." Frustration had me clenching my fists until my knuckles ached. "I'm still convinced Cob had something to do with Lillian's death. If he didn't kill her himself, he knows who did. Derrick, you and I got nowhere with him. But, Jesse, if you could arrest him, or bring him in for questioning . . ."

"On what grounds?" he asked with a shake of his head and a shrug.

"He was one of the last people to have encountered Lillian before she died, and he argued with her. He upset her." Even as I spoke, I saw the answer in Jesse's expression.

"Arguing with someone in broad daylight doesn't constitute a crime, I'm afraid. And we're going by the word of a man, your friend Angus, who's known for enjoying his grog—a lot. So yes, I might question Cob Hendricks on the basis of his having seen Lillian on her last day on earth, but I'm likely to get no more than that out of him, and I can't exactly threaten him with charges to loosen his tongue."

Silence, heavy with disappointment, fell over us. Then I said, "We should bear in mind that whoever killed Lillian must also have killed Edward Gorman. Or ordered someone else to."

"It's not as easy as all that to hire an assassin," Jesse said.

"It is when you're a member of the Four Hundred," I countered with a wry twist of my lips.

Derrick looked both concerned and wounded. "Is that what you think of us?"

"You just said you're not a member of the Four Hundred," I reminded him.

"A matter of semantics," he quipped in return. "Most of

us are law-abiding citizens." At the smirks Jesse and I sent him, he amended that to, "I said *most*."

I considered the claim debatable, but I didn't challenge him further. It had been a dilemma for me my entire adult life, from the time I first began reporting on the doings of the Four Hundred and others of their ilk. I had soon learned that even my own relatives, whom I had always esteemed and still did, were not blameless when it came to opportunism, profits, and using their considerable influence to their benefit. All I did know of a certainty was that Derrick was not such a man; indeed, a more fair-minded individual could not be found.

"If the same person murdered them both," Jesse said, picking up where I had left off, "they had to have gotten to Long Island and back in less time than you did."

"Perhaps not." I considered the timing. "The person might have gone down ahead of us and made it back before we ever sailed, or we crossed paths at sea without realizing it. The *carte de visite* found on Lillian might have alarmed whoever killed her, and he hurried down to Great Neck and back to Newport before anyone realized he—or she—was missing. Just about any of our suspects has access to sailing vessels—fast ones. Even a woman could have hired a boat to take her there and back."

"So what now?" Derrick appealed to both Jesse and me. "We're no closer to identifying the killer than we were the night Lillian was found."

I paced a few steps before coming to a sudden halt. "I have an idea. Tyrone Kerr was willing to help me once before by having Wallace Rayburn help him sail the boat he was considering buying. I wonder if he might arrange a similar opportunity for us to question Cob where he can't simply walk away as he did on the *Corsair*."

"Aren't you forgetting something?" When I didn't reply,

Jesse continued as though explaining a difficult concept to a child. "Tyrone Kerr is on our list of suspects. He may be the very person giving Cob his orders. What makes you think any help from him will be sincere?"

"I don't see that we have many other options." I blew out a breath. "We'll simply have to corner Cob and press him until he tells us . . . something."

Derrick nodded. "Let's just hope it resembles the truth."

"Hold on one moment." Jesse turned a stern expression on both of us. "The first time Tyrone Kerr helped you, Emma, you boarded a boat with him and Wallace Rayburn and set out past the harbor. I cannot allow you in similar circumstances with Cob Hendricks."

"Certainly not," Derrick agreed.

"Nor you," Jesse shot at him. "It's too dangerous."

A smile spread across my face. "I know how we'll do it. It might involve a boat, but I promise neither Derrick nor I need step foot on it."

Chapter 14

As it turned out, I had told Jesse a half lie. Two days after our discussion at the *Messenger*, the *Columbia* sailed out of Brenton Cove for the first of several practice runs it would make while in Newport. I remained on dry land, watching with Lucy Carnegie, the Morgan ladies, and Mrs. Delafield from the northwest corner of the terrace at Beacon Rock. It was a splendid sight to see, with *Columbia*'s white sails filled with wind and sunlight, and the flashing of the gulls that escorted her out to the harbor sparkling against a brilliant sky. Once clear of the cove, the yacht seemed to draw a breath, gather its energy, and soar forward, arcing wide as it headed south.

I found myself clutching the railing and leaning forward as my throat tightened from the sheer beauty of it. The word *Godspeed* sprang from my lips.

Oh, and the half lie? Derrick was aboard, as were the Morgan cousins, Tyrone Kerr, and Bernard Delafield. Also onboard were Wallace Rayburn and the entire racing crew, and one man who had been asked to fill in a spot—a spot invented by Tyrone Kerr for Cob Hendricks.

During the voyage, every nuance involved in racing the ship would be inspected, adjusted, and put to the test. We ladies were expected to entertain ourselves in the ensuing hours. As a New York Yacht Club member in her own right, and a *Columbia* backer, Lucy might have gone with them, but she chose not to.

"I know when to push and when to back away quietly," she told me only minutes before the *Columbia*'s anchor had been raised. "It's a tricky thing, dealing with men on their terms. They don't like to share power." She laughed. "There were quite a number who opposed my joining the yacht club, and I've no intention of fanning that fire if I don't have to. In the meantime, I'll enjoy Lizzy Morgan's hospitality."

Elizabeth Morgan's hospitality included a sumptuous lunch, card playing, and entertainment provided by a string quartet. The terrace's overhang had been extended with wide awnings, providing us ample space in the cool shade. Also cool were Mrs. Morgan's and Mrs. Delafield's greetings when I arrived earlier, but they didn't dare completely shun Derrick Andrews's fiancée. They didn't wish to risk losing a backer for their Cup challenge of the coming year. Although, Ruth Delafield did grumble a bit about there being too many of us to play bridge. We instead played euchre, hearts, and pinochle, in between chatting and eating.

The *Columbia* thrilled us with another appearance partway through the day. Sailing in through the mouth of the harbor on the Jamestown side, she arced close to us before looping back out toward the Atlantic. I thought I spied Derrick waving, although that might have been wishful thinking. But the sight once again brought a lump to my throat, and a kind of wordless mariner's prayer swelled in my heart.

"Men and their toys," Fanny Morgan said, though with a tolerant chuckle in her voice. "Thank goodness they have such pursuits to keep them busy and out of our hair. Am I right, ladies?"

Lucy didn't reply, but the other two nodded and voiced their agreement, though I heard in Ruth Delafield's murmured reply a sentiment approaching bitterness.

I played the polite and grateful guest for the rest of that day—even losing a couple of times when I might have won—until the *Columbia* made its way proudly back into Brenton Cove, its sails reflecting the soft pinks and oranges beginning to tint the western sky. There was still much to do onboard, and it would be some time before they disembarked, but the plan, again masterminded by Tyrone Kerr but eagerly approved by Edwin Morgan, was to have the entire crew up to the house for a celebratory dinner.

Two celebratory dinners, actually. The gentlemen and upper crew—skipper, first and second mates, navigator—were to dine with the ladies in the main dining room, while the others would eat in the servants' hall. Cob Hendricks was one of those others.

I waited until I saw the first of the rowboats set out from the Morgans' pier. Then I quietly separated myself from the other women, went through the house, and emerged onto the circular drive. From there I hurried to the staircase and zigzagged my way down to the pier, hoping the men on the *Columbia* were too busy to notice me, or if they did, they hardly spared me a thought. I also hoped Lucy hadn't seen me and decided to follow, as she had on the night we found Lillian.

With a quick look back at the stairs, I slipped into the boathouse and waited for Derrick to arrive.

Although the western sky blazed with the sunset, the dock between the boathouse and the craggy mound of Beacon Rock lay cloaked in smoky blue shadows. Inching the curtain aside on one of the front windows, I watched as the men climbed the many steps up the cliff face to the driveway, from where they entered the house. The gentlemen and head crewmembers entered through the front door. The others went around the jutting west wing to the service entrance. So far neither Derrick nor Cob had appeared, and I grew worried.

I needn't have. The last skiff bumped against the pier, and Derrick and Cob Hendricks climbed out, along with two other men and the oarsman. Again, I waited while they went to the steps, all except Derrick and Cob. Muffled through the glass I heard Derrick ask the other man to wait. Cob shrugged him off, told him he works only for J.P. Morgan, and started toward the steps. It was then I opened the boathouse door and walked out.

"Mr. Hendricks. Not so fast."

He spun around, his leering gaze sweeping me from head to toe. "You again. I mighta known there was a reason I was asked onto the *Columbia.* Thought there was something fishy about it."

"Then why'd you agree to it?" Derrick asked him in an offhand manner.

"Got paid for it, didn't I?" He scowled, then turned his head to spit something into the water. Chewing tobacco, I guessed, with a grimace of distaste. "And don't be thinking of cheating me out of a day's pay because I won't answer your infernal questions." Once again, he started toward the landward end of the pier.

"Stop right there, Mr. Hendricks." Derrick strode to him and grabbed his upper arm to stop him and spin him around.

The man's other arm came up, his hand curled in a fist, and I cringed in fright for Derrick's sake. I made a quick mental inventory of the inside of the boathouse. A bookend? A large magnifying glass? But the blow never came. Cob Hendricks seethed, but lowered his fist to his side.

"A good decision, Mr. Hendricks." Derrick spoke amiably, as if to a friend.

"I answered your questions already. I ain't about to tell you nothin' different."

"Had you actually answered our questions the first time, we wouldn't be here now." I swept across the dock to them. "Mr. Hendricks, a reliable friend of mine saw you arguing with Lillian Fahey the afternoon of the day she died. Now, we also know she left you very much alive, at least then. She hired a boat to bring her out here, to Brenton Cove."

"So? What's it got to do with me?"

"She was upset after leaving you," I persisted. "Why? What did you say to her?"

His chin came up, the bristling afternoon growth of beard matching the blue-black shadows gathering around us. "She stepped on my foot. I told her to watch where she was going or she'd end up in the water."

He spoke flippantly, with a mean grin that faded as I said, "She *did* end up in the water, Mr. Hendricks. Very much dead."

His mouth gaped and his gaze darted back and forth between us. I saw speculation behind his muddy brown eyes, as if, for the first time, he took seriously the notion that he might be a murder suspect. "I heard she did herself in."

"You heard wrong, Mr. Hendricks."

He ran a hand under his chin. "I don't want any trouble."

"Oh, I think you're already in it up to your eyes, Hendricks." Derrick slapped a hand on the man's shoulder, prompting him to shrink and pull away.

"We've given the police your name," I added. "But you can avoid having to deal with them by telling us who gave you your orders."

"Orders? Don't know what you're talking about."

"You didn't just argue with Lillian," I said steadily. "You

threatened her. Why else would she have been so upset after her encounter with you on the wharf?"

"You know how women are," he said with a sneer. "One harsh word and they fly apart."

"Not Lillian Fahey." I smiled slightly and shook my head. "Lillian was made of sterner stuff than that. We believe she came up to Newport to confront someone, and that someone silenced her permanently. We also believe you know who that someone is. If you don't tell us, if you continue to protect this person, Mr. Hendricks, you will be an accessory to murder and will soon find yourself on the inside of a jail cell."

"Or swinging from the end of a rope," Derrick added in a deadpan voice. "Tell me, were you paid enough to make it worth it? Or are you that afraid of this individual?"

"I ain't afraida no one." Cob began backing away from us. Only a flick of his gaze over his shoulder prevented him from taking one step too many and falling in the water. He stopped short and appeared at a loss. He opened his mouth and I expected an entreaty for us to leave him alone, to believe he had nothing to do with Lillian's death. But no words came.

Instead, he lurched forward. His hand shot out and he grabbed my arm, spun me around—much as Derrick had done to him minutes ago—and held my back to his torso. My arm throbbed when his grip released, but any relief I felt dissipated as his forearm lodged against my throat.

"Step away, or I'll snap her neck." His threat, growled at Derrick, rumbled against my back. The forearm tightened, cutting off my breath, while the other hand gripped the back of my head. He could easily make good his threat with very little effort. My eyes were wide as they held Derrick in a desperate gaze.

Derrick didn't hesitate in opening up space between us. "Let Miss Cross go, Hendricks. You're only getting yourself in deeper trouble."

"Keep moving. Over there." He gestured to the boathouse with a jerk of his chin. He inched us forward, his feet kicking mine with each step he forced me to take.

Derrick continued to back away, but with infinitesimal steps that kept him nearly within my reach. "Be reasonable, Hendricks. You don't want to compound your own sins to protect someone who'd toss you aside without a second thought."

We reached the juncture where the smaller boathouse dock met the larger pier. I expected Cob to force me to step up. Instead, my world tilted and I went over the side of the dock, to be swallowed by the churning water, made so by my own splash.

I slipped under and the world went silent. But only for a moment. Regaining my awareness, I shook away my disorientation and kicked my feet. My skirts twisted around my legs, but I kept kicking anyway. My arms reached upward and despite the drag of several layers of fabric, I broke the surface and drew a frenzied breath. I heard another splash, and then Derrick was in the water beside me. His arm closed tightly around me, while with the other he pulled us toward the dock. I stopped kicking but used my arms to paddle. Somewhere in the back of my mind, beneath my shock and fear, I thanked my brother Brady for having taught me to swim when we were children.

At the edge of the dock, Derrick grabbed hold of a piling and used it for leverage to help lift me out of the water. I reached up onto the dock and pulled with all my strength, dragging myself upward as Derrick pushed me from behind. Not the most dignified of circumstances, but it worked, and soon I was lying on my stomach on the boards and helping him roll himself up and out of the water. Only when I knew he was safe did I sit up and brave a glance upward.

Cob Hendricks scrambled up a few last steps and onto the service driveway. He disappeared into the gloom, but the sounds of disturbed brush told us Cob had scrambled beneath the bridge and into the landscape designed by Frederick Law Olmsted.

I swept my sodden hair back from my cheeks and brow. "Well, we made a hash of that, didn't we?"

"The pair of you are going to put me in an early grave." Jesse shook his head in disgust at Derrick and me, but I saw the relief lurking behind his exasperation.

After our drenching in Brenton Cove, we'd gone up to the house, explained I'd had a mishap that landed us both in the water, and set out for Gull Manor, dripping on the lovely leather seats of Derrick's carriage the entire way. While our poor excuse might have made us look foolish, we didn't wish to reveal our confrontation with Cob, or his hasty retreat, to any potential culprits at Beacon Rock. We were all but certain Cob took his orders from one of them, and we didn't want the individual in question to feel suddenly cornered and have a reason to lash out at the Morgans and their guests.

Tyrone Kerr did, however, follow us outside to the driveway and ask what had transpired with Cob down at the boathouse. "Did you learn anything?"

We were able to truthfully tell him we hadn't, and went on our way.

Now, we sat with Jesse and Nanny outside in my yard in the wooden chairs brought out from the kitchen, because Derrick hadn't clothes to change into and refused to drip on our floors and sofa, despite my insistence that my furnishings would be none the worse for it.

"You both might have joined Lillian in a watery death," Jesse continued grumbling, "and for what? He didn't tell you a thing."

"Whoever has Cob in his pocket has him in deep. And it's hard to reason with a poor man who has found a lucrative source of income." Though I had changed into a dry frock, moisture clung to my hair despite a brisk toweling from Nanny. I resisted an urge to shiver as the ocean thrust a cooling breeze across the property. One shudder and Nanny would send me back into the house.

"I thought perhaps he feared whoever is giving him his orders," Derrick added, "but the way he shook off that suggestion makes me believe it's a case of greed, not fear. Which, in my mind, rules out most of the women, who wouldn't have access to the kind of funds needed to keep Cob loyal—not without their husbands noticing."

"Unless she happened to know something about his past," Jesse said easily, "some secret that could put Cob Hendricks away for years, or send him to the gallows."

"Or perhaps the person giving the orders has threatened Cob's wife." Nanny spoke softly, her words almost drowned out by the ocean waves striking the boulders at the foot of the peninsula.

"Isn't he rough with her, though? Emma, didn't you say that?" Derrick reached down and yanked a few tall strands of hawkweed from the surrounding grass. Absently, he sat back and twirled the yellow blossoms between his fingers.

"She implied as much." I winced, even as I said, "I suppose that doesn't mean he doesn't care for her in his way."

"A man who shows his love with his fists?" Jesse made a sound of repugnance. "As I've said, it wouldn't pain me any if he turns out to be our guilty party. But at least your dousing tonight gave me a reason to launch a search for him." He came to his feet. "We should have him by morning. It's unlikely he'll find a way off the island tonight. Even if he does, we've alerted the mainland."

I looked up at him, grateful for his friendship. "You're leaving?"

"I need to get back to the station in case anyone brings him in or telephones with information on his whereabouts." He once more leveled a stern look on both Derrick and me, but spoke to Nanny. "Try to keep them out of trouble, if you can, Mrs. O'Neal."

Nanny reached up to place her hand in his as though making a pact. "I'll do my best."

News came early the next morning with the ringing of my telephone. I hurried down the stairs, securing my robe around me and with my hair trailing down my back. I'd had the contraption for several years now, but its jangling bell always startled me, especially in the early mornings or late evenings.

Nanny had already answered the call and was speaking quietly into the ebony mouthpiece when I slid my way into the alcove beneath the staircase. "Here's Emma," she said, and handed me the ear trumpet.

"We found him," Jesse's voice said across the wires. "Practically right where you left him, or where he left you. He's dead."

A jolt went through me. When Nanny saw my reaction, her expression mirrored my own shock. "He drowned in Brenton Cove?" I asked.

"No, Emma. We found him beneath the Beacon Rock bridge, his head smashed on the rocks. I'm at the house now. Can you meet me here soon? We'll need to ask you and Derrick some questions."

"Of course, Jesse. What about Cob's wife, Polly? Does she know yet?" My heart went out to the woman, who evidently cared for her husband, whatever he might have been in life, however he might have treated her.

"We sent a boat out to the *Corsair* to bring her to town."

After we ended the call, Nanny and I hurried back upstairs, where she helped me don my usual shirtwaist and skirt, and put up my hair in a simple twist. The day promised to be a hot one, the air moist and close, so I carried my jacket over my arm after pinning on my straw boater. Katie, meanwhile, had gone out to the barn to hitch Maestro to my gig, and by the time I hurried back down the stairs, horse and carriage waited on the drive.

Faces that showed both fatigue and shock greeted me upon my arrival at Beacon Rock. Jesse had gathered the Morgans and their guests in the drawing room, where my adventures had begun only days ago. Derrick was there as well. He stood as I came down the steps into the sunken room and met me partway.

Hand in hand we turned to face the others. I was glad of his solid presence beside me, especially as I perceived the anger seething in the room around us. The Morgans and the others had been awakened abruptly to the distasteful news that yet another death had occurred on the property. John and Fanny Morgan, the Delafields, and Lucy Carnegie had rowed ashore hours before they typically would have left their staterooms. But even for Edwin and Elizabeth Morgan and Tyrone Kerr, staying here at the house, being awakened by the police barely after dawn would issue a rude shock to their systems.

I would have expected their dismay, but I realized by their expressions that Derrick and I were somehow being held to blame. Only Lucy Carnegie's features maintained a semblance of neutrality. I couldn't help but recall her warning about how dangerous a man like Cob Hendricks could be. I should have listened to her.

Jesse walked to the center of the room. He took a small notebook and a pencil from his coat pocket. "Miss Cross, thank you for joining us. I'll get right to the point. You and Mr. Andrews met with Cob Hendricks yesterday evening, yes?"

"That's right," Derrick said, and I nodded.

"What happened during that encounter?"

Never one to stand silently by, I offered, "We asked him some questions concerning Lillian Fahey."

Before I could say more, Ruth Delafield cut me off. "Why?"

I met her gaze. "Because we believe he had something to do with Miss Fahey's death."

J.P. Morgan harrumphed, his barrel chest straining the buttons of his vest. "Why didn't I know anything about this? The fellow worked for me. I should have been consulted before anyone approached him."

Jesse held up a hand. "I'd appreciate it if everyone would allow Mr. Andrews and Miss Cross to continue." He turned back to us. "What kinds of questions did you ask him?"

Jesse knew quite well what had been discussed with Cob; he asked for the benefit of the others, who watched us with a combination of resentment and reluctant interest. Derrick said, "We had heard from a witness that Cob Hendricks argued with Lillian Fahey when she first arrived in Newport." He went on to describe our conversation with Cob, while I filled in some of the finer details.

"And then what happened?" Jesse asked when we fell silent.

"He became violent," Derrick said.

"He grabbed me and threatened to snap my neck if we didn't stop asking questions and allow him to leave," I replied, eliciting gasps from the women present—all except for Lucy, who watched intently from a corner of one of the sofas, her expression still one of impartiality. "He forced me to walk with him toward the steps up the cliff face, but suddenly shoved me into the water."

"He deduced, rightly," Derrick continued, his hand tightening around mine, "that with Emma in the water, nothing else but her safety would matter to me, and he could make his escape. Which he did."

"The police searched the grounds last night and didn't find any sign of him," Jesse said. "He must have come back later, in the early morning hours." He turned slowly as he addressed everyone in the room. "I'll need to know where everyone was between midnight and dawn, when Cob Hendricks's body was found here beneath the bridge."

With a small cry, Ruth Delafield shut her eyes. "Must you be so macabre, Detective?"

"A man is dead, Mrs. Delafield," he replied, not unkindly.

"That is hardly our fault." Her eyes opened and her gaze went to her husband, sitting across the room in one of two wingback chairs. The other was occupied by Tyrone Kerr, whose gaze shifted back and forth between the married couple.

I watched them as well. When their gazes met, Ruth's became accusing, while Bernard replied with a look of defiance.

Jesse apparently saw it, too. "We'll begin with you, Mr. and Mrs. Delafield. Where did you spend last night?"

"Onboard our yacht, the *Cassiopeia*." Mrs. Delafield sounded as though Jesse's question had offended her unforgivably.

He didn't let it deter him. "Is that so, Mr. Delafield?"

The husband shifted uncomfortably, uncrossing and then recrossing his legs. He cleared his throat. "It is true in my wife's case."

"And in your case, sir?" Jesse took on an expression of keen interest, the point of his pencil tapping his notebook.

"I spent the night in town. At Dover House."

"On Catherine Street, sir?" Jesse specified. "White clapboard with dark green shutters? Portico out front?"

"*Ahem.* Yes. I . . . er . . . keep a room there whenever we're in Newport."

I needed no explanation to understand what that meant. If he merely wished to put space between himself and his wife, their yacht was big enough. No, his room at the inn on Catherine Street was for discreet assignations, where he might indulge his pleasures without having to cross the threshold of a brothel.

"Were you alone, or accompanied?" Jesse raised an inquisitive eyebrow, as did several others in the room.

A fiery blush crept up Ruth Delafield's neck and flooded her face. Her eyes sparked with fury. Her husband said, quietly, "Accompanied. If you like, I can supply a name to corroborate that."

A guttural sound came from Mrs. Delafield's throat. Her pretty lips curled downward, and she stared into her lap. Her husband spared her a glance and shrugged, though she did not see the gesture. But the others did. Suddenly, Fanny and Elizabeth Morgan appeared not to know quite where to look, and in their discomfiture their complexions nearly rivaled Ruth's. I thought Elizabeth might have darted an accusatory look in my direction, as if I were the cause of everything unpleasant this morning.

"Yes, Mr. Delafield," Jesse said briskly, "I'll be needing that name." But he turned his attention next on Lucy Carnegie. "Mrs. Carnegie, did you spend last night on your yacht?"

Lucy didn't seem in any way taken aback by this manner of questioning, and said readily enough, "I surely did, Detective. I was onboard the *Dungeness* from eleven fifteen—sleeping soundly most of the night, mind you—until this morning when your men came and alerted my steward that my presence was required here at the house. Didn't so much as set a toe in the water, much less come ashore, before that."

"And you can verify that?"

"Ask any of my crew." She hopped up from her armchair, displaying her diminutive height, and held out her plump arms. "But surely you don't believe the likes of me could have overpowered a boiler room worker?"

Jesse only smiled and said, "Thank you, Mrs. Carnegie." She resumed her seat and Jesse turned to John and Fanny Morgan. "And you, sir? Madam?"

"We were on the *Corsair*. All night, same as Mrs. Carnegie. And any member of my crew will vouch for it." John Morgan's voice boomed through the room, reverberating against the high ceiling. I even imagined the windows rattled slightly as if from rumbling thunder. Unlike Lucy, he apparently did mind, very much, being questioned by the police.

"Now, John." Fanny Morgan laid a hand on her husband's arm. "The detective is only doing his job. Detective Whyte, if you think you should, you may certainly come aboard the *Corsair* and question any of our crew, not only concerning our whereabouts last night, but about this man, this Mr. Hendricks. I understand he worked in our boiler room. I believe his wife might also work for us."

"That would be Polly Hendricks, and yes, she does," I blurted. It irked me that a woman of Mrs. Morgan's standing wouldn't know the names of those in her employ. Yes, the *Corsair* was a large yacht and probably employed about sixty servants and crew, but it seemed only common decency that her owners would be acquainted with the names of all souls onboard.

"Oh, isn't she our chambermaid? Yes . . . I believe that's right." Mrs. Morgan looked unperplexed by my outburst. "Poor thing, she's a widow now. John, we must see to her future, mustn't we? And assure her of her position with us, if she wishes to stay on."

That redeemed the lady considerably in my estimate.

Jesse then appealed to Tyrone Kerr. "I understand you're staying here at the house, Mr. Kerr?"

Tyrone Kerr glanced down at his fingernails. "That's right. I'm here as Edwin and Elizabeth's guest."

"Were you here all night?"

The man smiled. "Indeed I was, Detective."

"Did you not go outside at all, say, for a breath of fresh air?"

"Well, Detective, now that you mention it, I did do just that. It was sometime after midnight, I believe. I came through this very room and out onto the terrace."

"Did anyone see you?" Jesse asked.

"In fact, I passed by the night footman on my way through the center hall. We wished each other good evening. I didn't see him when I came back inside."

"And you went directly back to your room?"

"I did."

Jesse paused as he jotted down these details. "Did you hear anything unusual on the property last night?"

"Not a thing."

"Mr. Kerr, you arranged the meeting between Mr. Andrews, Miss Cross, and Mr. Hendricks, correct?" Jesse asked next.

"What is this?" John Morgan sat up straighter in his chair, anger sending a rush of blood to darken his features. "Without mentioning it to me?"

"Now, J.P., don't go having an apoplexy." Mr. Kerr gave a roll of his eyes. "They merely wished to question the man, and he hadn't been cooperating. I arranged for them to speak under circumstances where he couldn't run off—at least not easily. Happened he did anyway, but he turned out to be cleverer than we gave him credit for. Or perhaps not, seeing how things turned out." He shrugged. "I would surmise my having helped corral this Hendricks fellow lets me off the hook suspicion-wise, Detective?"

"We'll see, sir." Without a moment's hesitation, Jesse asked Edwin and Elizabeth Morgan the same questions he'd asked the rest. They both claimed to have been in their respective bedrooms all night, not leaving them until Edwin's valet and Elizabeth's maid woke them at dawn. I tended to believe them, just as I believed John and Fanny. As for the rest . . .

Jesse's next question sent a jolt of surprise around the room. "Where were you all in the afternoon of the day Lillian Fahey drowned? Let's see . . . We'll start with you, Mr. Delafield."

Chapter 15

"I was . . . I was . . ." Bernard Delafield's stuttered attempt to answer Jesse's question faltered abruptly. His color rose.

Ruth Delafield, on the other hand, barely missed a beat. "We had only arrived in Newport that morning, Detective. Our yacht dropped anchor in Brenton Cove at about eleven o'clock. We were both onboard, and remained onboard until we were rowed to the Morgans' pier to attend their dinner party that evening."

"Neither one of you left the"—Jesse consulted his notes—"the *Cassiopeia* until that evening?"

Mr. Delafield compressed his lips, causing Mrs. Delafield to frown. "Did you? When?" she demanded.

"While you were napping." He sheepishly avoided her gaze. "After luncheon." Turning back to Jesse, he explained, "I had one of our men row me into town."

"For what purpose, Mr. Delafield?"

We were all interested to know, our attention riveted on the man's face. He cleared his throat. "I went to the Reading Room to check in with my acquaintances."

Jesse made a notation. "Did you go anywhere else, make any other stops?"

"I stopped at a tobacconist along Thames Street."

"Which one?"

"I don't know . . . I don't remember."

Mrs. Delafield snorted, managing to make it a pretty sound despite her obvious disgust. "One would think you'd had enough of tobacco after you lost all that money two years ago when the bottom dropped out of your American Tobacco stock. All the smart men sold out ahead of time."

Fanny Morgan gasped. Elizabeth Morgan's hand flew to her lips. And the men in the room, excepting Derrick, darted glances at one another from beneath their eyebrows. No one—but *no one*—ever discussed such losses among their peers. Not among the Four Hundred. A wife certainly never admonished her husband publicly in such a way.

Good heavens, the Delafields' marriage was truly in tatters.

After another question or two wherein Jesse established for the record that, according to Mr. Delafield, he returned to the *Cassiopeia* directly after leaving the Reading Room, Mrs. Delafield added a sullen, "I, for one, never left the yacht until we went ashore for the Morgans' dinner party."

"Thank you, Mrs. Delafield," Jesse said graciously.

"Wait one moment." Tyrone Kerr tugged the lapel of his linen coat. "If the death of this Hendricks fellow has to do with the young woman who drowned, isn't it obvious what happened?"

"Exactly what is obvious, Mr. Kerr?" Jesse further beckoned with an outstretched palm for the man to elucidate. Indeed, the rest of us looked at Mr. Kerr with eager anticipation, although I admit mine—and I suspect Derrick's and Jesse's—came laced with skepticism.

Mr. Kerr made a sound of exasperation, as though dealing

with a room full of imbeciles. "Obviously, Hendricks was guilty, or he wouldn't have pushed Miss Cross off the dock and run away. He murdered the girl—this Lillian Fahey—and her father murdered Hendricks out of vengeance. The man is staying in town, isn't he? That's what I've read, anyway."

"That's true, Mr. Kerr," Jesse confirmed with a nod. "It's quite possible that Cob Hendricks murdered Lillian Fahey. But if so, we believe it was on behalf of someone else. However, Mr. Fahey has witnesses who can place him in town last night."

"What Kerr is saying makes sense," Bernard Delafield jumped in. "Surely these so-called witnesses must have slept at some time during the night." He gave an amused laugh. "Fahey could easily have given them the slip."

"True." Jesse again nodded as if giving this theory serious consideration. "But there is no likely way Mr. Fahey would have known of yesterday's and last night's events: the practice run of the *Columbia* and how Cob Hendricks was included in the crew; his being questioned by Miss Cross and Mr. Andrews upon returning to Beacon Rock; his shoving Miss Cross in the water and running off. No, far likelier is that someone here had been watching, and later met with Hendricks in the hollows beneath the bridge. They might have arranged the meeting even before the incident with Miss Cross."

Lucy Carnegie spoke up. "Why would they have planned to meet?"

It was my turn to explain. "Precisely because someone noticed that Cob had been asked to fill in on the *Columbia*'s crew. Whoever had been paying him would have seen this as unusual since Cob was not a sailor, per se, but a workman. He—"

A stab of guilt halted my words. Whatever Cob Hendricks had been, whatever ill deeds he had performed in life,

his death was partly on my hands. Had I not been so adamant about questioning him, the events of last night would
never have occurred. Derrick apparently noticed or sensed
my hesitation and my thoughts. He eased closer, until his
shoulder touched mine. With a steadying breath, I continued, "His associate must have wished to get to the bottom of
why he had been asked to sail, and who he spoke with during and immediately afterward. Again, it had to have been
someone connected to the *Columbia* and to Beacon Rock."

Mrs. Elizabeth Morgan gasped. Managing to gather her
dignity about her, she rose from the sofa and clasped her
hands at her waist. "I resent the implication that anyone
connected to our home is responsible for this man's death.
He was a ruffian, an undisciplined troublemaker, as evidenced by his actions toward you, Miss Cross. Any hooligan from town might have followed him here after a jaunt
among the taverns, fought with him, and . . . and we know
the rest." She pressed her lips together primly and remained
standing, casting an imperious glance around the room. No
one dared challenge her.

"We've gotten away from the question at hand," Jesse reminded us, then turned to Mr. Kerr. "Where were you the
afternoon of Lillian Fahey's death, sir?"

"Aboard my yacht," he answered without hesitation.
"Which has since been sent up to Warwick for some engine
work, ordered before I left New York."

Jesse once again jotted a notation in his notebook. "May I
ask, sir, why you are having this work done in Warwick
rather than New York?"

"For the simple reason that having my vessel serviced in
New York would have delayed my arrival here. I did not
wish to miss these first runs with the *Columbia*. Besides, I
know a quite capable marine mechanic in Warwick. He's
done work for me before."

"And since then you've been staying here in the house?"

"I have."

Jesse's brows gathered in a subtle frown, as if he found this particular detail highly interesting. Mr. Kerr tugged at his lapel again, plucked at his sleeves, loosened the knot of his necktie. A small but defined ridge asserted itself beside the inner corner of his right eye. Jesse left him to stew. He turned the same line of questioning on the Morgan cousins and their wives. When he got to Elizabeth Morgan, she exhaled audibly and sank back onto the sofa.

I had begun to wonder what suspicions were running through Jesse's mind. Surely his questions were a matter of procedure, and he didn't believe any of the Morgans, the men or the women, had a hand in either Lillian Fahey's or Cob Hendricks's death. I felt the latter death also ruled out Lucy Carnegie and Ruth Delafield, as neither woman appeared to have the strength necessary to overcome a workman.

Tyrone Kerr or Bernard Delafield? Either struck me as far more likely than any of the others present. I silently assessed each man. Mr. Kerr always seemed so amiable, so confident and at his ease—except presently. Mr. Delafield, on the other hand, often exhibited agitated behavior, arrogance, and plain inconsideration.

But as I had learned in the past, guilty individuals could often put on a good face, while innocent ones could seem untrustworthy. So, which one?

Or—it suddenly occurred to me—could both be involved?

"Detective Whyte."

At the authoritative voice behind me, I released Derrick's hand and spun around to behold Jesse's fellow detective, Gifford Myers, descending steps into the room. I hadn't known he was here; Jesse hadn't mentioned it when we spoke on the telephone. He was followed by a uniformed officer, and a third man who shuffled between them, nearly tripping on the steps.

Even before I saw the handcuffs encircling his wrists, the clinking of the chain linking them together confirmed that Wallace Rayburn had been arrested.

"He has no alibi for last night," Gifford Myers announced to the drawing room as a whole. "After the dinner laid out for the crew in your servants' quarters, Mr. Morgan, he disappeared. His bed hadn't been slept in, according to the fellow he's been bunking with."

"I told you, I went into town, had too much to drink, and slept it off. . . ." Wallace Rayburn trailed off, looking uncertain. He also looked as if he had been in a recent brawl and had not emerged the victor. His clothes were rumpled and soiled, his hair matted, eyes bloodshot, and, in addition to several bruises on his face, he sported a gash across the back of his hand.

"Where did you sleep it off?" Detective Myers pressed.

Mr. Rayburn shook his head. "Woke up behind a shed on Thames Street. Near Howard's Wharf."

"How did you get into town?" Jesse asked him.

"Walked. With Jim Farrow and Will Comstock. They told you as much," he added with an accusing look at Detective Myers.

"They also said they lost track of you during the night and walked back to Beacon Rock without you." Gifford Myers regarded Jesse. "This Farrow is Rayburn's roommate here in the house. It's him that said Rayburn never turned up till this morning. The whereabouts of everyone else is accounted for."

"How'd you get that gash on your hand?" Jesse pointed at the wound.

"Fight," Mr. Rayburn replied succinctly.

"We'll need more than that," Jesse said.

Mr. Rayburn shrugged. "Can't remember much more than that."

The Morgan cousins both came to their feet. The younger of the pair, Edwin, came forward and gestured at young Mr. Rayburn. "This man is a part of our racing crew. We can vouch for him."

"You can vouch for his whereabouts last night, Mr. Morgan?" Jesse asked, almost as a challenge. One neither Morgan seemed willing to accept.

"Well . . . no." Edwin conferred silently with J.P. The elder man shrugged and tugged at one shaggy side of his handlebar mustache. "I suppose we can't at that, but Rayburn has never given anyone a moment's grief. He's quiet, hardworking, a knowledgeable sailor, and a dependable crewmate."

"Mr. Morgan." Jesse addressed the elder cousin. "As we've already established, Cob Hendricks was employed on your *Corsair.* To your knowledge, were he and Wallace Rayburn acquainted?"

"How the blazes should I know a thing like that?" the financier blustered, his face reddening in annoyance. "What a man does in his free time is his affair. They don't work together, that I can tell you. Wouldn't be on the same vessel at the same time. Except for yesterday." His eyes narrowed on me. "And whose doing was that?"

"Actually, it was mine, if you'll remember, John." Tyrone Kerr huddled deeper in the wingchair, as if his admittance put him in bodily danger. "I arranged it."

"That's right. And for the life of me, I still can't understand why," the elder Morgan grumbled.

"You did this?" The chains of the handcuffs jangled as Wallace Rayburn raised his hands to point at Tyrone Kerr. "We all knew Hendricks shouldn't have been on the *Columbia* yesterday. He didn't *do* anything useful, mostly just hopped out of the way of the rest of us. Why, Mr. Kerr? Why'd you do it?"

"To help find the truth of who caused that poor girl's

death," Mr. Kerr said sadly, his gaze on the floor. But then he looked up sharply. "You admitted you knew her, Rayburn. How well?"

"You say *admitted* as though knowing her is a crime." Wallace Rayburn flinched and nearly lost his footing, if not for Detective Myers steadying him by gripping his biceps. "I told you I met her the one time. Same time you did, onboard the *Columbia* when she came with her father."

Yes, I recalled, Mr. Rayburn freely admitted having met her. But Mr. Kerr hadn't remembered her. At least, he claimed he hadn't.

"Then tell us, Rayburn, why was she wearing a ring with your initial engraved on it?" Gifford Myers's voice held no pity. "And carrying a picture of herself addressed to you, which you apparently handed back to her in a most caddish way when you broke off the relationship."

I stared at the detective with something approaching shock. Was this the same man who had insisted Lillian killed herself out of grief? Apparently, this most recent death, as well as that of the photographer, Edward Gorman, on Long Island, had proved to Gifford Myers and his superiors that there was more going on here than a young girl's broken heart.

"What?" Wallace Rayburn attempted to back away from the rest of us, but the detective's hold on him prevented him from taking more than a step. "I never gave her any ring. And she certainly never gave me any picture. And what does any of that have to do with last night?"

"We'll discuss it down at the station." Detective Myers turned him roughly and gave him a shove to start him walking. The uniformed officer assisted Rayburn up the steps. They disappeared across the central hall.

"Well then." Edwin Morgan let out a long sigh. "I supposed you're quite finished with us, Detective Whyte?"

"For now."

"I hardly see the point of upsetting us all the way you have, Detective," Elizabeth Morgan said with no small derision. "Goodness, the things that were said here."

"It's all right, Lizzy." Ruth Delafield rose and swept to the other woman. She clasped Elizabeth's hand and cast a brief glance over her shoulder at her husband. "I didn't learn anything I didn't already know or suspect."

"I'm so sorry, Ruth, dear."

"I know."

Linking arms, the women faced the rest of us. Anger blazed in Elizabeth's eyes, though whether directed at Bernard Delafield on behalf of her friend, or at Jesse and me for bringing such unpleasant tidings to spoil the day, I couldn't say. Perhaps both. Mrs. Delafield, on the other hand, looked abashed and as though her hold on her composure could crumble at any moment.

"We're finished here for now," Jesse announced to no one in particular. "But we may need to speak with some of you again."

"Really, Detective," Edwin Morgan declared, "can you not be satisfied with the results of this fiasco without making matters worse? As it is, we've lost a valuable crewmember, one we'll be hard pressed to replace in the coming months. Will you not leave us in peace now?"

Jesse made no reply. He flipped his notebook closed and placed it, with his pencil, back in his coat pocket. As he passed me on his way out, something in his expression told me he wasn't at all satisfied with today's results.

And neither was I. Circumstances certainly did make Wallace Rayburn appear guilty.

Circumstances . . . and coincidences. I didn't like it.

Our welcome more than worn out, Derrick and I also made our way outside. Once there, I lamented our having come separately, as now we had no choice but to leave in our respective carriages.

"What did you think?" I asked him as he walked me to my gig.

"I think Edwin was right. It was a fiasco, from start to finish."

His answer startled me. "Are you blaming Jesse for mishandling things?"

"Not at all. Although I do wish he and the rest of the police force would stop treating my brethren with kid gloves." He added mocking emphasis on the word *brethren.*

"You know he'd like to, but it would probably make more problems than it would solve. Better he use caution and appease the sensibilities of your set."

He offered me a humorless, lopsided grin. "You mean their egos."

"Yes. I can afford to ruffle their feathers. He can't."

We reached my carriage, and Maestro turned his head toward us in greeting. I walked past the buggy and stroked the length of his muscular neck. Reaching into my handbag, I proffered the treat I'd brought him as a thank-you for waiting here so patiently for me. He gobbled the small apple in one good bite.

"You know, Emma, seeing the Delafields at each other's throats—"

"It wasn't *that* bad," I protested, though I nearly squirmed at the memory of Ruth having heard her husband's confession of where he had spent last night. And then I remembered what she had said about his financial losses. "Then again, perhaps it was. My goodness, do you think they'll have a frightful row once they're alone? He wouldn't hurt her, would he?"

Derrick shook his head and put his hand on mine in reassurance. "No, he's not the violent type, at least not with women."

"But if he murdered Lillian, then he *is* the type to become violent with women. Oh, Derrick, perhaps we should do something."

He grasped my shoulders and drew me closer. "Don't worry so. Even if he's guilty, he wouldn't push his luck by harming Ruth. His guilt would be too obvious. No, theirs will be a war of words, a loud and lengthy one."

Feeling relieved on that point, I frowned. "What were you about to say when you brought them up? There seemed to be something more."

"There most certainly is." He leaned his forehead against mine, knocking my hat askew despite the pin holding it. "Seeing the Delafields like that made me realize how *happy* you and I will be, and that we mustn't waste any more time before setting a date. I want to be married to you as soon as may be."

I couldn't help chuckling as I leaned slightly away to look up at him. "Their *un*happiness as a married couple brought this on? I would think it would make you run for cover."

"No. We'll never be like them. They're wasting their time being together. Having no children, they should end their farce of a marriage as soon as possible. On the other hand, you and I . . . what we feel for each other is the very reason for marriage. Emma, what are we doing? Why are we still waiting? You've mourned your uncle Cornelius, and Alice approves. Let's set a date. Today."

I smiled up at him. "Today is a bit short notice for a wedding, no?"

"You know what I mean." He brushed his lips against mine, setting off a multitude of sensations within me. "What do you say?"

My heart and the pleasure of his lips, of his hands on mine, made me want to cry out that we'd be married before the week's end. But then the old hesitancy descended on me like a wool blanket on a hot summer's night, stifling and restraining. Why should I feel that way, when time and again Derrick had proved to be the kind of man who was unafraid of an independent woman, who valued my opinions and my abilities and never sought to thwart me?

Perhaps it had to do with my conversation with Brady back in New York. His questions popped into my mind: *Is that realistic? What about children?*

I had agreed to marry Derrick without a moment's hesitation nearly a year ago when he had surprised me with the ring I wore on my left hand. Neither then nor now did I doubt my love for him, but . . .

I did continue to doubt my suitability to become his wife. Never mind the disparities in our backgrounds, or his parents' disapproval. What if I couldn't manage to be a wife, mother, and journalist? Would I disappoint him? Would I disappoint myself? Would I feel limited, suffocated? Would I miss the freedom to come and go at will, or feel crowded in my own home and begin to pull away? Good heavens, would I ruin everything between us, until we ended up little better than the Delafields?

"Emma . . . ?"

I owed him an answer. I owed myself an answer.

"Miss Cross!"

The call came from the courtyard behind us. Derrick stepped away with a groan as Mrs. Carnegie emerged onto the driveway, her skirts flurrying around her ankles in her haste.

"Yes, Mrs. Carnegie." I suppressed a sigh. "Can I do something for you?"

"You most certainly can." Lucy Carnegie stopped a few feet away and surveyed the two of us, her eyes alight with speculation. "It seems I've interrupted something."

"Not at all," I lied.

"*Hmph.*"

"What is it I can do for you?" I asked, hoping to distract her from her assumptions.

She relaxed her posture, pinched her lips together, and shook her head. "You can explain to me what the devil went on in there." She held up a hand when both Derrick and I started to speak. "Don't give me any more rigmarole. I want the truth. Yes, Wallace Rayburn has been arrested, but this isn't over, is it? Your detective friend still suspects one of us, doesn't he?"

Chapter 16

"To be perfectly honest," I replied to Mrs. Carnegie, who appeared in no mood to be pandered to, "I don't know what Detective Whyte is thinking. He didn't confide in me."

Though only partially true, that last detail irked me. I had grown accustomed to Jesse freely expressing his thoughts concerning cases and asking my opinions. This time, however, he had given me no indication of whom he suspected, if anyone, among the Morgans' guests. But I believed Mrs. Carnegie was correct that Jesse wasn't satisfied with the arrest of Wallace Rayburn. Neither was I.

What made today different from other times was the presence of Gifford Myers. With him as coinvestigator on the case, Jesse had little choice but to make it appear he no longer valued my insight. He had been warned once, and if he openly went against his superiors, he could very well find himself wearing a uniform and walking a beat.

Derrick cleared his throat. "Perhaps I should leave you two to discuss what went on inside. Emma, I'll see you at the *Messenger* in a little while?" Though his question was a casual one, his expression held so much more, filling me with both anticipation and perplexity. It seemed the two most important men presently in my life, Jesse, my friend, and Derrick, my beau, had reached decisions that nudged me off balance and into a world of uncertainty.

How much easier, in that moment, to face Lucy Carnegie's questions. I nodded to Derrick. "I shouldn't be long."

He kissed me again, regardless of Lucy's watchful eyes, and climbed into his carriage. The Cleveland bays started off at a trot, stepping high as they made their way down the drive. Once he'd disappeared over the bridge, Lucy turned to me.

"Do you think I did it?"

Her bluntness startled me. "I . . . uh . . . no, of course not."

"You're sure about that?" Her eyes narrowed, her head turning slightly to the side as she regarded me. She meant this as a confrontation, no mistake, and she wanted an honest answer.

"Mrs. Carnegie—"

"Lucy. And I'll call you Emma. Or do you prefer Emmaline?"

"No, it's Emma." I smiled and relaxed a fraction. I held out my arm. "Shall we walk?"

She linked her arm through mine and we strolled along the drive toward the bridge. "I thought we had the beginnings of a friendship, Emma. But something has changed. I see it in your eyes. What happened?"

The same thought as moments ago popped into my mind: I owed her an answer. And I deserved to hear her reply.

"I did come to have a slight suspicion against you, Lucy. I'm sorry, but it's true. You see, I'd asked you if you knew Eben Fahey, if he had formulated improvements to your *Dungeness*. You said no."

Whatever she had been expecting, this was not it. She remained silent for several long moments, her body stiffening beside me. Then, she quietly asked, "How did you know?"

"I didn't. But Derrick did, when he and I were on the *Dungeness* for your luncheon."

She kicked at a bit of loose gravel on the driveway with the toe of her side-buttoning boot. "I might have known. I tell you, the pair of you are too clever by half."

We reached the bridge, a masterpiece of engineering that resembled the great Roman aqueducts with their broad, arching supports, but in miniature. Below, Frederick Law Olmsted's graceful landscaping hid all evidence of the murder that had taken place only hours ago, and with the foliage growing far beneath us, it felt as though we were walking among the treetops. From here, we could see out beyond the cove to Fort Adams, sprawling on its peninsula, with Jamestown an undulating line of green in the distance. Closer, only the masts of the vessels anchored in the cove were visible as they reached for the sky.

"Derrick saw the similarities to Fahey's other work immediately," I disclosed, "then went around to confirm what he suspected. He found plenty of examples of Fahey's innovations. Why did you hide it?"

"Why did I lie to you, you mean?"

I sighed, not liking to call it that. Not when it pertained to a woman I had admired—still admired. "All right, yes. Why?"

"Because I didn't like the idea of being linked to the father of a dead woman."

"I don't understand. Eben Fahey has worked with many a yacht owner. That simple fact certainly doesn't link you to his daughter or what happened to her." A wave of dismay washed over me. "Lucy, did you know Lillian? Is that it? You knew the girl and for some reason didn't wish that to become general knowledge?"

Good heavens, I hoped not. The night we found Lillian,

when Lucy had jumped in the water to hold the body in place, she had exhibited not the slightest sign of recognition. She—and Wallace Rayburn as well—had treated Lillian as a complete stranger. As it turned out, Mr. Rayburn *had* met her previously and freely admitted it once he learned of her identity. He had claimed not to recognize her at night, in her sodden, disheveled state. Could that have been the case with Lucy? But then why continue to deny it?

"Did you know her?" I repeated, and held my breath as I awaited the answer.

"No, I swear to you I never met her."

"Then I'm afraid I don't understand why you didn't reveal your acquaintance with her father."

She leaned her arms on the stone parapet, gazing out over the cove and the harbor. "Acquaintance is stretching it a bit. I barely knew the man. In fact, he dealt more with my captain and head steward than with me."

I compressed my lips and considered that claim, then shook my head at a recollection. "You said so before, when I suggested Eben Fahey might have worked on the *Dungeness*. You said he hadn't to your knowledge, but your captain might have consulted with him."

She skewed her lips. "You do have an awfully good memory, don't you?"

"A reporter isn't much use without one." I placed the flats of my hands on the parapet, the stones warm beneath my fingertips. "Why did you lie? How could you possibly think you wouldn't be found out?"

"I simply didn't think it mattered much. I didn't kill his daughter." She paused and turned her face toward me. "I didn't, you know. But after the girl was identified, along with the ring and the photograph found on her person, I didn't want to be linked to any kind of scandal, even third hand."

"How on earth would you be linked to a scandal involving Lillian Fahey simply because her father helped make improvements to your yacht?" Surely there was something she wasn't telling me, some other connection between her and Eben Fahey that she didn't wish society to discover.

"Oh, Emma. Are you that naive, or does the notion of a reputation mean nothing at all to you? If so, bravo you. The rest of us women aren't nearly so cavalier. We cannot afford to be."

Those words astounded me. Did she truly believe I cared not a bit for how my neighbors, family, and friends perceived my character? Did she think I held myself to no moral compass?

Whether she did or not, I realized, was not the point—at least not at that moment. I made a sound of frustration in my throat. "I still don't understand."

"Do you know what it took for me to earn my place in the New York Yacht Club—what it really took? Me, a woman. They were all against me at first. All of them. Only by appealing to their egos and assuring them a mere woman surely had no wish to upset their rules and traditions did I slowly chip away at their reluctance. Ha!" Her sharp laugh made me jump. "Reluctance? No. Downright refusal to take me seriously. But ever so slowly, by seeking their advice, then their approval, and finally their friendship, did certain members of the yacht club come to have a grudging respect for me. Not all of them, mind you. No, not by a long shot. But enough to gain my membership."

"What does knowing Eben Fahey have to do with any of that?" Was Lucy leading me in circles, trying to distract me with her tribulations in the yachting world in hopes I would never arrive at the heart of the matter? "He's certainly done work for most of the members, hasn't he?"

"That's all well and good for the men, but my knowing

Eben Fahey, having done business with him, could very well be used as a means of ousting me, not only from the club but from my social circles. I am a widow, and yes, that affords me some measure of independence, but it's a precarious independence. Society can turn its back on me at the slightest misstep. Surely even you know that. You, who seem impervious to mores and standards and public opinion."

I slowly took my hands off the parapet, scraping my palms slightly against the stones, and eased away from her. Beyond Beacon Rock, the vista of harbor and land formations blurred behind the veil of anger that swept over me. "Mrs. Carnegie, no friend of mine would ever say such a thing, much less think so little of me. You believe I have no morality, no self-respect?"

"That isn't what I said."

"Then what?"

"I admire your courage." She hadn't donned her hat before following me outside, and now she gathered strands blown loose by the wind and tucked them behind her ears. "It far exceeds my own."

I laughed outright. "You, who took on the New York Yacht Club and won?"

"Only because I played by their rules and didn't seek to shock. I would never have knocked on the door of the Newport Reading Room, but I admired you for doing so."

Ah. A few years ago, I had climbed the front steps of that exclusive gentlemen's club on Bellevue Avenue and, as Lucy said, knocked at the door. It was something women simply didn't do. But someone I needed to speak to had been avoiding me, and I took this action as a last resort. Again, I laughed, though ruefully. "It didn't exactly turn out well for me. For my pains I lost my position at the *Newport Observer*."

"Yes, only to be hired by the *New York Herald*, quit that,

and find a position at the *Newport Messenger*, first as its editor-in-chief, and now reporting on real news." Well, she certainly knew a bit about me. She raised one eyebrow as if challenging me to refute these facts. "The point is, you're willing to take the risks, while the rest of, most of us, dare not. I have daughters of marriageable age, Emma. Sons as well. I must think of their reputations as well as my own."

During most of her explanations, I had only half listened, finding them flimsy and being certain a deeper truth lay hidden beneath them. But mention of her children—goodness, she had nine!—prodded me none too gently toward a realization: I cared about doing right, about helping people when I could, about staying true to my sense of integrity, but I seldom cared what high society thought of me because I didn't consider myself part of that society. Yes, I had my Vanderbilt cousins and others like them who had taken me under their wings because of the services I had done them, but the society I valued consisted of Nanny and Brady, Derrick, and the friends and acquaintances I'd grown up with here in Newport.

But Lucy Carnegie was very much part of the higher echelon that lived by its own standards, rules, traditions, and, perhaps most of all, its pecking order. I had witnessed firsthand how fragile a woman's reputation could be, how easily society could turn on her, how she could be shunned simply for being in the wrong place at the wrong time. Raise eyebrows once, and no one ever looked at a young lady—or mature widow, for that matter—the same again. What seemed to me ludicrous, that Lucy should lie about knowing Eben Fahey, was to her a matter of her children's future well-being.

"You see, Emma . . ." She paused, and I realized she had been speaking during my ruminations. I blinked, eliciting a tolerant smile from her. "As I was saying, had it merely been a matter of Lillian being Eben Fahey's daughter, without all the rest, I wouldn't have thought twice about admitting I knew him. But with the photograph and the ring, and the implication that she jumped from the ferry because of a broken heart brought on by indelicate behavior . . . it all seemed rather sordid and I couldn't know what more might be discovered. What part he might have played. How shocking it might become."

"Yes, I suppose I see that now." Even as I nodded my understanding, a whisper of suspicion continued to blow a cool breath across my shoulders. I chalked it up to habit, learned these past several years, rather than to any real disbelief in Lucy's reasoning.

"May we remain friends, then?" She drew closer and reached for my hand.

In all honesty, I didn't quite understand why she wished to be my friend. We were at least two decades apart in age, and of very different backgrounds and lifestyles. Yet I nodded again. "Of course."

"Good. Because I don't know where I might find another like you." She tugged me closer and gave me a kiss on the cheek. "Now go and tell that nice Mr. Andrews when you plan to marry him. And don't forget to mention the Adirondacks."

Lucy had me smiling all the way into town. A weight had lifted from my mind where she was concerned. Though I never truly suspected her of murder, especially in Cob Hendricks's case, I came away from our talk reassured about her reasons for never mentioning her connection to Eben Fahey.

And then there was that other matter. . . .

Midmorning traffic of carriages, wagons, carts, and pedestrians choked Spring Street when I arrived in town. With no hope of finding an empty place along the curbstone at which to park my buggy, I signaled to one of the *Messenger*'s newsboys whom I spied coming around the corner, a stack of folded papers peeking out from the messenger bag slung across his shoulder. I fished a few coins out of my purse and handed them to him. "Would you bring my buggy to Stevenson's Livery, Freddy?"

"Sure, Miss Cross." The eagerness that lit his eyes made me pause.

"Straight to Stevenson's, Freddy, and nowhere else. Mind?"

"Oh, sure, Miss Cross. Right away."

"By the way, did you happen to see Mr. Andrews inside?" I couldn't help asking in my own eagerness to speak to Derrick as soon as possible.

He climbed up into the buggy, gathered the reins, and glanced down to regard me. "You might want to avoid him, Miss Cross. He's in a prickly mood."

"Is he?" He hadn't seemed particularly perturbed when he left Beacon Rock earlier. I wondered what had happened at the *Messenger* to so alter his mood.

"Yes, ma'am, as prickly as a hive that's been poked. Well, I'll be getting along to Stevenson's now."

"Thank you, Freddy," I replied absently, and made my way inside.

Only Mr. Sheppard sat in the front office. He saluted me but barely glanced up from the papers strewn in front of him. I bid him good morning and pushed through to the rear corridor.

Voices drew me toward the back of the building, where the physical work of producing each day's edition took place. At the moment the presses were quiet, the morning papers having been printed and sent out, some on delivery wagons, some with our newsboys. Soon they would start up again to produce the afternoon extras. The voices grew quiet a moment, then I heard Derrick's voice alone.

"It's not acceptable. We can't be late with our morning

edition. Whatever happened, make sure it doesn't happen again."

I stopped in midstep. Derrick never spoke to his employees that way, especially not to Dan Carter, our head press operator. Yet it was Mr. Carter who replied, "Yes, sir, Mr. Andrews. It won't happen again. . . ."

He said something more, but just then Ethan Merriman stepped out of the office we shared. "He's in a right foul mood, Miss Cross. You have any idea why?"

"I don't, Ethan. He seemed just fine when I last saw him, which wasn't all that long ago."

"Well, he laid into me for a mistake he found in the morning edition, in the article on the Wileman girl's coming out ball. I left an E off one of the guest's last names. I told him I'd put an apology in the afternoon extra, but really, it was someone of little note and no one is going to care."

"Except perhaps for the family in question . . . and Derrick."

"And he hollered at two of the newsies for horsing around while they collected their papers."

I frowned. "Not the newsies." I wondered if Freddy had been one of them. It would explain his comment about Derrick being prickly. "So what's wrong with the presses?"

"You know, just a bit of gumming up in the works. Stopped things for a few minutes while Dan and his assistants cleaned it out, and they were off and running again." Ethan sighed and ran a hand through his dark hair. "I don't like to talk ill of Mr. Andrews, and this isn't like him at all, but . . ."

I patted his arm in reassurance and continued toward the press room.

"If I can't trust you to inspect the lines before trouble happens, then—"

"Derrick," I interrupted. Dan Carter stood before Derrick, his cap in his hands, his two assistants flanking and a little behind him, all three of them looking bewildered. Scowling, Derrick whirled around to face me. Before he could demand what I wanted—I could see sharp words forming on his tongue—I said, "A moment, if you please."

"I'm in the middle of something."

I shook my head subtly. "It's important."

He hesitated, the scowl persisting another few seconds before fading and leaving him looking nearly as befuddled as the employees he had been scolding. He blew out a breath and approached me. I took firm hold of the crook of his arm. "Outside." I didn't add a "Now, mister," but I'm sure he sensed the stern command by how tightly my fingers curled around his arm.

Chapter 17

Derrick and I went out the back way and stepped into the alley. Instead of rounding the corner onto Spring Street, I tugged him in the opposite direction until we reached Touro Park on Bellevue Avenue. Barely a word passed between us along the way. His posture remained defiant, his features stony, until the park and the Old Stone Tower came into view. We made our way along one of the footpaths to an iron bench facing the tower with its rough stone construction of eight columns and archways, reaching nearly thirty feet above us. The tower continued to confound those who would define it. Was it a windmill, built by early settlers? A defense tower, erected by ancient Vikings? No one seemed able to decide. I liked the mystery of it and hoped it continued.

Beside me, Derrick let out a long breath that finally relaxed his torso and long limbs. His shoulder brushed mine, then pressed against it and remained. He reached for my hand and threaded our fingers together. "I was beastly back there, wasn't I?"

"According to all reports, yes." I turned to grin at him. "Why is that?"

He regarded the tower and shrugged. "Things weren't running smoothly this morning. Of course, that doesn't mean I should—"

"No. I don't believe that's why at all. Let's think about it and start again."

"Now who's being contrary?"

"I was hoping to be honest." Crows and a few blue jays dotted the park, pecking at the ground, swooping through the air, and coming to land in and on the tower. "Are you angry with me?"

"You?" He seemed startled. Then he raised my hand to his lips. "Why would I be angry with you?"

"For not answering your question. For not setting a date for our wedding."

"Ah. That." He nodded, continuing to hold my hand. He brought it to rest against his thigh. The easiness of the gesture, and the familiarity that should have shocked me, instead filled me with a deep and heart-racing sense that if I didn't seize this chance, if I didn't marry him, I would never find it again—this entwining of love and friendship, of safety and adventure, of being an individual yet part of something larger.

"St. Paul's," I whispered. It was a commitment, and while it frightened me, it elated me, too. "A simple service."

"Yes."

"You won't mind that it's not Trinity?" Although most society weddings took place in New York City, when members of the Four Hundred did marry in Newport, it was always at Trinity Church, beautiful in its white clapboard with its graceful bell tower, and its floating, chalice-shaped pulpit overlooking the congregation in their private, cushioned boxes. By comparison, St. Paul's, the Methodist church I had attended all my life, was modest and unadorned. But I found it lovely and honest, like Methodist Sunday services.

"I won't mind," he said without hesitation. "Why would I?"

Encouraged, I went on. "We could have a small reception downstairs, in the meeting room." Some years ago, the entire church had been raised so that the sanctuary occupied the upper floor, allowing for a large space downstairs used for meetings, receptions, and dinners. "Would that be all right with you?" Would he find such an arrangement paltry, a disappointment?

"I think it will be splendid. Do you think we could entice Nanny to supply us with her apple ginger cake?"

"Hmm, not a traditional wedding cake, but if you ask her, I'm sure she would."

"She could layer it in tiers and cover it in white cream frosting."

I laughed, his enthusiasm warming me to the core. "Yes, and whatever else you'd care for."

"We don't want her working too hard," he said in all seriousness.

"No, but we also mustn't let her think we don't want her doing for us."

"Good heavens, no." His eyes widened in mock horror. "She must never think that."

I sat back, enjoying the solid set of his shoulder against mine and the hardness of his thigh beneath my hand. "I'd like to invite Neily and Grace. If they're in the country at the time, I'd like them to be there."

He was silent a moment, then remarked, "If they come, Alice probably won't."

"I know," I said with a resigned nod. "But I can't not invite people I care about. It's up to them whether or not they'll come. I do hope they will, all of them." Pausing, I contemplated the matter hovering over us, wished it needn't be discussed, and decided there could be no avoiding it. "Will your parents attend, do you think?"

He compressed his lips, that stoniness reclaiming his features, etching lines across his brow and at the corners of his eyes. "As with Alice, we'll invite them. Whether they come will remain up to them." Then a smile softened his expression. "Judith will be ecstatic."

"Oh, Derrick, will she?" He spoke of his sister, Mrs. Judith Kingsley, a widow who had been living in Italy ever since an indiscretion had forced her to seek refuge from the snide whispers and finger pointing of the Four Hundred. Like Derrick, Judith had also fallen out with their parents, who disapproved of the choices she had made. But that had brought brother and sister that much closer, despite the physical distance between them. That a member of his family would be happy for us filled me with unexpected joy. "Do you suppose she'll be able to come?"

"Truly, I doubt it. Robby is still so young, and the cost of traveling . . . And then there is everything she crossed the ocean to escape."

I nodded, trying not to let my disappointment show.

"Of course, where Judith lives in Tuscany is beautiful year-round, except perhaps for the dead of winter and the middle of summer, when it's either too cold or too hot. But were we to marry in, say, September or October . . ."

"Italy . . ." I had told Lucy I hadn't given our wedding trip a thought, but now, tantalizing images of gently rolling hillsides, temperate shores, and fragrant vineyards—all described to me in Derrick's letters while he had visited his sister—filled me with eagerness. Of course, it would mean crossing the Atlantic. . . . The memory of our trip across Long Island Sound replaced some of my enthusiasm with trepidation. "Do you think I'd be terribly ill on the voyage over and back?"

"I think that's something to worry about later." His dark eyes lit with amusement. "For now, the larger question is, do you wish to be married in the fall? Or would you prefer a Christmas wedding, or will you leave me on tenterhooks by insisting on waiting until spring?"

The topsy-turvy emotions of the past several minutes suddenly calmed, like the ocean at sunrise on a clear summer morning. Questions, concerns, fears—they suddenly were of no account whatsoever as conviction took their place. I leaned my cheek on Derrick's shoulder, tipping my boater askew on my head. "October, I think. Indian summer, after the September rains and before the chill sets in. While the leaves are aflame. And when the apples are at their perfect ripeness for Nanny's apple ginger cake."

He plucked the pin from my hatband, removed my hat, and rested his cheek against the top of my head. Then he shifted to plant a kiss on my hair. "October it is, then."

Derrick followed me home that evening and we broke the news to Nanny and Katie together. We still hadn't set an exact date, but the church schedule would have to be consulted for that. We enjoyed a celebratory dinner of roasted chicken with Madeira sauce and savory mushroom bread pudding—a concoction of Nanny's own making. This of course being a sudden change of plan from the simpler dinner she had planned, we ate late in the evening, having calmed our rumbling stomachs with cheese and fresh-baked bread until the roasting had been done.

I didn't know if I had ever seen Nanny so happy. She even splashed a bit of that Madeira into a glass and joined us in toasting our future happiness. Katie never imbibed alcohol, but her flushed face and shining eyes almost belied that fact tonight. The dinner consumed, the dishes done and put away, and the kitchen swept, Derrick finally left us around midnight.

I walked him to his carriage, enjoying the balmy night air against my skin and the gilding of his dark hair in the moonlight. The ocean sang a gentle but constant melody in the background, as the leaves overhead, forming a black frame against the night sky, whispered of summer contentment. Derrick took me in his arms and pressed me tightly against him, until our breath mingled and I wished October wasn't so far off. His kisses were deeper and more profound than any I had experienced so far, suggesting, for the first time, the intensity of what we would soon share. There was still so much I didn't know, about him and about the *us* we would become, but when he climbed up into his carriage and blew a kiss down at me, I felt at peace, but for the rippling desire he had awakened inside me.

I all but floated back into the house. In a happy trance, I helped Katie finish tidying up, humming to myself as I did, prompting Katie to comment that I seemed in an exceptionally good mood. Her sly smile conveyed she knew the reason. That night I slept soundly, and if I dreamed at all, I didn't remember them in the morning. I only knew I awakened with a warmer sense of well-being than I had experienced in a long time. And then the ringing of the telephone beneath my staircase startled me out of my bliss. I grabbed up my robe, found my house shoes, and hurried down.

"Emma, it's Lucy. Can you come to Beacon Rock?"

Confusion and lingering sleepiness made me stammer. "L-Lucy? What . . . what is it? What are you doing there at this hour?" Then again, as a seafaring woman she probably rose early most days, except perhaps when balls ran into the wee hours.

"I want to show you something and see what you think. Can you come?"

"See what I think?" What could she mean? "I suppose I could be there within the hour."

"Sooner, please, if you can." Her excitement and eagerness filtered through the wires. "This could be of vital importance. Or not. I'm not certain. That's why I need you."

"Is this something the police should know?"

"Again, I'm not certain. Come as quick as you can. I'll be waiting at the boathouse."

The boathouse? We had been all through it when we searched for evidence linking Lillian to Beacon Rock. Apparently, we must have overlooked something. I yearned to ask Lucy and ease my curiosity, but I realized, as she must have, that telephone lines offered little privacy.

After we ended the call, I stood for some moments listening to the dead static crackling in the ear trumpet. Slowly I placed it in its cradle, still contemplating Lucy's words. A sudden impulse prompted me to snatch up the ear trumpet again and turn the crank.

Since I hadn't exactly endeared myself to Mr. and Mrs. Morgan, each time I approached Beacon Rock's gatehouse I worried I'd be turned away. But this time, as in the past, the gatekeeper waved me through, having become familiar with me and my gig. With a sigh of relief I crossed the bridge and drew Maestro to a halt on the circular drive, well away from the house. I supposed it was to the Morgans' credit that they hadn't denied me access to their boathouse and their guests' ships anchored in Brenton Cove. Perhaps Lucy had intervened by reminding them that, while they found me a nuisance, she welcomed my company.

I hurried down the staircase that spanned the cliff face, disturbing several gulls feeding along the ledges who in turn startled me when they flapped their great wings and swooped off. At the bottom of the steps, all was quiet. No sounds but the slapping of the tide against hulls and the tugging of lines against masts drifted across the water from the anchored vessels. Several more gulls perched along the gunwale of the *Bessie Rogers*. A few plump, brown-spotted sandpipers picked among the rocks lining the shore farther along the cove.

The boathouse, too, seemed overly quiet, not that I had expected Lucy to come bursting out the door to greet me. Not a light shone inside, but then again, since my telephone summons from Lucy, the sun had risen and cast its slanting rays across the island. I made my way along the dock and found myself stepping lightly to muffle my footsteps. At the door, I hesitated, then knocked softly.

"Lucy?" I leaned close to the window beside me and cupped my hand to the glass to peek inside. The interior was dusky and still. With a frown, I tried the knob, finding the door unlocked. I stepped inside.

"Lucy, are you here?"

No reply came. Strange. Could she have gone up to the house? Perhaps back to the *Dungeness*? I peered out the back window to the steps that led down to the water. A rowboat sat tied to a piling, but neither Lucy nor her oarsman was in it. Perhaps they *had* gone up to the house. While I didn't relish the notion of going up there myself, I reasoned that at this early hour the Morgans weren't likely out of bed yet. At any rate, I was accomplishing nothing here, on my own.

Yet, when I turned back toward the room, the sight that met my eyes held me in place. Above the fireplace, the painting depicting the vessels belonging to the guests assembled here hung askew. Only slightly, but enough that I noticed it no longer quite hung straight against the brickwork behind it. Who had touched it, and why? Judging by the immaculate cleanliness of my surroundings, someone cleaned here every day, dusting and straightening to ensure the boathouse was always presentable. That meant whoever had moved that painting had done it recently, because a maid wouldn't have left it to hang crooked.

Very recently. Lucy?

I walked closer. By now the steamers depicted were all familiar to me. In the shadows, I couldn't read the names emblazoned in tiny letters on the hulls, but I no longer needed to see those names to know which was which. The *Dungeness*, the *Corsair*, the *Cassiopeia*, the *May*, and, in the center, like a crown jewel surrounded by the others, the *Columbia*. A sixth, which I'd forgotten about, stood closer to the mouth of Brenton Cove, as if the owner hadn't wished to come any closer to shore, perhaps to be able to make a quick getaway.

The idea made me chuckle, but only for an instant. One of those ships *had* been here initially, and had left. Gone to Warwick for maintenance. *After* Lillian Fahey had been found in the water.

But what could that mean? Yes, Tyrone Kerr had sent his ship away, but he had made those plans before sailing from New York. Or so he had claimed. He himself had stayed behind, had helped me question two men: Wallace Rayburn and Cob Hendricks.

One of whom was now dead.

Had Tyrone Kerr merely wished to ingratiate himself to me by being so accommodating? I never had checked his story with the marina in Warwick. It would have been so easy, a telegram, even a ride up on the train. But I had believed him. I had thought the story *so* simple to verify, that of course he wouldn't have lied about it.

Reaching up, I took hold of the frame in two hands and lifted it from its hook. I placed it on the sofa and opened the window curtains wider, then turned on the two closest lamps to flood the room with light. The vessel whose name I wished to make out was farther in the background than the rest, and the artist had remained true to proportion. The lettering depicting its name was so miniscule as to be impossible to make out. I hunched lower, grasping the painting again and raising it closer to the light.

E. The name appeared to begin with an *E. EL,* perhaps. Then there was a space, indicating the name consisted of two words. A *D* took shape. The rest were so small, I despaired of ever deciphering them.

Did it matter at all? What could this ship have to do with Lillian Fahey's death? Did she die onboard, and been tossed over the side? But no, the coroner concluded she had died of drowning; he had found no other injuries on her. She had died in the water, perhaps forced in and held there below the surface, but certainly in the water.

EL D; El D . . . The second word was considerably longer than the first, made up of several letters. Could there possibly be any meaning here? I went over the circumstances of Lillian's death, the clues found on her body. The photograph, the ring . . .

The name in the photographer's register: Walter Raleigh. We had theorized it to be a moniker for Wallace Rayburn. The initials fit, and he had been in the wrong place at the wrong time, compounding his possible guilt, enough to convince the police.

Walter Raleigh . . .

I began to consider what I knew about the historical figure who lived during the time of Elizabeth I. Among his accomplishments, he had been a poet, a politician, an explorer . . . He'd traveled to Virginia and helped pave the way for England's first colony.

When the answer came to me, I gasped out loud and once again held the painting up to the light. Could the name of the vessel be *El Dorado*? Had Tyrone Kerr named his yacht after the mythical city in South America Walter Raleigh had sailed in search of in the 1590s? But if that were so, why hadn't any of the others mentioned this to me, or to the police? Why had no one suspected?

Because, I realized with a start, they might simply not

have known of the connection. Many women of the Four Hundred were schooled at home, for the most part, and not many tutors would see the use in educating young ladies about mythical cities and Tudor-age explorers. Wealthy young women were educated in language, music, dance, etiquette, and those skills needed to oversee their households. Even for the men, Harvard and Yale educated, such subject matter would have been dismissed in favor of courses geared toward business and finance.

Again, I wondered where Lucy was. She had telephoned me nearly an hour ago. Had she grown tired of waiting for me, and either returned to the *Dungeness* or gone up to the house?

Footsteps sounded on the dock, startling me. I dropped the painting back onto the sofa and hurried to the door. I flung it open.

"I believe I've figured it out. . . ." I trailed off, my breath catching in my throat, then leaving my lungs in a great heave as I realized the newcomer was not who I had thought it was.

"Miss Cross, good morning." Tyrone Kerr paused on the dock. At first, I hardly recognized him, he looked so different from his usual self. Gone were the tailored coat and trousers, the smart-fitting vest, the straw boater. Now he wore the garb of a workman: denim pants rolled up at the ankles, a dingy cotton shirt covered by a corduroy vest, and a woolen flat cap. He doffed the cap and bowed to me with a flourish. He carried a cloth-wrapped bundle under his arm. "What is it you've figured out?"

Before I replied, I scanned the staircase behind him. Not another soul appeared on the way down. My stomach sank. "Oh, nothing important. I thought you were Mrs. Carnegie. . . ."

He beamed at me as if we shared an uproarious joke, but only he knew how it went.

When he didn't say anything, but simply stood there grinning, I asked, "Have you seen Mrs. Carnegie this morning?"

"Why, yes, as a matter of fact I have."

"Where is she?"

He started toward me again, his footsteps reverberating against the trestles of the dock. They shuddered with each step he took, the vibrations traveling down the pilings and sending little ripples over the water. I shivered as well, and wished I had room to retreat. But there was nowhere to go, only the *Bessie Rogers* or the boathouse. I thought of the rowboat tied out back. Could I make it there and manage to row away before he caught up?

I doubted it very much.

I summoned a smile and repeated my question. "Where is Lucy?"

"Were you to meet her here?" He stepped down off the main dock onto the smaller one in front of the boathouse, only a few feet away from where I stood. I studied his clothes again, wondering where he had gotten them, and why.

"Yes." I thought fast. "She was going to bring me on board the *Dungeness* for breakfast. Apparently, she's been detained. I hope there isn't anything wrong. Oh, but you say you saw her? Is she well? Perhaps she's up at the house?"

Mr. Kerr stood between me and the staircase that led to safety. "I'm afraid Lucy has been tied up this morning." His grin turned frightening, a baring of the teeth that left me little doubt as to who had killed Lillian Fahey. And Cob Hendricks. As for the photographer on Long Island . . .

"Why don't we go inside?" He held out an arm and gestured to the boathouse.

"I really must be going." I started to take a step, but he blocked my path. I almost wished he would shove me into the water, where at least I could attempt to swim away. Or should I simply jump in?

But then he was there, inches away. The feral grin had subsided into a once-more pleasant smile, and I thought perhaps I'd only imagined the sinister aspect of moments ago. He held out the crook of his arm to me.

"Let's do go in, Miss Cross. I have something I've been longing to discuss with you."

"Couldn't we speak up at the house?" I suggested as innocently as I could. But we both knew I wasn't fooling him.

"I wouldn't want the others to overhear. It has to do with the *Columbia*. It's a special secret I wish to share only with you." He took my hand and linked my arm through his, turning me toward the boathouse door as he did so.

"Then I'm afraid you've sought out the wrong person, Mr. Kerr. You know I'm hopeless when it comes to yachting. We firmly established that the night of the Morgans' dinner party."

"Ah, yes. The others weren't particularly kind to you when they learned of your lack of boating experience, were they? Oh, they were subtle, but we both heard the undertones of their comments. Didn't we, Miss Cross?"

He opened the door and gave me a nudge over the threshold.

"Yes, I admit you're right, Mr. Kerr. I didn't mind so very much, though."

He seemed to ignore that as he continued, "You're especially good at detecting the subtleties of a situation, aren't you?"

"I beg your pardon?" I knew what he meant, but I decided to play ignorant as long as possible and keep him talking. However, in the boathouse, the painting greeted me from its perch on the sofa, the bottom of its gilded frame sure to leave an indent in the seat cushions. Again, my breath caught in my throat. If only I had placed it back on its hook before running outside, I might have continued my show of innocence.

Mr. Kerr let out a cordial laugh as he stepped in behind me

and locked the door. "Ah, I see you've been examining it. No, subtleties cannot get past you, Miss Cross. You're too good a journalist to allow any detail to go unnoticed."

"It's a lovely painting." My throat had gone dry and I fought to keep my voice from trembling, only just succeeding. "Yes, I took it down to study it. It's almost like gazing out a window at the yachts in the cove, it's so realistic." I held up a finger to point, astounded that it didn't shake. "There is Lucy's *Dungeness*, where I was to go today. The artist was frightfully skilled."

"You weren't examining the *Dungeness*, Miss Cross. No, it's the one in the distance that captured your attention, isn't it? Clever, clever lady. But perhaps not clever enough."

Chapter 18

The room around me seemed to darken, as if the sun had decided to sink back into the eastern horizon. My heart hammered, my vision wavered, and my knees turned to putty. How I remained standing, I'll never know. Especially when Mr. Kerr dropped the bundle he was carrying, dragged a silk scarf out of his coat pocket, and wrapped it around his two hands, leaving a length between them.

A length sufficient to encircle a person's neck.

"Would you like to sit, Miss Cross?" His voice carried enough force to convince me this was no question. I settled beside the painting, never taking my gaze off him. As I had learned to do in countless situations before this, I visualized the room around me, mentally searching for a weapon. One of the lamps? One of the two crossed oars hanging on the far wall? Could I reach them before he did? Would he snatch one up first and bludgeon me to death?

As I attempted to compute the odds, taking into account that I faced an experienced sportsman in the prime of life and in fit physical shape, he stared down at me, the smile flitting about his lips filled with malice. What did he want? Why hadn't he dispatched me yet?

Our odd standoff ended when he unwound the scarf from one hand and leaned down close, prompting me to shrink farther into the cushions behind me. My throat closed in fear. Yet it wasn't me he reached for, but the painting. He lifted it in one hand, glancing down at it briefly before setting it on the end table beside the sofa. "I'll have you know I commissioned this painting for the Morgans, just last winter. Yes, indeed, it was my gift to them, intended for that very spot." He jerked his chin at the space above the fireplace. The scarf dangled from his left hand, swaying gently as he spoke. He shook his head. "I never dreamed what trouble it could cause me."

"You're Walter Raleigh," I whispered, seeing no point now in pretending. *"Wally dearest."*

His eyebrows went up, not in surprise, but with a wistfulness. "I am. I'm a descendant of the great Sir Walter Raleigh, you know."

"Are you?" My voice came as a murmur. My spine had turned to liquid, my head felt shrouded in cotton.

"We're very much alike, he and I. Both adventurers, sportsmen. Ladies' men."

"Why did you kill Lillian?"

"I didn't."

Why would he deny it now? Surely he didn't mean for me to live. Then I knew. "Cob did."

He nodded slowly, thoughtfully. "She got in my way, even when I tried to end it between us. Stubborn woman. Too tenacious for her own good."

And Mr. Kerr, obviously, had killed Cob to prevent him from talking once he saw that Derrick and I were getting closer to the truth. Perhaps Cob got what he deserved, but

Lillian Fahey did not. "You used her. Convinced her to steal her father's formulas."

"Lillian didn't steal anything," he contradicted me, much to my surprise. "I tried to persuade her that her father hadn't earned her loyalty, that he never gave her the credit she deserved. Many of those formulations were hers, you know. But she refused to help me, foolish girl. So I stole them, while her father was away at one of his deadly dull meetings. Ever met him, have you? Yes, I recall you saying you did. Such a colossal bore, didn't you think?"

While he rambled on, a sensation akin to triumph leaped inside me. Lillian had been innocent; she hadn't betrayed her father after all. With no small measure of satisfaction, I said, "And she came after you, demanding them back."

"Again, such a foolish girl. Yet I thought she might, so I had Cob on the lookout for her the very day she arrived. I met with her that evening before the dinner party, right here." He held out his arms to encompass the room. The lamps I'd switched on sent shadows of that dangling scarf dancing on the wall behind him. He shuddered dramatically, like an actor on stage. "Such a scene. Yelling, tears, recriminations . . . I feared at one point they'd hear us up at the house, or out on the water. Tried to let her down gently. Finally, I had Cob row her back to town."

My blood ran cold. "She never made it there—was never intended to make it. He pushed her overboard."

"Held her under off the side of the dinghy until she stopped thrashing. Damn his bones, though, he should have emptied her pockets first. But who knew the chit would float back into the cove?"

The way he spoke about Lillian sent bile rising in my throat. "Was it worth it, Mr. Kerr? Two people dead—no, three. The photographer in Great Neck. How on earth did you manage that?"

He laughed. "I sent someone to take care of our good Mr. Gorman at the same time I sent the *El Dorado* north for maintenance."

"There's nothing money can't buy," I intoned in a flat voice.

"So true. As soon as you pulled that photograph out of Lillian's pocket, I knew it was only a matter of time before someone went asking the man questions. I'm afraid, Miss Cross, that you left me with no choice." I refused to react to that accusation, as if I were responsible for the crimes this man had committed. "As for your other question. Yes, it will indeed be worth it when I sell those formulations."

"To whom? Yacht clubs from rival countries? Whom else can you sell them to without being caught—" I broke off, realizing this was exactly his plan, and that there were men willing to ask no questions if it meant winning. Because winning didn't simply mean taking possession of an ornate silver ewer designed by Gerrard and Co. Oh, no, there were also wagers made, small fortunes at stake. And obviously, Mr. Kerr didn't care who won, didn't care if he betrayed his own fellow yacht club members. "It all goes to the highest bidder," I concluded with a weary sigh.

He shrugged and wound the scarf once more about both hands, leaving that neck-sized span between them. "I'm sorry you and Lucy became such nuisances. Your Derrick, too, but I'm hoping I won't have to do to him what I'm forced to do to you. After all, he'll be too frantic about you to think of much else. I'm sure your disappearance will prove just the distraction I need to be free of him. A shame, though. I truly do like you, Miss Cross. You've got spirit, for a woman. And brains. Even your share of beauty. But as for breeding . . . well, one can't have everything."

"Is Lucy dead?" The question came from some part of me that already felt hollow and lifeless.

"Not yet." He made an upward jerking motion with his hands, as though I were a puppet and he held the strings. "Get up, please."

I gripped the arm of the sofa beside me and pushed slowly to my feet. Once upright, I wobbled as the room spun slightly. "Poor Lucy. I wish that painting never existed. I wish she hadn't figured it out."

"You should worry about yourself." Then he shook his head, looking puzzled. "It wasn't the painting, I don't think. I'm not sure how she knows." He stepped back, making room for me to move around the sofa table.

I once more contemplated snatching one of the oars mounted on the wall. But he stood between me and it. "Where are we going?" I asked.

He raised his hands to point to the storeroom door. "In there."

"Is Lucy in there?" If so, how was it she hadn't made a sound? Was she truly alive, as he claimed, and merely unconscious? I hung on to that hope.

"Open the door and find out."

I did as he bade me. The room smelled of wood and dampness. It took a moment for my eyes to adjust to the dusky interior, before shelves lined with supplies took shape around me. Bright strips of daylight outlined another door at the far end of the room. This, I knew, led out to the steps where the boat I had seen sat waiting. Then I saw Lucy. She lay on her side atop a pile of folded sail fabric. She appeared to be sleeping peacefully, one hand beneath her cheek, the other draped over her waist, as though she had simply decided to take a nap.

"What have you done to her?" I demanded.

"Nothing. Yet." A rap of his knuckles urged me farther inside.

I stumbled before taking several more steps. I went to

Lucy and crouched at her side. "Lucy?" Reaching out one hand, I nudged her shoulder. When I didn't receive any response, I gave an insistent shake. "Lucy. Wake up. You must wake up."

"She won't, you know."

I started and let out a gasp, not having heard him move so close. He stood only inches behind me. I stroked Lucy's face with the backs of my fingers. "Why won't she?"

"Laudanum." He moved away then, unwrapping the scarf from his hands once more and taking something down off one of the shelves. A bottle, from which he slid the stopper, and a cup. He poured a measure of liquid and set the bottle down again.

I eyed him in the darkness. Suddenly, I understood his plan—the workman's clothes, the rowboat, the laudanum. With Lucy and me incapacitated, he would row us out beyond the bay, into the ocean, and dump our bodies overboard. If anyone saw him, his disguise would help pin the blame on some anonymous deckhand. "Lillian. You used that on her, didn't you?"

"Yes, before I handed her over to Cob. It made his work all the easier."

"I won't drink it," I told him, and clamped my lips shut.

"Oh, you will."

I sprang to my feet and lunged for the door, but he reached it first and slammed it shut. He grabbed me one-handed by the shoulder and hurled me against the nearest shelves. Pain shot through my ribs and reverberated up and down my spine. He wasted no time in pinning me in place, his legs wedged against mine, his left hand encircling my throat. He forced my head back and brought the cup closer. A slight adjustment brought his fingers off my neck and to my mouth, where they dug between my lips to force them open. I fought back, shoved, punched, tried to kick, but he held me too tightly against the shelves and I could find no leverage. I started to bite down. He pulled his fingers free, and covered my nose with his hand, cutting off my breath.

With no choice, I opened my mouth to drag in air. Bitterness coated my tongue, burning on its way down my throat. Then more of it, until I coughed and gagged and sent liquid spraying out of my mouth. Still, enough went down and my stomach threatened to revolt.

Tyrone backed away, smiling maliciously as he wiped his face with his coat sleeve. "How do you feel, Miss Cross?"

At first, all I felt was relieved to be able to breathe again. Then it seemed as though molasses moved through my body, my brain, and I felt myself plummeting from the very apex of Beacon Rock, slowly, slowly falling head over heels, waiting for a violent landing that never came.

Though I seemed to be swimming in darkness, I yet remained conscious. Perhaps I had spit out more of the concoction than either I or Tyrone had realized. His hands clamped around my upper arms, preventing me from simply collapsing to the floor. I wondered why he bothered—why take care with someone who would soon be dead?

He swung me about like a rag doll. My head lolled backward, as I hadn't the strength to keep it steady on my neck. I was lowered onto my side, as Lucy lay, and became aware of the warmth of her body at my back. She and I had been reduced to a small pile of humanity atop the heap of sails. Somewhere, in the part of my brain still able to reason, I supposed Tyrone would now ready the dinghy and dump us into it before rowing us out into deep waters.

In my fight to stay conscious, I pressed my fingernails into my palms and concentrated on the pain. It wasn't enough, and a warm void beckoned, enticing and hard to resist. How easy to tumble into it, to find peaceful respite after all the days of worry and danger.

At sounds from beyond the boathouse walls, I pricked my ears. Voices! Or did I only imagine them? Perhaps, but I didn't imagine the swear words Tyrone cut loose, followed by the creak of the storage room door opening. I waited for his footsteps to signal his exit from the room, but he seemed to be hovering on the threshold. Summoning every ounce of strength left to me, I peeled one eyelid open. Yes, Tyrone stood with his back to me, the door into the main room cracked an inch or two. He swore again, a whispered oath. My pulse leaped as I heard my name.

"Emma! Emma, are you here?" The shouts were followed by a fierce pounding, a rapid rattling, and another voice calling my name.

Derrick. Jesse. Outside. Attempting to break through a locked door. I tried to call to them. Opened my mouth, drew a breath . . . The most I could manage was a whimper, like that of a newborn kitten. The pounding and rattling at the boathouse door continued, a cacophony I wished I could drown out, until I remembered they were here for me. But it also occurred to me they didn't know what had happened, or who had Lucy and me under his control. For all they knew, she and I were in here alone, Lucy with a gun to my head.

A door much closer to where I lay opened with a shudder, as if from disuse, and daylight flooded the space behind my eyelids. I tried opening one eye again, but the light was too glaring, too painful. Hands grabbed my wrists. I was dragged off the sails, onto the hardwood floor. My hipbones took the brunt of it, yet I felt no pain, at least not then. More dragging, across a short span of floor, over a sash, and then a drop onto another hard surface, before I was pushed, rolled, pushed again, landing with a hard thump, this time on my back. Harsh light pierced my eyelids as the surface below me dipped and rocked, then steadied. A salty breeze rolled over me. Dampness seeped through my clothing.

Tyrone had me in the dinghy. Refusing to be thwarted by my own limited capacities, I forced both eyes open. A blur of cloud-studded sky arced above me, framed by the chipped blue paint of the boat's gunwale. Though Tyrone was beyond my line of vision, I sensed his movements close by, heard the rustle of his clothing. I saw the oars being lifted from the deck and placed in the oarlocks. Felt the little boat pushing away from the dock.

Footsteps thudded against the dock, sending vibrations into the water and rocking us gently. The motion should have made me queasy, I thought, but I was as a babe in a cradle, being lulled into oblivion. The boat surged forward, cresting each wave before dipping in the trough of the next.

"Emma!" Derrick called out again, his voice edged in panic.

"Halt! Drop those oars." Jesse's order skittered out over the water, echoing against the moored yachts. "Drop them and don't make another move."

We kept going, rising and dipping with each wave. A blast of gunshot ricocheted like thunder across the cove, slapping against Fort Adams and rebounding against Beacon Rock. The forward movement of the boat stalled, and I rejoiced that Tyrone should give up so easily. Or had he been hit? Except that, having released his grip on the oars, he now thrust his arms around me and lifted me roughly to a sitting position. I sagged against him. Something encircled my neck and pulled tight. I remembered Tyrone's silk scarf. In a corner of my brain, fear blossomed.

"Don't try that again. I'm warning you." His voice, rumbling against my back, sounded deeper than normal, and strained. He was attempting to disguise it. In the distance—so much greater than I expected it to be—two blurred forms took shape on the boathouse steps. One reached out his arms as if to lift me from the boat. Tyrone stiffened against

me as he yelled, "Don't come after us. She'll be dead long before you reach us."

Would I? The notion sent anger burning in my gullet, just
as the laudanum had. But what could I do? I could barely
keep my eyes open. I certainly couldn't muster fists and
swing them in self-defense. Nor could I grab an oar and
swing it at Tyrone's head—not with any accuracy. Even if I
managed to jump overboard, I wouldn't have the strength to
stay afloat, not long enough for Derrick to swim out to me.

Would Jesse summon the Lifesaving Service? With its
kerosene-powered cutters, one of their vessels would over-
take this one in moments. But it would take time to alert
them. The telephone in the boathouse only connected to
the main house. Jesse and Derrick would have to climb the
steps, make their way inside, wait for the connections to be
made . . . Much could happen in that time.

And yet, the explosion of Jesse's firearm had helped
sharpen my wits. Perhaps only slightly, but I felt I had a
firmer hold on clarity. Again, I considered that I had expelled
more laudanum than I had swallowed. What else might I be
capable of doing?

Tyrone released me, letting me fall against the deck, and
took up the oars again. I wondered where on God's green
earth he thought he was going. Where could he hide? Would
he attempt to span the bay to Jamestown? Circle the island
to some secluded inlet in Portsmouth? From there, it was
but a short distance to Tiverton or Bristol on the mainland.
Would his strength hold out that long? Of course it would.
He was, after all, a sportsman and an avid boater. But long
before we reached the mainland, I would be dead.

At least his need to get away in a hurry had prevented him
from bringing Lucy with us. She would live . . . A chill
gripped me. Yes, Lucy would live, provided he didn't over-
dose her with the laudanum. But perhaps even now, help was

on its way to Beacon Rock. As for me, I would have a better chance of surviving on my own than if I'd had an incapacitated Lucy to look after.

Forcing my eyes to open again and stay that way, I tried to scan the deck of the little boat. Was there anything I could use to fight Tyrone? I tried to find the leverage to lift myself upward, fighting the weight of my own body. I heard a laugh above my head.

"That's right, Miss Cross, expend your energy. That will make the end quicker and easier."

I stilled. Blast him, but he was right. I was doing myself no favors with my struggling. If only I knew where we were . . .

Not only my body lay immobile now, but I willed my mind to calm as well—no easy feat. I needed to think logically, needed to remember everything I knew about the island I'd grown up on. Which way was Tyrone taking us? I realized I had already felt the arc as the little boat had swung southward. It made sense. North meant rowing past Thames Street's many wharves, the plethora of boats anchored in the harbor, the Navy War College. He would not be heading up to Portsmouth that way. By heading south, we'd clear Fort Adams in moments. It was unlikely any soldiers who happened to be perched on its defense walls would take notice of a fisherman rowing past. If anything, I would appear as a bundle of blankets and sacks tossed to the deck.

"They'll catch you, you know." The words slurred beyond my control, but perhaps my best chance was to get him talking again. "You left Lucy behind, and she'll tell them everything."

"Feeling chipper, Miss Cross? Your cordial wasn't strong enough then, apparently. No matter. Lucy's was. I doubt very much she'll be alive much longer, but if she is, she likely won't remember a thing." His chuckle jarred me with its bit-ing edge. He dipped the oars, swung them quickly in the air, dipped again. The dinghy thrust forward. I could feel the speed in the rush of the waves against the wooden hull beneath me. "I doubt very much you'll be able to swim. But just in case, I brought something to help you along to your maritime grave."

He kicked something that made a metallic sound. A chain, perhaps. Attached to an anchor? A ball of panic spun inside me.

No. Focus. Whatever his plan for me, I had to remain calm. Where was he taking me? Where would he go afterward?

I visualized the coastline. It wasn't very difficult. Brady and I had rowed these shores countless times, often with Angus. I knew the coves and beaches, the inlets and cliffs, as well as I knew my own face in the mirror.

How long had we been on the water? Not long, I estimated. Time was Tyrone's enemy, for it meant authorities alerted, boats launched. No, he had to be rid of me soon, where no one would see and where he could disembark and take cover on land. I wondered . . . I remembered the small bundle he'd carried when he reached the boathouse. He must have brought it with us. He'd obviously hidden the workman's clothes he wore somewhere on the Morgans' property, and changed into them on his way down to intercept me at the boathouse. He'd probably stolen them from one of the *Columbia*'s crewmen staying in Beacon Rock's servants' quarters. The bundle I saw must be his normal clothes to change into once again. How long had he planned this? Perhaps since two nights ago, when he'd found it necessary to murder Cob. Yes, it made sense that, if he felt the need to silence his lackey, he would see the same necessity for me.

Where would he put in? The coast between Fort Adams and Castle Hill was rocky, but fairly even; there wouldn't be much opportunity there. But Castle Hill itself . . . There, a long, narrow inlet turned the Castle Hill property practically into an island. He could go deep into the cove and find ample places to hide. Perhaps he'd set the boat adrift, change clothes, and make his way inland at his leisure.

But to make this work, he needed to be rid of me in open waters. That meant swinging wide, away from the coast, where I would have nothing to hope for—no boulders sticking out of the water, no shoreline to swim to. If only he would keep going south and then east. There, a dangerous shoal might rip into the bottom of the dinghy, but I would rather take my chances with the vagaries of the sea than with Tyrone Kerr.

Chapter 19

He did as I thought he would, which was to swing the dinghy out into more open waters. Once again, I tried to lever myself up so I could see beyond the sides of the boat. I almost succeeded. This time, however, Tyrone saw no humor in it. He released one oar, leaned forward to grasp my shoulder, and shoved me back down. As earlier, I felt no real pain, only the force of his rough treatment, but it was enough to send my head bouncing against the bottom of the craft.

"Don't try anything or you'll be sorry."

"Why shouldn't I? You're going to kill me anyway." I sounded drunk. My limbs felt numb, my stomach queasy. With a bizarre bit of humor I hoped I threw up all over him.

The chain rattled as he moved it. The chilling sound erased all humorous thoughts from my mind and filled me with terror. Yet at the same time, resolve coursed through me. I had nothing to lose. Only my life.

I pushed myself upright into a sitting position. This time, Tyrone let me, as it only made it easier to wrap the chain around my waist. He did this so quickly I hadn't time to resist, even if I'd had the room to try. My gaze followed the heavy iron links to their far end, where the chain connected to a steel girder that would quickly drag me under. He held a padlock in his hands.

Suddenly, he dropped the lock and snatched up the oars again. His features turned frantic as he struggled to get the dinghy moving again. I managed to glance over my shoulder. Though my vision doubled, I made out a few other boats—a schooner, a clipper, and a barge being hauled along the channel into the mouth of the harbor. None was close enough to signal to, or I would have tried. What had put Tyrone in such a state?

I looked around again, twisting at the waist. A sailboat, perhaps forty feet long and similar to the sport craft I'd sailed in with Tyrone and Wallace Rayburn, headed in our direction. It wasn't a huge craft, but much bigger than ours. The three men onboard were tugging lines, twisting the wheel this way and that, but nothing they did had any effect. Even in my state, I saw how inexperienced they were, how they had no notion of how to adjust the sails to control the wind currents. The boat continued to cut through the water straight for us. In his panic, Tyrone, too, couldn't seem to gain control over the dinghy. Both vessels became caught in the channel, and neither was manned by someone familiar enough with the currents to fight them. Perhaps if Tyrone had manned the sailboat, he might have managed to change its course. But he was attempting to row an unwieldy dinghy, and I doubted he had much experience with oars.

It soon became apparent the three men on the sailboat were drunk, despite the early hour. One of them staggered to the gunwale and was desperately waving his arms as if he might magically change our course. The distance between us grew smaller with each passing moment. Surprising myself with my sudden agility, I shook the chain from around me. Tyrone cast me a half scowl, half look of astonishment. Somehow, the sailboat had come around and was now aimed straight on at our port side. It came on full fury, like a summer squall. I waited until I deemed it seconds before we would collide.

Then I leaned, gripped the gunwale, dragged myself closer, and rolled myself over the edge. The weight of my clothing sent me plunging into the waves. Tyrone's shouting filled my ears, but only briefly. The water closed around me and blocked out all sound. The water's chill brought a shock to my senses. I'll never know how I swam, but swim I did. Not fast, not frantically, but slow and methodical. One arm up, over, in . . . then the other. I didn't bother kicking; I knew my skirts would hinder those efforts, tire me more quickly, and drag me down. Somewhere in my mind floated the thought that I should wriggle my way out of them, but with whatever nimbleness I'd gained, I needed to keep moving.

Up, over, in . . .

The surf crashed in my ears . . . no, not merely the surf. It was the two boats hitting, splintering, cracking. There were shouts and thrashing, the sounds of panic . . . while I continued, my eyes mostly closed, my arms reaching for a shore I didn't know if I would find. Up, over, in . . .

And then I did the thing that probably saved my life. I rolled over onto my back, spread my arms out to my sides, and floated. The tide now controlled my fate.

Can one stay afloat while sleeping? I would have sworn I dozed, rocked to sleep by the rolling waves. Then I'd open my eyes to the glaring brightness of the wide sky above me, relieved occasionally by tall banks of clouds with flat, steel-gray bases. I wondered vaguely if that meant a storm approached. I should have been worried, but the burst of energy that took me from Tyrone's dinghy had long since drained into nothingness. At least I had grown accustomed to the temperature of the water, and no longer shivered.

Had Tyrone and the three sailors survived the crash? Were they close by, swimming to shore, and would Tyrone find me, hold me under, and make good his threat of a watery death? I listened for voices, but I heard only the arguing of gulls.

Gulls. Did that mean I had drifted close to land? On my back, I could see nothing but water and sky, and I didn't dare turn over to see what lay behind me. My limbs could no longer be trusted to have the strength to support me in the water. I had no choice but to continue floating, other than to pray someone on the water spotted me. But a person dressed in blue, in the midst of the ocean? They'd likely run into me before they'd ever see me.

My shoulder came up against something. I gasped and nearly went under as a bout of panic went through me. I reached up with one hand and felt the roughness of stone against my fingers. Joy replaced panic. Grabbing hold, I turned in the water, reached out with my other hand, and dug my fingertips into pits and cracks. The rock stood perhaps two feet out of the water, and extended like a tiny island for several feet. Had I reached one of the formations near Brenton Reef? Seal Ledge or Black Rock?

I found a foothold beneath the water and tried to haul myself up. The toe of my boot slipped, and I went under. But I hadn't let go, despite the pain in my fingertips, and pulled myself up again. Perhaps I couldn't get myself out of the water, but I could hold on.

Or should I? Would clinging to a rock make me less visible in the water? Should I push away and continue my aimless floating? Neither prospect filled me with hope. No, I must climb up, onto the rock. It was my only hope.

The deep, bass note of a steam yacht's horn startled me. Peering over my shoulder, I shook the streaming hair from my eyes and saw the vessel about a hundred yards out, heading for the mouth of the bay. I waved a hand in the air. Had they seen me? Is that why they'd blown their horn? I cried out for help, but the ship kept on its course.

Foolish of me to have thought otherwise. With both hands gripping the rock now, I ignored the pain, the blood, the tearing of the pads of my fingers and palms, and pulled for all I was worth. My feet slipped again and again, and my knees hit the jagged surface, but inch by inch I reached higher, until my hands were on top of the rock. I used up the last of my reserves in one violent pull upward, dragging skirts and bloodied knees up the side and onto the craggy surface.

There I lay on my stomach, my cheek against the inhospitable rock, out of breath, gasping, spitting salt from my mouth, as spent as the remnants of last night's boiled chicken. I wondered how long before my rock, my island, would become submerged by the tide. My head began to spin. . . .

Hands clasped my shoulders and immediately I began to fight. Even before I opened my eyes, I kicked my feet and thrashed with my fists. I shouted at Tyrone that I would not be his victim, that I'd see him dead before another person, me or otherwise, died by his hand.

And then I realized the hands were gentle, and a voice pleaded with me—no, not pleaded, exactly. What he said was, "Emma, Emma, please, you're safe now. You've nothing to fear anymore."

My arms and legs went limp. My head fell back against the rock with a jarring crack. I opened my eyes. Through a blur of brine and sunlight and yes, tears, I made out Derrick's face—his beautiful, steady, soothing face—and knew it was over. Knew I had lived. *Would* live.

When I awoke next, I was lying in a bed, the covers pulled to my chin. A white wall stood a couple of feet to my left, with a window looking out onto treetops. To my right, a curtained screen blocked my few of the rest of the room. But I knew immediately where I was. I tried to sit up, but an instantaneous bout of nausea sent me prone again.

From somewhere beside my head came a voice, and then Derrick was once more at my side. "Emma, don't try to move. You're safe now, my darling."

His hand searched beneath the covers for mine and wrapped it in warmth. "How long?" was all I could manage.

"You've been here since yesterday. You're fine, though. Miraculously." He laughed softly and bent over to plant a kiss on my forehead. Before he pulled away, he brushed another across my mouth. His lips were as much a balm as anything the hospital could have given me. "You were passed out all the way from Brenton Point in the Lifesaving Service cutter. You woke briefly when we got you here, but you've been sleeping ever since."

"Nanny?" She must have been frantic.

"Yes, she's been here as well. All night. Katie too. But I sent them out in my carriage to have some breakfast." His fingers stroked mine as he spoke. "If I know them, they won't be gone long. How about you? Are you hungry?"

I shook my head, finding a smile for him. "You found me."

"Of course I found you. What on earth did you think would happen?" He spoke gruffly. His crumpling features startled me, as did the glistening of his eyes. He took a moment, his head bowed, as he swallowed and hardened his jaw. "I don't know how you managed to find your way onto that rock, but thank the stars you did."

With a gasp I tried to sit up again. Derrick gently pushed me back down. "Don't. Not yet."

"Lucy," I said, panic rising in my throat. "Is she . . . ?"

"She'll be fine. She's here, in a private room. The doctor thinks she can leave tonight or tomorrow morning."

"The laudanum." I squinched my eyes tight as memories flashed of Tyrone forcing the noxious liquid down my throat. "It could have killed her."

He nodded. "It could have killed you both. Luckily, it wasn't quite enough to do so. Lucy was out a good long while, but I'm told she rallied before we brought you in. She's tough, Lucy Carnegie is."

"I spit most of mine out, I think."

Derrick laughed again, but the sound carried a hard edge. "Of course you did. A man like Tyrone Kerr could never get the best of you."

"Tyrone . . . what happened to him?" The sound of the two boats colliding echoed in my mind, and I flinched. Before he could answer me, I blurted, "There were three men in a sailboat. Oh, Derrick, were they hurt? Did they live?"

"Yes, the yawl. By the time we came upon them, their boat was half sunk and going down fast." He pinched his lips and shook his head. "Don't waste too much time feeling sorry for them. Soused, all three of them. Had no business being out on the water. They might have killed you. The cutter picked them out of the water. They're fine."

"I thought they'd been drinking. They were ridiculous, trying to avoid Tyrone's dinghy. Still, if they hadn't come along and distracted him the way they did, I might not have gotten away." I studied him, a frown forming between my brows. "You didn't answer about Tyrone."

He shrugged. "There's no definite answer, actually. We found pieces of what looked like a rowboat tangled in the sails of the yawl. The rest of the boat must have sunk. We saw no sign of it, and no sign of Tyrone. It's highly doubtful he survived." He flexed a fist. "But if he did, it's only temporarily."

I relaxed and let my head sink into my pillow. What ironic justice if Tyrone died of drowning. I took a moment to search my conscience, but I couldn't dredge up an ounce of sympathy for him. He had used an innocent girl—one with so much promise—to further his greed, and then took her life when she stood up to him. It didn't matter that Cob had done the actual murder. Tyrone was equally guilty; perhaps more so for having planned everything.

"Has Wallace Rayburn been released?"

"And exonerated," Derrick assured me. "Poor lad. Jesse found him weeping in his cell one night." He held up a hand. "Don't worry too much about him either. He perked up considerably when the Morgans assured him he still had his place on the *Columbia* crew."

"Good, I'm glad. Oh, but we're forgetting something," I said with a start that brought me half upright again. "The photographer. Neither Cob nor Tyrone killed him. Tyrone's got someone else under his thumb, someone willing to earn his pay any way he must. And I have no notion of who it is."

Without releasing my hand, Derrick leaned toward me until his elbows rested on the mattress beside me, his face close to mine. "Emma, leave it alone. Let the police find this one. Tell Jesse everything you learned from Tyrone. Lucy will do the same. He'll relay it all to the police in Great Neck, and together they'll find the scoundrel who murdered Mr. Gorman. But you—stay out of it."

It wasn't quite a command. Neither was it a request. A

protest bubbled up inside me, but the look on his face—so fearful, so imploring—banished any dispute I might have made. My heart turned over. I gave his hand a squeeze and surprised even myself with two simple words. "Yes, Derrick."

He pulled back, peering down his nose at me through narrowed eyes. "'Yes, Derrick?'"

I nodded. "Yes."

"Is this a trick?"

"No, of course not. Why would you think that?" I knew very well why he would think it, but if I was going to abide by his wishes, I was certainly going to tease him about it.

As I knew he would, he said, "Because I know you. I know you like to be in the thick of it. Like to be the one who cracks the case, even if you let Jesse take the credit."

Yes, that was all true. Still. "Jesse deserves the credit. I only help when I can."

"Indeed." He let go of my hand, crossed his arms over his chest, and let go a laugh that was more of a snort. "I'll have my eye on you, Emma Cross."

I grinned. "I certainly hope so." Reaching out, I grasped his lapel and pulled him close, craning forward until our lips met.

"Emma, is that your voice I hear? Thank goodness you're awake!"

Derrick and I pulled apart at the sound of Nanny's voice and her hurrying footsteps. In another moment she came around the privacy screen, Katie behind her, both of them beaming with joy and relief. Derrick pulled away as they flanked either side of the bed, and Nanny gathered me in her arms and rocked me as she had countless times when I was a child.

I went home the next day with strict instructions to rest. I did my best to comply, but could I help it that a steady stream of well wishers stopped by all day? Jesse was among them, come to take my official statement about my ordeal with Tyrone Kerr. A good dozen of Nanny's friends who worked at nearby cottages also came bearing gifts of food, from stews to casseroles to baked goods. Nanny and Katie wouldn't have to touch a pot or pan for the next week at least. Hannah, my friend who worked at the hospital and who had helped nurse me back to health while I was there, also stopped in to check on me. She had no sooner left than someone else knocked at the front door. By then I had found myself ensconced on the sofa in the parlor, a rug tucked around my legs, sipping what had to be my tenth or eleventh cup of tea that afternoon.

At the sound of the new voice in the foyer, I set the teacup on the table beside me and started to rise.

"Emma, don't you move from that sofa," Nanny ordered, and led my latest guest into the room, the top of her beribboned hat barely clearing Nanny's shoulders.

"Lucy!" I was delighted to see her. I had wished to speak with her before this, but she had left the hospital before me. That she hadn't stopped in to visit me first had left me fearing she didn't wish to see me, or that she didn't wish to discuss what had happened to us at Tyrone's hands. Her smile banished those fears from my mind.

"How are you, Emma?" She came and perched at the end of the sofa. I shifted my feet to make room for her. "Are you quite recovered?"

"Almost," Nanny answered for me. "We're taking good care of her."

"I'm glad for that," Lucy said with a hearty grin.

"And you? No lingering effects from the laudanum?" I scanned her from head to toe. She appeared sound enough, if slightly pale. "Was he violent? Did he hurt you?"

"No, he didn't really. But he did put his nasty hands on me when he forced me to drink the laudanum. If that isn't adding insult to injury, I don't know what is." She drew a breath and continued, "I wanted to explain to you what happened, why I called you to come to Beacon Rock. You see, I'd discovered a clue left for us by Lillian Fahey."

"Did you?" My eyes went wide. "Then it *wasn't* the painting that made you realize Tyrone murdered her?"

"Well, yes, it *was* the painting. In a manner of speaking." She snapped open her handbag and fished out a small notecard. A calling card, I discovered as she handed it to me. It simply read, *Lillian Fahey*, with a small sketch of a spray of lilies beneath her name.

I studied it, then turned it over. The back was blank, as calling cards usually were. "I don't understand."

"Lillian had tucked it behind a corner of the painting, with a tiny sliver of it peeking out. I was down there that morning looking for anything we might have missed when we searched, and suddenly, why, there it was, tucked between the painting and the brickwork, discreet but visible. I'm surprised we didn't see it sooner." Lucy leaned closer in her eagerness to explain. "I believe it was her way of telling whoever found it that she had been there, at the boathouse. She must have known she was in danger, but couldn't leave a more obvious sign for fear Tyrone would find it."

"But how did you know it was Tyrone and not Wallace Rayburn or someone else?" I peered at the card again, looking for a further clue.

"The lilies," she said, and pointed to the card. "They were obviously her favorite flower, which makes sense, given her name. You and Derrick hadn't arrived yet at Beacon Rock the night of the dinner party, but Tyrone had brought a bouquet of lilies for Elizabeth. I thought nothing of it at the time, didn't give it a second thought but that it was a considerate gesture. But when I discovered this card and saw the lilies, I realized the bouquet must have been meant initially for Miss Fahey, perhaps to help placate her when they met. As if a young woman like Miss Fahey could be mollified with flowers after what Tyrone did to her and her father."

"Yes," I said as I worked it out. I suddenly remembered the lilies that had graced the center of the Morgans' dining table the night of their party. "Perhaps he'd hoped to forestall a fiery row with Lillian and convince her to go along with his plans. And when that didn't work, he forced laudanum on her and had Cob Hendricks row her out and leave her to drown." The deviousness of it, the cold-blooded scheming, sent a shudder across my shoulders. "Poor Lillian. She never stood a chance against him." But then I tilted my head at Lucy. "But how did Tyrone realize you had figured it out?"

A blush crept into her stout cheeks. "I'm afraid I gave myself away. After I telephoned you, I went back down to the boathouse to wait for you. He must have seen me go in, because it wasn't long before he came strolling in after me. I admit that upon finding myself alone with a murderer, my poker face failed me entirely. I gasped, I stammered, I backed away, and I stared at him with saucer-sized eyes. Foolish, I know. Apparently, I'm not cut out for detective work. I nearly got us both killed."

"Well, you didn't." I reached over and took her hand. "I'd do it all again to find justice for Lillian."

Lucy stayed a few more minutes, and we chatted about more pleasant topics. Then she consulted the watch pinned to her bodice. "I must be off. I'm leaving soon, but I wanted to make sure I saw you at least once more. We're disbanding for now and plan to regroup in a few weeks' time in New York. Until then I'm heading home to Cumberland Island. Some of the children are there with their little ones."

"Isn't Georgia awfully hot this time of year?" I wondered aloud.

"For you Yanks, probably," she said with a laugh. "But we have those wondrous ocean breezes and the house was built to catch them all." She patted my knee through the blanket. "I'll miss you, I'll have you know."

"You know where to find me."

"I do at that."

"In the meantime, I wish you and the *Dungeness* smooth sailing."

Lucy leaned in closer. "I'm thinking of selling her. Got my eye on something newer and sleeker. Something to make the men positively salivate with envy."

I would miss her, too. Very much, I decided.

"I cannot thank you enough. Both of you." Eben Fahey held my hand in his veined, pale one, and bowed over it as he raised it to his lips. He seemed to have aged since his arrival in Newport, his thinning hair appearing stringier, his eyes more bloodshot behind his spectacles, his back more stooped. He released my hand and shook Derrick's.

Around us, the usual activity of Long Wharf swept clouds of dust into the air, laden with the odors of fish and brine and perspiration, while the acrid smoke of the coal that powered the steamships and northbound trains stung our eyes.

Despite Mr. Fahey's thanks, I wished I could do more for him. Wished I could have returned his daughter to him. As it was, her casket had been loaded onto the ferry. On the mainland, it would be placed onto a southbound train and brought home to Long Island. What a heartbreaking journey ahead of him. What a cruel end to such a promising life. Had I had the chance to meet Lillian, I felt sure I would have liked her, that we would have found ample ground on which to build a friendship.

With little more to say, Derrick and I wished Eben Fahey well. His part in all that happened had ended. While the police continued to search for the individual who murdered the photographer, Mr. Fahey would move on with his life, as best he could. We watched him board the ferry and returned his parting wave before he made his way inside.

We turned toward Derrick's carriage, waiting for us not far away. He offered me his arm. It was more than a gentlemanly gesture. Four days had passed since my ordeal with Tyrone Kerr. I had suffered from exhaustion and hypothermia, but I had adamantly refused to remain home with my feet up another day, despite Nanny's urging. Only Derrick's repeated vow to look after me had reassured her, at least partially, but we had left Gull Manor with her parting words nipping at our heels. "You take care of my lamb, Derrick Andrews, or you'll have to answer to me."

"Back to the *Messenger*?" I asked as I linked my arm through his.

"Eventually, but not quite yet." We reached the carriage and he handed me up. "There's a story I'm pursuing, and I need to get the scoop."

"Oh, what story's that?"

"The one about you and me getting married." He stepped up and slid onto the seat beside me. Leaning, he took my face in his two hands, tilted it to allow him to duck beneath my hat brim, and kissed me soundly. I gasped against his mouth. Good heavens, was anyone looking? On second thought, I decided I didn't care and melted into him. Before his lips had quite left mine, he kissed me again. "It's time we had a look at the church schedule, Miss Cross, wouldn't you say?"

"You know, Mr. Andrews, for once I'm in full agreement." I grinned. "I think we'd better, before people begin to talk."

Author's Note

Beacon Rock was designed by Stanford White, of the architectural firm McKim, Mead and White, in 1887. Modeled after the ancient Athenian Agora and Stoa of Attalos, the house took three years to complete and opened in 1891. It soon became known as the Acropolis of Newport. As Emma recalls in the story, Beacon Rock was originally a small mountain overlooking Brenton Cove, and as such was not an ideal building site. Still, its magnificent views commanding Narragansett Bay and the surrounding countryside proved too tempting for Edwin Morgan, who became determined to build his summer home there. Solution: have the top of the mountain blasted away and leveled. All evidence of this upheaval would be well disguised by the artistry of landscape designer Frederick Law Olmsted. The original formation can be seen in a painting by John Frederick Kensett. The house is located on Harrison Avenue on the west side of Aquidneck Island. Though it can't be seen from the road, the views of the house from the water are breathtaking.

Edwin Morgan was a distant cousin of John Pierpont Morgan, and made his fortune in business, livestock, and mining. Both men were avid yachters and members of the New York Yacht Club, and each served at various times as the club's commodore. As in the story, they did join forces, along with others, to form a syndicate and enter the America's Cup yacht races. The *Columbia* won those races in 1899 and again in 1901, coming up against the *Shamrock* and the *Shamrock II* respectively, of the Royal Ulster Yacht Club. The NYYC enjoyed a winning streak from 1870 until 1983. Although the US challengers ultimately lost that year against the Australian team, it was an exciting time in Newport. I remember specifically listening to reports on one of the races—one we happened to win—while lunching on the patio of the Black Pearl Restaurant on Bannister's Wharf, and feeling the pride of cheering for the home team.

Lucy Carnegie is taken from history. Born Lucy Coleman, she married Thomas Morrison Carnegie, the younger brother of steel and iron magnate Andrew Carnegie, whom Thomas joined in business. He then went on to become successful in his own right. Lucy herself was the daughter of Pittsburgh iron magnate William Coleman. As industry turned the Pittsburgh skies more and more gray, Lucy and Thomas went looking for a more healthful atmosphere in which to raise their nine children. They found Dungeness, a ruined plantation on Cumberland Island off the coast of Georgia. Together, she and her husband commissioned a Queen Anne style mansion to be built there, but Thomas didn't live to see its completion. He died in 1886 of pneumonia, leaving Lucy a wealthy widow. An outgoing woman with an adventurous spirit, Lucy purchased a steamer yacht, named it the *Dungeness*, and, after a persistent campaign to be accepted into the New York Yacht Club, became its first female member in 1894. By 1900, the time of the story, however, Lucy had sold the *Dungeness* and purchased another yacht, the *Skibo*, named for her brother-in-law's estate, Skibo Castle, in Scotland. I decided to use the *Dungeness* in the story because I felt that vessel, having been instrumental in Lucy's being accepted into the New York Yacht Club, personified her independent spirit.

The two other members of the racing syndicate in the story, Tyrone Kerr and Bernard Delafield, are both fictional, as are Wallace Rayburn and Cob and Polly Hendricks.

The incident concerning Lillian Fahey's death was also taken from history, from a newspaper article I discovered in the *Newport Mercury*, dated July 14, 1900. The body of a woman, Lillian Foye, had been discovered floating in Narragansett Bay near the Jamestown shore. She wore clothing as I described in the story, and a tintype photo was found in her pocket depicting Lillian and a young man of her acquaintance, William C. Rich. Additionally, she wore a love-knot ring with dangling hearts, on which were inscribed their last initials. Evidence suggests they had planned to meet in Fall River, Massachusetts, and continue down to New York City together on the ferry. A porter who inquired whether she needed assistance remembered Lillian saying she was there to meet a female friend, but she later admitted she was meeting a young man. When Rich failed to turn up, Lillian, clearly upset, continued on alone, believing she would find him on the ferry. This, too, proved to be a disappointment for Lillian, and it was assumed she jumped from the ferry in despair.

Yet there was more to the story, as I would discover in a subsequent article written after William Rich had been found and interviewed. He admitted that Lillian had been pregnant, and that on a recent trip they'd taken to New York together, he had tried to find work in order to be able to marry her. His search proved fruitless, and the couple returned home, telling their families nothing. This was only days before her death. In the article, he made no mention of any plan to meet in Fall River. Did Rich deliberately leave out this information to avoid being blamed for her death? Did Lillian misunderstand his intentions? Or had she planned to run away to New York alone, but took her own life long before arriving?

These questions, to my knowledge, were never answered. I chose to omit the details from the later article in *my* Lillian's story, focusing instead on the mystery of a well-to-do young woman at the wrong place at the wrong time, and on the types of assumptions authorities often made in those days when dealing with the unexpected actions of a determined female.

The glorious mansions of Newport in the Gilded Era house many mysteries—murder, theft, scandal—and no one is more adept at solving them than reporter Emma Andrews...

1901: Back from their honeymoon in Italy, Emma and Derrick are adapting to married life as they return to their duties at their jointly owned newspaper, the Newport *Messenger*. The Elms, coal baron Edward Berwind's newly completed Bellevue Avenue estate, is newsworthy for two reasons: A modern mansion for the new century, it is one of the first homes in America to be wired for electricity with no backup power system, generated by coal from Berwind's own mines. And their servants—with a single exception—have all gone on strike to protest their working conditions. Summarily dismissing and replacing his staff with cool and callous efficiency, Berwind throws a grand party to showcase the marvels of his new "cottage."

Emma and Derrick are invited to the fete, which culminates not only in a fabulous musicale but an unforeseen tragedy—a chambermaid is found dead in the coal tunnel. In short order, it is also discovered that a guest's diamond necklace is missing and a laborer has disappeared.

Detective Jesse Whyte entreats Emma and Derrick to help with the investigation and determine whether the murdered maid and stolen necklace are connected. As the dark deeds cast a shadow over the blazing mansion, it's up to Emma to shine a light on the culprit...

Please turn the page for an exciting sneak peek of Alyssa Maxwell's newest Gilded Newport mystery MURDER AT THE ELMS now on sale wherever print and ebooks are sold!

Chapter 1

Newport, RI, 1901

The aromas of ink and newsprint. The rumble of the presses emanating from the rear of our little building on Spring Street. The murmur of voices and the tap-tapping of my colleague and officemate working away on his latest article, his shoulders hunched and his dark hair flopped over his brow as he hunted and pecked faster than most people typed using all ten fingers.

Home. The word filled me with overwhelming satisfaction and a sense of peace. After weeks away, I was back where I belonged. Where I felt most myself. Where I presided over the news stories that would inhabit the pages of the Newport *Messenger,* the small but growing paper owned by my husband and myself. I was now officially the news reporter, but that distinction, of course, was tempered by my being the *only* news reporter on staff. My colleague, Ethan Merriman, currently engaged in capturing the tastes and textures of the latest to-dos along Bellevue Avenue, was our society columnist.

Wait. Did I say husband? Yes, indeed I did, for I was now

Mrs. Derrick Andrews, although here, in these offices and in the byline that accompanied the articles I wrote, I continued to be Emma Cross.

We were married in October of the previous year in a quiet, heartfelt ceremony at St. Paul's Church here in town, attended by close friends and family, followed by a luncheon in the large room below the sanctuary. My parents being unable to travel here from France, my half-brother Brady walked me down the aisle, and my longtime friend, Hannah, who was also Brady's sweetheart, served as my bridesmaid. At Derrick's request, darling Nanny, my housekeeper, friend, and surrogate grandmother, had made her special apple ginger cake in several layers and iced it with snowy cream frosting. My aunt Alice Vanderbilt attended, as did her daughters Gertrude and Gladys, and sons Alfred and Reggie. In their jewels and finery, they'd appeared the teensiest bit out of place against St. Paul's plain surroundings, but they had done their admirable best to pretend otherwise. Neily and Grace— *dearest* Neily and Grace—had stayed away so that the other family members would come, but the schism in the Vanderbilt family is another story altogether.

Derrick's parents had vowed to boycott our wedding, a threat his mother made good on but which his father, in the end, did not. It had been our first meeting, and I found him distinguished if a trifle austere, gracious if somewhat melancholy. He had kissed my hand and wished us well, and gifted us with a lovely set of china that had belonged to his mother.

At the suggestion of a friend, a trek to the beautiful, rugged Adirondacks had served as our wedding trip. Then, when spring came, we boarded ship and ventured across the sea to Italy. It had been touch and go for me, the journey over, but Derrick had plied me with chamomile tea and oyster crackers to settle my stomach, and somehow I made the crossing without an excess of misery.

We disembarked in France and spent time with my parents, who were overjoyed to see us. Tuscany, our eventual destination, was glorious, as was visiting with Derrick's sister, Judith, and reuniting with a small friend from several years ago, her precious five-year-old son, Robbie. Upon learning that as an infant he had spent time at my home, Gull Manor, he had professed to remember me, but I knew that to be impossible at his tender age.

Now, on my first day back at the paper, I stepped into Ethan's and my cramped office, made even smaller by the two desks, chairs, and typewriter table. His index fingers went still on the keys. With a swoop of his head to flip the hair back from his brow, he glanced up and broke into a beaming grin. "Miss Cross. Um, that is, Mrs. Andrews. You're back."

"Yes, I am. And it's wonderful to see you. But really Ethan, Emma will do."

His eyes filled with mild alarm. "Oh, now, that wouldn't be right. I couldn't."

No, we had established that some months ago and Ethan was nothing if not consistent.

"Why, you're the boss's wife," he went on, still enumerating the reasons we must avoid undue familiarity. His agitation widened a grin of my own. "And I'm . . . I'm just . . ."

"Just the best society columnist Newport has ever seen." I included myself in that assessment. I'd once held the very position he did, except at a different publication. But where I had bristled at assignments covering the antics and excesses of the Four Hundred, Ethan relished them and put all his energy into recording every detail. "Tell me, how did it go for you covering hard news while I was away?" A sudden qualm gave me pause. "Will you miss it terribly, do you think?"

"Not a speck. It's all yours, Miss Cross." He caught himself at the last minute. "Mrs. Andrews. Anyways, speaking of hard news, there's something already here for you. Mr.

Sheppard brought it in just a few minutes ago." He waved a hand toward my desk and the torn piece of paper that sat square in the middle. "Seems there's trouble brewing down the Avenue."

He meant Bellevue Avenue, of course, that long, straight thoroughfare that traveled the southeastern portion of Aquidneck Island overlooking the cliffs and the Atlantic Ocean. Once mere farmland, one by one the families of the Four Hundred had built their summer cottages—palaces, really—and transformed the area into their exclusive playground for eight to twelve weeks each year.

I picked up the paper and read the terse message in our editor-in-chief's sharp, tilting handwriting. An instant later I slapped it back down on the desk. I'd already slid the pin from my straw boater. Now I slid it back through, securing it to my coif, and headed out of the office. "Ethan, we'll catch up later."

At the front of the building, in the room that served as both our administrative office and lobby, I stopped long enough to tell Derrick where I was off to. I started to explain the situation, but he stopped me as he rose from the desk that faced out over Spring Street. "Stan told me. He stepped out for a minute. Do you want me to come with you?"

"Don't be ridiculous. You've got your own work to do." I took advantage of having the front office to ourselves, albeit with the risk that passersby might swing their gazes in our direction, and gave Derrick a quick peck on the lips. "I'll see you after. Now I'm off for my first-ever look inside The Elms."

"You probably won't get farther than the kitchen but good luck." He grasped my arm as I started toward the door. "Be careful."

"I always am," I replied, and ignored his grunt of skepticism.

The weather being fine and clear, Spring Street teemed with activity. The sidewalks were jammed with pedestrians while the street juggled carriages, wagons, and the oncoming streetcar. I almost left my buggy where it was along the curbstone, thinking it might be quicker for me to walk the block up to Bellevue and then head south on foot.

One look at the heatwaves shimmering from the dusty road convinced me to take the buggy rather than arrive at The Elms covered in a sheen of perspiration and my skirt and shirtwaist a study in wrinkles.

Its construction only recently completed, The Elms sat along the upper portion of Bellevue Avenue only a few blocks from town. Once I drove past the Casino with its row of shops, the trees, mostly elm, closed overhead to offer sweet, reviving shade and a cooling breeze. Kingscote, a neo-Gothic structure with an almost fairytale aspect, stood to my right. I wondered if the Kings were back in town after spending the winter and spring in Europe. I thought about leaving my calling card, but decided I'd best be about the business that had brought me to this part of town.

The Elms came soon after. Designed by Horace Trumbauer in the style of an eighteenth-century chateau, the house comprised a columned center section with long, recessed wings on either side. The façade revealed only two stories, but a limestone balustrade wall along the roofline concealed a third story that housed the servants.

It wasn't to one of the three front doors framed in columned arches that I went, but instead I turned down Bellevue Court, a side street that skirted the north side of the property. There I turned in at the service driveway. Approaching the delivery entrance was like venturing into another world entirely from the one the owners, Edward and Herminie Berwind, inhabited. Gone were the statues, the exotic trees, and the carefully designed flowerbeds that graced the rest of the property. Here, it seemed the sun ducked behind thick clouds. That was only an illusion. Dense and tangled vines of wisteria grew like a roof above the circular drive, shielding the delivery carts and wagons from view of anyone gazing down from the first- or second-story windows. Likewise, coal deliveries were made at the mouth of a tunnel that opened onto Dixon Street beyond the stone wall on the south side of the house. As far as the family or any of their guests were concerned, The Elms ran as if by magic.

Yet it wasn't magic that had brought me there that morning. As soon as I passed through the delivery hall and into the cold-preparation kitchen, the tension wrapped like tentacles around me. The house had been open a mere few weeks, but even so, by now the staff should have fallen into a seamless rhythm as they went about their tasks. I felt no such rhythm, no harmony of a well-tuned orchestra.

Footmen, maids, kitchen staff—even the butler and housekeeper, judging by their clothing—stood gathered two and three deep around the long, zinc-covered table used for the preparation of cold dishes. A quick glance through the wide windows looking into the main kitchen—normally the heart of any great house—revealed a stillness I found astonishing, especially at that time of day. Only one man hovered over the cast-iron range with its many burners and oven doors. His white tunic and tall hat identified him as the Berwinds' chef. No assistants chopped food or mixed ingredients at the worktable, no scullery maids collected used pots and pans to scrub at the long sink.

If I hadn't known better, I'd have ventured to guess that nearly all the servants, over forty of them, were planning to . . .

"That's it, then," the butler said with a sigh and a yank at his necktie, "we are going to strike."

I swallowed a gasp.

"Do you think that'll get through to 'em, Mr. Boreman?" someone asked.

"Yeah, what if it doesn't?" another challenged.

"It has to." The assertion came from somewhere in the middle of the crush. "Where will they find enough servants to replace us all on such short notice?"

Despite the butler's assertion that "this was it," the debate raged on around the table while I watched, listened, and took notes. I tried to be discreet, keeping well to the back of the assembly, but it wasn't long before a housemaid spotted me.

"You're Miss Cross from the *Messenger*, ain't you, ma'am?" At that, the room fell silent.

"Aren't," the housekeeper corrected, then turned her sights on me. "Do you intend running this story in your newspaper?"

"I . . . uh . . ." Suddenly feeling cornered, I took a half step backward. My shoulder blades came up against the cold surface of the rectangular white tiles that lined the walls.

"I certainly hope so," the butler said with a sniff. "It's the reason I telephoned your office. Come closer, Miss Cross. Or . . . did I hear you'd married recently?"

"Miss Cross will do." The crowd parted and I stepped up to the edge of the table. "You're truly planning to strike? You know it's never been done before. Not by house servants here in Newport."

"We have as much right to air our grievances as any long-shoreman or rail worker or coal miner," a liveried footman said.

I couldn't help frowning as I remembered the violent results of a miners' strike only last September. I set my notebook and pencil on the table in front of me. "I was led to understand your wages here are among the highest in Newport. And that many of you enjoy rooms to yourselves, and two full bathrooms with hot and cold running water at your disposal. Forgive me if I inquire what it is you're asking for."

"A little time off, is all." This angry retort shot at me from a young woman in black serge sporting a crisp, white pinafore and frilled-edged cap.

"You're a housemaid?" I took up my writing implements once again.

"Head parlor maid," she said with an Irish lilt. Her chin lifted proudly.

"And the Berwinds allow you little time off?" I queried.

"Little? How about none?" Fiery color swept her porcelain complexion from chin to hairline.

My pencil went still. Had I understood correctly? "None? As in . . ."

"Never," the housekeeper clarified. She was a stout woman with severely swept-back hair, round spectacles, and a dignified air. "When we are not sleeping or eating, we are working. Seven days a week, with time off only for meals and church Sunday morning."

"I worked eighteen hours yesterday," the head parlor maid supplied. "As I do most days."

Murmurs of agreement rose in volume, echoing off the tiled walls.

"We've had about as much as we can take, Miss Cross," said a handsome young footman. "A fella needs some time to himself once in a while."

"And to *her*self," the parlor maid added.

"I certainly agree." I addressed my next question to the butler. "Have you talked to the Berwinds, tried to reason with them?"

"On more than one occasion." Mr. Boreman shook his head sadly. "I'm afraid my words have fallen on deaf ears."

"There's nothing left to be done but walk out." The parlor

maid spoke as if ready to lead the charge out through the service entrance doors. "We'll see how they get on without us."

"You do realize that once you leave, there's no guarantee you'll ever enter this house again." While my sympathies lay entirely with them, my hopes for their success were rather less enthusiastic. Call me a realist. I hated to see anyone put out of work.

While they continued their planning, working out exactly when and how they would walk off their jobs, I noticed one young woman backed off into a corner by the electrical circuit box. Her frightened eyes darted from one colleague to the next, and her hands fisted around her cotton apron. I went to stand with her.

"You don't look particularly confident about this plan."

She shook her head rapidly and spoke with an accent I recognized as Portuguese; there were many families from Portugal, or of Portuguese descent, living on Aquidneck Island. Her dark hair and eyes spoke of her southern European origins. "Only ill can come of it, ma'am."

"And you don't wish to follow their lead," I guessed.

"No, ma'am. No trouble. I wish only to work."

"You're from Portugal?"

"I am, ma'am."

"You're far from home. I understand your trepidation. Have you family here?"

"No, ma'am. No family. No one. Only me. I am Ines."

"I'm Emma Cross." I almost corrected myself, until I remembered that since I'd come here in a professional capacity, my maiden name would do. "I'm pleased to meet you, Ines. Your English is quite good for someone who hasn't been here long." I stopped myself from adding that her language skills would help in securing her another position, should it come to that.

Her eyes grew large with fear, as if I'd accused her of something. She backed up until she came up against the glass case that housed the circuits. "There was a wealthy English-woman in my village. My parents worked for her. She taught English to many of the children on the *propriedade*." She shook her head again, then translated, "On the estate."

"I see. That must have made things easier once you arrived in this country."

"Yes. But now . . ." She shook her head. "Miss Cross, I do not wish to strike. I am afraid. I don't want trouble," she repeated. She was shorter than me by several inches. She tipped her oval face up at me, the cheeks wide and smooth, the chin gently pointed, mouth bowed pleasantly. An exotic beauty, by American standards. Behind a thick fringe of lashes, her eyes reddened and she blinked away tears.

I reached for her hand. "You can't be forced to strike, Ines. They are doing what they believe is right. You must do the same, even if it is to remain behind when the others leave."

She returned the pressure of my hand, holding on tightly. Almost desperately. "May I truly?"

"Ines, you are free to make your own decisions."

"What's this? What are you telling her?"

The cross voice startled us both, and we glanced up to see the parlor maid standing close, her features taut with anger. Ines pressed herself farther into the corner and half behind me. I let her use me as a shield as I stared the housemaid down. "I'm simply confirming that she has choices, just as the rest of you do."

The maid held up a fist. "It's all for one and one for all. Everyone must agree to strike. If one of us backs out, the rest of us will fail." Her Irish accent thickened as she spoke.

"That's not fair," I told her calmly but firmly. "Ines has no family in this country and nowhere to go should she lose her position. Are you prepared to help her if you're all fired from The Elms?"

"We won't be fired if we stand together." She half turned and spoke to no one in particular. I noticed that several servants were watching us. "Isn't that right?"

Heads nodded, but I shook my own. "That's not how it works. The Berwinds might concede to your requests or they might send you all packing, as they see fit. It won't matter to them if one or all of you decide to strike."

Yet, even as I spoke, I again recalled the miners' strike of last autumn. Those men were quickly replaced by nonunion workers. An easily done solution for the mining company—one that ended tragically when the union miners opened fire on their replacements at a terminal of the Illinois Central Railroad.

Was I helping to put Ines in a similar position, with her coworkers so resenting her that they would take out their anger and frustrations on her?

I pointed into the main kitchen. "What about the chef? He doesn't appear to be interested in striking either."

"Monsieur Baudelaire is an exception," the maid informed me in a tone that implied I was something of an idiot. Her lips flattened in disapproval. "He has time off whenever he isn't cooking, and he's never considered himself one of us."

I turned back to the Portuguese woman. "Ines, if you should lose this position, you can come to me for help. You're to go to Gull Manor on Ocean Avenue and tell whoever answers the door that Miss Cross sent you. Do you understand?"

She nodded vigorously. "Thank you, Miss Cross. But I hope it will not be necessary."

"I hope so too."

"Traitor." Scowling, the housemaid started to move away, but I placed a hand on her shoulder.

"The same goes for you. For any of the women here who might find themselves in need of shelter. They'll be welcome at Gull Manor."

The maid pressed her face close to mine. Her complexion turned so red I fancied I could feel the heat wafting off it. "No one here needs your charity. Not them, not me, and not her." Her finger shot out as if to pin Ines to the wall. "We're willing to work for our livelihood, and work hard. All we want is a bit o' respect and working hours that wouldn't kill a donkey."

"I'm only saying that you'd be welcome, if you needed—" I tried again, but she cut me off.

"Besides, I've a family on the island, and family sticks together. Just as everyone here is a family, or should be." She aimed another spiteful look at Ines, who cowered with her chin to her chest.

"Bridget," the handsome footman called over, "leave Ines alone and come over here if you want in on this vote."

"Did I hear something about a vote?" A man in street clothes pushed his way in through the delivery entrance and stood poised with a notebook and pencil. He wore a brown tweed coat with patches at the elbows and a battered derby, his pale blond hair in such need of cutting it stuck out in tuffs all around the brim.

"Hello, Mr. Brown," I said with a sinking feeling. Orville Brown owned—and almost single-handedly staffed—the *Aquidneck Island Advocate*, a newspaper I had found to be of more sensationalism than substance. If Mr. Brown didn't believe a story had what it took to sell newspapers, he had no qualms when it came to exaggeration, embellishment, and, I had seen with my own eyes, downright fabrication.

"What have we here, hmmm? I hear tell there's worker discontent here at The Elms." His weasely gaze took in the room. "It seems everyone is here. So, who is going to give me tomorrow morning's front-page story?"

I wished the little man would go away. Behind him, other reporters filed inside, among them a journalist from the *Newport Daily News*, one from the *Mercury*, and Ed Billings, my former coworker and, to put it honestly, my nemesis at the *Newport Observer*. I put Ed Billings in the same category as Orville Brown, but with rather less creativity.

Ed walked in my direction. "Emma," he said in terse greeting. "Always the first on hand, aren't you?" He spoke with his typical resentment, prompting me to shrug.

"Sorry, Ed. Can I help it if I got the scoop earlier than you? From what I understand, the staff here called me in specifically. How did you find out about this?"

He looked me up and down. "I see marriage hasn't improved your manners." I didn't rise to the bait but stood waiting for his next comment, a faint smile on my lips. He harrumphed. "Word always gets around."

Yes, that was Newport. I couldn't have expected to keep a story like this all to myself, as nothing stayed confidential for long. Tell one person, and you've told everyone. I gestured to the group around the table. "Would you like to listen to them, Ed, or do you want me to fill you in later?"

It was a subtle poke at how he had often taken credit for stories I'd fleshed out when I worked for the *Observer*. His excuse had always been that he held the *Observer*'s official news reporter position, while I was merely the society columnist.

He scoffed and moved away. I set my pencil to paper, ready to record what happened next.

The butler held up his hands for silence. "All in favor of going to Mr. Berwind this very day and presenting him with our demands and ultimatum, raise your hands."

"One moment." The French chef leaned in from the kitchen, his arms crossed over his chest. In his thickly accented English, he asked in a mocking tone, "Do the women get to vote, too?"

"I say no," a footman said.

"Oh, you do, do you?" The housekeeper challenged him with a heft of an eyebrow.

"Well . . ." The young man compressed his lips and seemed to deflate. In the next moment, he regained his bravado. "Women aren't allowed to vote, generally."

The housemaid, Bridget, raised her fist once again. I didn't doubt she'd use it if she felt the circumstances warranted it. "We're in this as much as any of you men."

Mr. Borman raised his hands again to halt the debate. "That will be quite enough. Mrs. Sherman and I are still in charge here. Everyone will vote." At the titters of disagreement this roused, his eyes blazed. "Everyone or no one. Is that clear?"

Once again titters filled the air, but these were a slightly more agreeable kind.

"All right, then," Mr. Borman said loudly. "All in favor of carrying on with our plans today, raise your hands."

Everyone did. Except Ines, who had remained in her corner, not exactly cowering, but not with conviction, either.

Well, I'd say the ayes have it." Mr. Boreman sighed deeply and clasped his hands behind him. "There's no sense in putting it off. I'll go up now."

He started for the service staircase, but stopped when a small voice cried out his name. "Mr. Boreman, may I come, too?"

He turned, searching for the source of the voice. His gaze lit on Ines. "You, Ines? Why?"

Her arms hugging her middle, she stepped forward timidly. "I wish to tell the Berwinds that I do not strike, sir."

"Why, I should . . ." Her fist again curling, Bridget whirled on the Portuguese maid. I stepped between them.

"That's enough threats from you." I held out the flat of my hand. Anger rose in several of the faces around me, and I braced for their outbursts. None came. They turned away and gathered among themselves to speculate on what the next minutes would bring.

Mr. Boreman held out a hand to beckon to Ines. "Come along, then, I suppose." He didn't sound happy about it, but at least he didn't forbid her to go.

Ines started toward him looking like a convict walking to the gallows. The chef put his feet in motion, as well. "I am going up, too. I must make clear to the Berwinds that I am not a part of this nonsense."

Mr. Boreman nodded, then faced his coworkers one last time. "Wish me luck."

He looked as though he believed he would need it.